GOOD-BY AND KEEP COLD
(Apologies to Robert Frost)

a novel

by Barbara Stiles Donnelly

This book is a work of fiction. Any references to real people and places are used fictitiously. The author's imagination is solely responsible for the other names, places and events and any resemblance to actual names, places or events is entirely coincidental.

ISBN 9781980924869

GOOD-BY AND KEEP COLD

Robert Frost

This saying good-by on the edge of the dark
And the cold to an orchard so young in the bark
Reminds me of all that can happen to harm
An orchard away at the end of the farm
All winter, cut off by a hill from the house.
I don't want it girdled by rabbit and mouse,
I don't want it dreamily nibbled for browse
By deer, and I don't want it budded by grouse.
(If certain it wouldn't be idle to call
I'd summon grouse, rabbit, and deer to the wall
And warn them away with a stick for a gun.)
I don't want it stirred by the heat of the sun.
(We made it secure against being, I hope,
By setting it out on a northerly slope.)
No orchard's the worse for the wintriest storm;
But one thing about it, it mustn't get warm.
How often already you've had to be told,
Keep cold, young orchard, Good-by and keep cold.
Dread fifty above more than fifty below."
I have to be gone for a season or so.
My business awhile is with different trees,
Less carefully nurtured, less fruitful than these,
And such as is done to their wood with an ax—
Maples and birches and tamaracks.
I wish I could promise to lie in the night
And think of an orchard's arboreal plight
When slowly (and nobody comes with a light)
It's heart sinks lower under the sod
But something has to be left to God.
When slowly (and nobody comes with a light)
its heart sinks lower under the sod
But something has to be left to God.

**"I only hope that when I am free
As they are free, to go in quest
Of the knowledge beyond the
bounds of life. . ."**

**from MISGIVING
Robert Frost**

Journal entry

Today I spent two hours with the specialist. How I hate the sympathetic attention and the oblique glances that shout the unwelcome prognosis and break the serenity and peace I treasure. What can they do to change the outcome? It turns out—not much.

Ah, well . . . I am thankful for small comforts however ministered.

I've often picked up this old journal and written, more in an attempt to identify the ignominious ramblings than to etch the mere thoughts for posterity, for they will never be seen by anyone else. Even though I am the only one to write in this old Morocco-leather-bound volume, it looks and feels old and is of a different age when everyone wrote with pen and ink and was obliged to think before writing as it's practically impossible to eradicate the inked word.

Just as often, I'm puzzled. Retrospect tells me that I have filled pages with prattle. I am almost at the end with only a few pages to be inked in before the last page is turned. I'm glad things will come out even—like a satisfying meal with one last delicious bite finishing the plate—no unsightly mounds of potato or Brussels sprouts to spoil the empty symmetry. I wish I had been more consistent in my recording of these bits and bites but I'll have no more to say when the final page is filled.

I think about a time, a hundred and more years ago, when everyone from St. Augustine to Samuel Pepys, kept a journal. Certainly some of the most telling insights into the lives f heroes and heroines, saints and sinners, have been through the diligent recording of the everyday reflections of trials and loves, petty, insignificant musings and intimate, never voiced, thoughts. It has been the communion of blank page and secret word that has prompted revelation after revelation. Did the elucidations shock the writers, as I have been shocked by my own, with shadowy inclinations and dispositions?

That I haven't even the most vague clue to the why of life—my life—saddens me. I know I'm not alone. Each of us wishes to leave a mark, to be remembered for something: a painting, a poem, an essay, or a song, a good deed or perhaps a bad one. That reminds me of Dostoyevsky's sinner who remembered at the final reckoning that once he tossed an old onion to a beggar—thereby almost saving himself from the eternal lake of fire. In the end, the onion wasn't strong enough to overcome the strain of the sinner and the many who grabbed onto his coattails in a futile attempt to be pulled from the inferno and be saved. They all perished. What is the moral here? Who knows what the saving clemency might be.

There is still time for me. Perhaps I can find a poor beggar to save from a miserable existence; it would be a kindness to relieve a solitary and boring life. That's another Dostoyevsky illusion I often think about—ridding the world of that despicable pawnbroker.

Time is a continuum they say, but I have my doubts. It seems to have stopped to let me off, out of the mainstream, for a while and then picked me up again, ticking off the minutes, to resume its journey—my journey?

Where will it end?

It is the ageless question.

What have I learned in this dewdrop of eternity?

The only constant in life is love; charity is the better word: "Tis a consummation devoutly to be wished . . . ."

Of course, Hamlet was speaking of death when he uttered those words . . . . to die, to sleep . . .

"This saying good-by to the edge of the dark
   And the cold to an orchard so young in the   bark
   Reminds me of all that can happen to harm
   An orchard away at the end of the farm . ."

. . . .

"How often already you've had to be told,
Keep cold, young orchard, Good-by and
   keep cold."

from GOOD-BY AND KEEP COLD

Robert Frost

PROLOGUE

Edward paused at the flyleaf of his most treasured possession: a small blue, linen-like, hard-cover volume, faded and worn, pages thumbed thin, notes and scribbles in the margins; his fingertips barely grazed the spidery inscription: *Edward, of a fruitful orchard, good-by and keep cold.* The signature was unmistakable.

Edward Lawrence Whitman closed and tenderly placed his silent but wordy companion on the corner of his desk to keep it separate from the less revered volumes on the emptying shelves. To always have it close by to pick up, read a few lines, and, if needed, adjust his perspective was no small comfort.

How, for instance, could one fail to find joy in, "In a Girl's Garden?"

Several times already he had pulled out the top drawer of his tired, utilitarian, time-worn oak desk and absentmindedly did it again. The front of the drawer was strewn with the usual paperclips, pencils, pennies and dimes, and ballpoint pens he seldom picked up; he always used the fountain pen he kept in his inside jacket pocket. The gold Waterman with ELW engraved on the cap was a present from Ann when he had accepted the honor of the first Robert Frost Chair many years ago when it was a newly endowed Fellowship. He could confidently reach for his pen and it would be there where it belonged—in his pocket— unlike all the other lost and strayed pens that went before. Ann was good at finding ways to keep Edward free from frustrating and time wasting pursuits like searching for wayward pens. As a result he had not misplaced this pen in forty-five years.

Elbows resting on the desktop, chin cradled in his cupped hands, Edward closed his eyes for a moment. He had threaded his way through a maze of memories all morning and was weary from the strain of sorting and packing and remembering. He felt like he was looking through the wrong end of a telescope; everything seemed drawn out and distant and small. The red leather-cornered desk blotter, fraying at the edges and almost worn to holes, recorded backward-slanting words blotted on it; he could make out his name. Ann had always taken care of new blotters so it hadn't been replaced in years. The rest of the set—the leather hand blotter and pencil holder had disappeared, but the scissors and letter opener in their leather case was within easy reach. He thoughtfully picked them up, looked them over, and placed them in the box with other odds and ends to take home where they would gather dust in the dreaded basement; and in the end probably be thrown away.

As he shifted his now considerable bulk in the comfortable swivel chair to glance at the clock on the wall behind, it protested with a squawk and brought him back to the present and the chore at hand.

Almost eleven o'clock and he had been here since early morning erasing his years in the seat of his pride.

I should toss this junk into the trash and be done with it; nobody will want any of this stuff. I certainly don't.

In fact, someone would—the university archives were always accepting of what others called junk, especially junk from Nobel laureates. Priceless notes and letters with amazing revelations had been found amongst such rubbish in the past. He couldn't see anything of redeeming value in front of him so he doubted it would happen here.

They can have this jetsam if they wish.

A broad smile crossed his face as, in his mind, he pushed the years back to that unparalleled, transcendent first day he sat at this desk in this esteemed institution. He had been honored and proud and alive with inspiration and, best of all, Ann had been there to complete his dreamscape.

"*Forty-five years*," he said out loud, though there was no one to hear. The thrill came rushing back and he mused about his insatiable infatuation with Erato. Modern lyric poetry had been an all-consuming flame. The pride, the excitement, the ambition, and the purpose set him afire with fervor he couldn't have imagined sustaining. Couldn't have imagined then—or now. It was hard to believe he had logged in so many miles on that less traveled road. All those years and passion devoted to a jealous mistress who demanded his undivided attention and left the rest of his life in a shamble, somewhat orderly only because Ann, who was not a jealous wife, saw to it that Edward left the house each day prepared with, at least, his calendar up to date, an appropriate tie, and socks that matched. A kiss on the forehead sent him on his way to this small space in academia with a song and cadence in his full heart.

Inspired and ambitious is how he had thought of himself then—not without some degree of pride nor "stepping o'er the bounds of modesty" as the Bard would have said. He frowned.

But have I made an impact in the world of poetry?

The clock on the wall ticked an answer: tick, maybe; tock, maybe not.

Have I even cracked the heavy door of tradition to allow a fresh breeze, an unheralded voice to infiltrate this ivory-towered league? A faint smile crept along his pursed lips. *I think I have* and his heavy sigh filled the room.

Edward had given little thought about how his life might have been had he not taken a "road less traveled." There was only one lane for him and he had navigated the stormy seas and found himself in the catbird seat of modern poetry. His books were required reading in classes across the country and cited by scholars the world over. A glance around the tired room confirmed his endowment. His heart and soul ebbed from between the shelves, slipped out of the drawers and hung on the walls for all to see in the dusty framed diplomas and awards and the books with his name on the spines.

I should be happy to be retiring.

His literary legacy was considerable and renowned. Those bindings were available in many more languages than he could speak.

Do I have more to say? Another deep sigh edged into the dense silence. *I'm almost seventy-five years old it's only right to step down to make way for a new generation and a fresh outlook.* It was something he often thought about.

Ann was gone and so was his inspiration. She had been his faithful muse and even though he had learned to live without her, he wasn't sure how he would survive with neither Ann nor the deep rooted habit and reason to get up and come here each day.

His blond hair had faded to almost white, his large athletic frame had gained many pounds, filling in the sharp corners of youth, and lending him a portly, wise bearing. And though his students thought him eccentric, he was merely an aging *persona grata* who never found it necessary to conform. It wasn't that he wouldn't; the issue simply never arose in his mind.

I feel like the last steam engine puffing on to the end of the line to be put into mothballs and viewed as an interesting relic whose time has long past. The image tickled him. He was reminded of the **Thomas the Train** books and "Mr.Topham Hat" the jovial conductor. His boys had loved Thomas' escapades particularly the one with the tiger who had hidden in the car barn.

With one finger, he traced the faint outlines of rings left by coffee cups. With his other hand he pushed his glasses onto the top of his head, old-fashioned aviator style, where they spent most of their time out of his pocket. He needed those glasses for reading but not for looking out the window or into the past.

A bittersweet sensibility overcame him as he picked up the silver-framed photo that had graced the left-hand corner of his desk for as long as he could remember. When he thought about Ann, it was as she looked in this photo. She was young and fair with an enticing, entrancing smile. Carefully he placed Ann-in-the-silver-frame into a SAVE box as he had placed Ann in her coffin years ago. He still found it hard to accept that she had left him when he still needed her.

With another resigned sigh, he turned back to continue sorting. One by one he picked up and inspected mementos that lay scattered in the back of the old deskdrawer. They were like crumbs from a satisfying meal: too small to save and too big to ignore. And like leftovers pushed to the back of the icebox, many had dried up, faded and become unrecognizable. Most he tossed out. He picked up a key ring with two dangling keys. He shook his head—didn't remember them. They jangled as he turned them over in his hand. *Office keys?* He had never locked his door in all these years so he wasn't sure. He would add them to the boxful of keys in the basement: skeleton keys, safe keys, padlock keys and all sorts of metal lock openers. He never could bring himself to throw away keys even though he hadn't a clue about what they would lock or unlock, so he pushed them aside to keep. Some old reviews of his books fastened with a rusting paperclip got tossed out along with some schedules that were so faded he couldn't make them out. He chuckled.

Way in the back of one drawer he found his old calendar-address books held together with rubber bands. They, along with Ann, had kept him moving forward so he always knew where he should be even though he wasn't always there. As he picked up one stack, the elastic fell apart and the small booklets tumbled onto the desk. He picked them up, put them in chronological order and wound a new rubber band around them. Every now and then someone had asked about a seminar or a class or the year he and half of the department were snowed in. He'd refer to his calendars and tell them when and where something had happened. It was reason enough to keep them. The wastebasket was already overflowing with memories and reminders—of classes, seminars, proofs, and academic responsibilities, along with a few sentimental mementos, like conference nametags and dusty tassels. And like many who salt away little scraps, he didn't know why he kept them; he just did.

Before he placed the calendars into the SAVE box, he pulled one out and fanned the pages. It was from before he and Ann were married. Ann's telephone number was written in red across the front—as though he would ever have forgotten it: UNIversity 4-0088. The old 'phone numbers were easy to recall. He remembered them with the old exchanges and wished they still used them; it was so much easier to remember TRObridge, UNIversity, CAPitol, and STAdium than the numbers that bore no relation to each other. It's funny how some things never fade with the years. He started humming: *"How many cookies did ANDrew eat? ANDrew 8-8000."* He had forgotten the name of the rug company that had advertised on the radio, but its telephone number was etched forever in his memory along with the silly tune. He hummed and drifted.

Ann's image never faded either; it popped into his head at the slightest nudge a dozen times a day. Traces of her smile shimmered through the pages of his books and her soft voice echoed through the chambers of his mind. She was never more than a reflection away.

His face tightened into a frown. *Without Ann and without my work at the University, what is there? There is nothing.* He didn't look forward to not coming to his cubbyhole in these halls of ivy each day. The autobiography he had promised his publisher only loomed before him as a tedious chore. He wasn't eager to chronicle his life in defining prose. *It's not my style.* There is so much that should be included in it; things he didn't want to think about—out of sight, out of mind. Like the twins. *Where are they?* He would have traded all of eternity to relive a few of the happy times, and there hadn't been many, when he and Ann and their difficult children had celebrated being together. Uneasily he shifted in his chair and tilted it back—it protested again with another squawk. He'd rather think about the idyllic days before they were married, before those burdensome responsibilities.

Ann had lived at 888 Massachusetts Avenue in a tired looking but substantial, yellow-brick building that had housed hoards of young people who would have been called Yuppies a few years later. He had never been comfortable about her living there. The corridors were dark and impersonal: green walls with green and black tiled floors, and worse, the floors and corridors were all alike. Sometimes, and he smiled to think of it, with no elevators, he wound up on the third floor where Ann lived and sometimes on the second where she did not. One Valentine's Day had he stuck a red-heart sticker on Ann's door to distinguish it from the other characterless portals. Did anyone else ever have trouble with floors and doors? He wondered: had his red heart been scraped off the door by a new tenant or had it been left like a heart carved into a tree?

The springs in his chair gradually tightened coaxing the chair back into its upright position and his glasses slipped down onto his nose again. Instead of pushing them back onto his forehead, he tossed them onto the desk.

He liked to think he had rescued Ann from 888 and a graceless life of dull green and black corridors; and she let him. They both knew, though, that it was she who had liberated him from the dreary halls of a monastic academic life. When he thought of life before Ann, it was as thin and transparent as tea that hadn't steeped. It was as though he had been biding time before Ann. Even his considerable accomplishments had seemed wanting, a sham, a pretty box done up with ribbons, secreting emptiness. Ann was the gift. She had delivered him from a black-and-white, two-dimensional existence into full color 3-D. Her hand had embellished and embroidered the fabric of their lives with vibrant threads into a freestanding *object d'art*. Together they were complete—*beau idéal*.

How I miss her. How could she have left me before our story was finished?

Theirs was not the frivolous romance of youth. At thirty they had seasoned and drawn back from the superficial trappings that lure and flirt with emotions. They discovered each other as they would a new book of poetry: intrigued and captivated by each Promethean revelation.

He closed his eyes and leaned back again into the creaking and protesting old chair. He could see the short wrought iron fence where he and everyone else parked their three-speed Raleighs in front of 888. It had been a long time since he had pedaled a bicycle. He used to take the twins on the Charles River loop when they were young. Five miles was a long way for six-year-olds, but they loved the challenge and always pedaled harder and faster to better their time to the ice cream vendor who spent the summer near the Hatch Shell.

Cycling used to be *the* mode of transportation around Cambridge. There were few ten-speeders or Kryptonite locks back then. Bicycles had three speeds and locks were flimsy, if used at all, and bikes were frequently "borrowed" only to wind up in the basement of the police station in Central Square. Edward had been there several times to retrieve his or Ann's bicycles. That was how he and Anthony Argus, who subsequently became Commissioner Argus, had first gotten to know each other. A professor and a police commissioner who otherwise might never have crossed paths became good friends. Just thinking about Anthony made Edward chuckle.

Edward's reverie was jolted back into the present by heels clicking loudly and purposefully down the outside corridor, becoming louder and, seemingly, more purposeful as they approached his corner of academia.

The door flew open and Catriona exploded into the office.

"Ready?" She was straight-backed and held her head high as if to say that it didn't matter that her inches didn't measure up. She glanced at her watch and then at

Edward. "Nice tie—a bit somber, though. Didn't I give you one with spring colors? I did--a beautiful Liberty print. Perfect for a nice day like today!"

It was a rhetorical question and did not require, nor did she expect or wait for, an answer. She whirled, cast an eye around the office and began rearranging the untidy stacks and clearing the almost vacant shelves.

"We have time to take a load or two to the car now and can finish up after lunch." She was quick with both word and deed and proceeded to take command like a drill sergeant spitting out orders he knew would be obeyed. "I'll help you separate the archive stuff from your personal stuff," she said without looking at him, and instead, surveyed the room.

The air was charged with her presence and inanimate objects seemed to yield to her, to say nothing of the animate ones, like Edward, who were always awed by her energy and stunned by her quick execution of a task. What had taken Edward hours was finished in minutes. She said, "There!" brushing her hands together.

I did the lion's share Edward thought but did not say it. *It's easy to put things into boxes. The hard part is sorting and throwing out.*

Still, he was glad to have her hurrying things along and he hastily swept the remains into a box, placing the motley mixture on the top of a pile. "Let's go," he said trying to match her vitality by bolting out of his chair and hurrying into his coat. She pointed to his glasses. Edward grimaced, nodded and jammed them into his jacket breast pocket. There was no handkerchief to hide them behind. That was the kind of thing Ann had always seen to.

Together they crammed her old VW with about forty-five years worth of Edward Lawrence Whitman stuffed into boxes and plastic bags. They locked the VW and set off on foot for the Faculty Club. Catriona said she had made a reservation for them for this momentous day

Catriona, called Cat by everyone, was Edward's most promising grad student. He worried that she didn't have the stature or the take-me-seriously presence of a consummate, contemporary poet. It wasn't that she didn't write brilliant verse; she did. Edward encouraged her to focus on getting published. It would certainly help to establish the seriousness of her aims, he often told her.

"But I'm happy with my lot," she had once responded by throwing out her hands with a dramatic flair, "and I don't have to wear a hair shirt and starve in a garret to write. I want my poetry to reflect the joy and promise in life." She wrote from somewhere deep inside her soul that astounded everyone. More so, perhaps, because she looked like a pretty, dizzy, scatterbrain.

Her short curly blond hair haloed a round freckled face, huge brown, questioning eyes and a quick, impish smile. She was always in a frenzied rush between social and political causes.

At the Faculty Club, Cat steered her mentor around a corner and into a private room. Friends and colleagues stood as the surprised Edward entered.

I should have known I couldn't just slip out unnoticed. He admonished himself for not foreseeing the inevitability of such an occasion.

The Department was there *en masse*. He glanced around the room feeling embarrassed and touched at the same time. He was, in fact, glad to see everyone; though he was amazed there were so many. The department had grown in forty-five years.

Looking over the familiar faces, he stood in contemplation for a few moments. "I'm truly honored," he mumbled, "and I'm unprepared to respond." He pushed a few strands of his faded blond hair back from his brow. Then he spoke about his friendship with Frost, the honor of being appointed the first Robert Frost Fellow and how forty-five years in this department of prose-run-mad had lured time into the drama, and it had sped by. He said a few words in praise of the new Fellow, Joshua Canfield, and ended with a quote from Emerson: ". . . the true poem is the poet's mind."

Some of his first students were there. Among them was Robert Ambrose, who had made a name for himself with his tart and terse reviews column in *The New York Times*. He had come with a large, leather-bound scrapbook tucked under his arm.

He stood and with a flourish of his hand, eloquently waxed "I started amassing this capacious tome after my first conference as a student, those many years ago, with this paragon of wisdom and intellectual vigor." He presented the album to Edward. Everyone applauded and then took turns thumbing through the pages of the chronological arrangement of clippings and reviews of Edward's books and lectures.

Police Commissioner Argus, the only non-academic present, but without whom the gathering would have been incomplete, then stood and proposed a toast to his staunch comrade who had helped him think out complicated dilemmas.

In a chair at the head of the table, next to the one left vacant for Edward, sat Edward's most cherished friend Lew— Laurence Edward Woodridge. When Lew stood to contribute his words about the retiring professor he had known since childhood, he opened Edward's first book of poetry and read from it with emotion that hushed the room and brought everyone to a standing ovation.

It was a fitting end to an illustrious career.

**". . . And my heart owns a doubt
Whether 'tis in us to arise with day
And save ourselves unaided . . ."**

**from STORM FEAR
Robert Frost**

Chapter 1

In the two years since Edward's retirement, he hadn't picked up his pen nor written a single verse A flurry of speaking engagements had carried him over the reality of infinite leisure--no small chore. Lately the invitations were fewer and, he felt, less enthusiastic; he certainly was less enthusiastic. "I guess they thought I wouldn't be around much longer, and wanted to see if I really had anything more to say," he said and poked at a piece of Styrofoam with his walking stick as the two friends traced their steps through the familiar pathway in the Quad on the way home from their customary Monday lunch in Harvard Square, "but as Tennyson said, 'men may come and men may go but I go on forever.'" He paused, "What a dreadful thought."

It was a beautiful early spring day—the kind poets write verses about. Edward motioned to an empty bench in the Quad. They sat under an almost budding apple tree in the welcome spring sunshine. Robins chirped and flitted back and forth with twigs and bits of grass.

Lew chuckled, ignoring the deeper implications of Edward's words, and keeping his tone light, said, "Everyone enjoys an old bumbler like you parceling out sagacious gems even though he may have written them all down in some voluminous tome." His spoke in a gravelly voice. He cast a sideways glance at Edward and they both began to laugh. "It's the human, and certainly the poetic, nature. Youth fawning on the romance of the past and the wisdom of the aged."

Lew had seen Edward's spirit ebbing over the past two years. He often found Edward sitting in his kitchen long after breakfast, with the newspaper before him, staring off into the afternoon. Edward had dredged up the cliché about solving the problems of the world, but his old enthusiasm and humor only sparked when he was prodded, and he fell short of wholehearted involvement in anything; even his chess game had slipped to mediocre and that was a generous assessment. Edward sometimes joked a bit but often there was a dejected edge to his humor. There was none of the Edward who used to poke fun at himself and most everyone else. He seemed a lethargic lump who had relinquished his claim on life.

A young couple ambled along the brick pathway, in step and with twined hands, searching for a free bench to open their Au Bon Pain lunch bags and enjoy the spring sunshine. Lew and Edward gave up their bench and continued their short walk home.

"Have you had your sulfur and molasses and spring check-up yet? I think you could use a vitalizing elixir." Lew said. "We all could. I've had my check up, and took the car in too. It needed some help. That old suit of yours could use some help too—throw it out and get a new one."

"What's the matter with this?" Edward reached down and shook baggy knees. I've got all the clothes I'll ever need. In fact I mean to bundle some up for the Friends Service Committee; someone might as well get some use out of them. I'll die before I can wear out what I've got. I hate trying to buy clothes—Ann always did that." He paused. "And I hate going for a check-up. All those prying questions and prying eyes and probing fingers that I can live without!"

Lew smiled. It was promising when he could stir Edward up a little. And he understood some of the soul-stirring pathos he imagined Edward was battling. He and Edward were the same age, born within three weeks of each other, so he, too, felt the vagaries of age and the loss of a beloved mate. His wife Sarah had died shortly before Ann.

They crossed the street and Edward stumbled on the curbstone, Lew asked, "Are you limping?"

"No, I just stubbed my toe. It's my mind that's limping. I sometimes think it would be better to have Alzheimer's so I wouldn't know how miserable I am."

Lew pretended not to have heard that and quickened their pace a little.   Since their retirements, the two old friends had slipped more and more into each other's lives. It seemed natural because they had grown up like brothers sharing books, lunches and intimacies. Each was a worthy devil's advocate and Lew longed for a good argument, like they used to have when they were young: unanswerable philosophical questions . . . cause, purpose, result. But, try as he might, Edward would never take the bait or even nibble at it.

There were times, Lew thought as they walked along in comfortable silence, when he, too, felt like sitting on the sidelines. But, there were other times when he felt so good he was tempted to take out his old single, put it in the water and row to Newton. He didn't give in to the whim because he knew that the following day there would be aches and pains he wouldn't want to cope with, but he carried the exhilaration in his memory and he was content with, and understood, his limitations. It seemed there were more and more of them with each passing day.

It worried him that Edward had foundered and the purpose that had given his life meaning had washed into a sea of ennui. He had stopped writing. Edward had forgotten how to be Edward. It had practically become Lew's *raison d'etre* to initiate a topic and prod until he got a response. Always pushing and pulling, nudging and goading, urging and prompting. By the end of an evening Lew's own humor was often dangling by a spidery thread.

Since long before Ann and Sarah died, Monday night was chess night just as Sunday evening for the four friends was a night out at a favorite restaurant and a concert or theatre or a movie. They seldom allowed anything to interrupt their routines. Chess night included dinner at Edward's. Over the years Lew had provided dessert. It was always something special from The Black Forest or The Blacksmith Shop and he still executed his part with gusto. Cat had taken over the cooking managing to whip up gourmet meals in very short times in the kitchen that was still Ann's kitchen with Danish and French cookware and Henri Diat's French cookbook. Lew wished Edward, who hardly touched the sometimes exotic, but always tempting and tasty dinners, would take more notice of Cat's creations.

They turned the corner to Berkeley Street, and Lew passed the bakery box he was carrying to Edward, "Dessert--special for Cat. I think she said *coq au vin* is on the menu tonight. I'm looking forward to it." Lew walked the few steps between their houses, opened his own back door and walked into his living room where he tossed his coat onto a chair and turned on his stereo. Beethoven's **Pastorale** was just what he needed to relax and maybe have a little nap.

Later that evening, after Cat's gourmet *coq au vin*, they adjourned to the living room for Lew's dessert and coffee and chess.

"Where's Mark tonight?" Lew asked as he watched Cat cut into the Linzer torte. She smiled at Lew. "Shall I cut some of this beautiful torte for you two?" They both nodded..

The two friends settled themselves at the three-week-old chess game with coffee and token slices of torte. Lew took a bite. It was good, but he didn't care if he had it or not. Cat had scoffed when he said, "Just a sliver for me, it's very rich."

"Nothing's too rich for me!" Cat said, "the only reason for having dinner at all is for an excuse to have a really good dessert," and Lew always remembered that when he picked out the richest or most chocolaty or creamy delicacy in the bakery showcase.

She answered his question about Mark as she poured her coffee. "He's dropping by later--had a late seminar or something. I saved him some dinner. Maybe there'll still be some Linzer torte or . . . maybe not," she said as she finished cutting a giant slice and put it on her own dessert plate.

Cat had been living on the third floor since before Edward retired. The rambling house, he had said, was too big for him. It turned out to be a good move for everyone. Cat ran the household without Edward's even being aware of it. Even though she was over-committed with her graduate program and all her other projects--feminist movements, saving the whales and the seals and the rain forests and anything else that needed saving, she ran things efficiently and within budget. Edward never asked to see an accounting of how she did it—he had faith in her choices and was never disappointed. She took care of the repairs and the snow removal and the yard work and everything else that Edward had never thought about when Ann was alive. She kept the pantry stocked with foods Edward might like to find if he fancied a snack; there was always peanut butter and raspberry jam and if he opened the icebox door he would find ham, cheeses, lettuce, tomatoes. English muffins and sour dough bread. She encouraged him to try a yoghurt now and then. In return, Edward had agreed to be available for consultation on Cat's first book of poetry, soon due for publication with

photographs by an inspired young photographer named Mark
Collins.

"Is everyone of that generation named Mark or Eric?"
Lew asked hoping to get a little feedback about Mark. He
thought Cat and Mark seemed to be having just a spot of trouble
and wondered if there were more to the relationship than the
joint book. No one ever said. The times Mark had joined them
for dinner, which was often, gave no indication of anything more
than a mutual-gain, professional collaboration. Still, Lew
thought he sensed an electricity—maybe it was only static--
between them.

"Huh?" said Cat not looking up from her dessert.

"I was just being silly, but the names do seem to be
overworked," Lew said, and settled back in the worn leather
chair. "Your move," he said to Edward. Lew watched closely
and hoped a power move, like the ones Edward used to surprise
him with, was coming--though he certainly couldn't see one on
the horizon. This game had gone on too long for a game that
was going nowhere. Though he was getting impatient, he didn't
want Edward to feel rushed, so he picked up his piece of torte,
took a bite, got up, poured himself more coffee and walked
around the room stretching his legs and sipping coffee.

He strolled from one end to the other of the comfortable
living room that graced the length of the house. Tasteful
groupings of chairs and tables--two wing chairs and a Queen
Anne table here, an easy chair with footstool and lamp there, the
chess table and chairs, where the two friends sat every Monday,
nearer the French doors that led to the small terrace, and the

comfortable sofa in front of the fireplace which Cat had completely taken over--had been arranged years ago by Ann and still made a harmonious setting for two or three things going on at the same time. The grand oak mantel over the fireplace was bare except for brass candlesticks and a bowl of fresh spring flowers--Cat's arty influence. A sandy-beach scene, with wild roses and dunes in watercolor, reached to either end of the mantle and mirrored the rest of the room in its glass. Lew watched the reflection of Edward's hunched form over the chessboard superimposed on the beach. A lamp was growing out of the roses in a dune.

Cat sat on the over-stuffed, flowery chintz-covered sofa amid scattered papers, sipping and munching, seemingly absorbed with a manuscript and making notes in the margins.

"There," Edward sighed.

Lew walked back and looked over Edward's shoulder at the chessboard. "I can't believe you did that! Cat, come quickly. Take Edward's pulse or his temperature! He must be sick." Lew's voice took on an animated tone as he rushed to Cat and gave her a good-natured shake.

"Oh, I didn't see your bishop," Edward apologized.

As Lew sat down, he bumped the leg of the table jiggling the chessboard and the men toppled and rolled off the board onto the floor. "What a clumsy oaf I am," he said as he started to pick up the men, "Let's just start over. I can't remember where they were anyhow. Can you?"

"No." Edward shook his head, picked a crumb off his lap and deposited it in his saucer.

"I am so tired of this dreary winter! Even though it was nice today, spring probably won't really be here for ages!" Lew said, taking his time setting up the board again. "Let's go off for a holiday in the sun. We could throw a couple of things into a bag and leave tomorrow." Cat's head popped up from her work and she stopped writing to listen. It sounded too impromptu for Lew and she was sure he knew tomorrow wasn't realistic but it gave the notion immediacy. "Maybe Florida or even some more exotic clime." Cat smiled at Lew as though she could see into his mind and knew he was trying to prod Edward.

"I don't think so. I never really liked sun vacations; you know that. There's never anything to do." Edward slumped in his seat. "And I hate trying to anticipate what I need. I don't pack very well. Ann always did my packing."

"I'll help you pack," Cat offered.

Lew went on as though he hadn't heard the protest, "We wouldn't need much and we could go where there *are* things to do--like Central America. We could go to the Mayan ruins-- you've always wanted to do that. I've always wanted to go there, too. We almost went once--remember? But Sarah and Ann said no, and we couldn't talk them into it. They always chose more cosmopolitan holidays with museums and opera and cultural events. Too hot, they said, and too buggy. Lizards crawling the walls." He was hoping Edward would join in the reminiscence. But he did not.

There were other reasons that Lew thought were at the root of Edward's doldrums in the first place, and he wanted to broach the subject of the twins carefully and the last trace of them had been in Central America. Maybe this was not the time. He went on: "In fact, we wouldn't have to pack much of anything. We could buy what we need as we go along and then throw the dirty and used things away! I've always wanted to do that. We wouldn't have to carry clumsy bags around. Probably the best idea anyway—neither one of us has much in the way of a safari wardrobe either." He mimicked putting a hat on his head and cut across his knees with his hand to indicate shorts. "It would be so easy."

Cat said, "I think it's a great idea. I wish I could go."

There was no reaction from Edward.

"In any case, the very least a vacation would accomplish, would be to make us happy to come home." Lew said. He thought that warranted a chuckle or two. He searched Edward's face for a response--nothing. In truth, the atmosphere around here lately was not anything anyone would choose to come back to. Edward shook his head as though nothing could make him change his mind or his thinking to a more innovative stance.

The front door chime sounded and, like a time-out call, stopped the conversation as they all looked toward the double doorway leading to the hallway.

Seconds later, Anthony Argus breezed in leaving a wake of rustling papers and fluttering curtains. Commissioner Argus was a whirlwind in a rumpled grey flannel suit. He tossed his coat onto a chair before he strode over to Edward and Lew. His amber eyes glowed from deep sockets on either side of his magnificent Roman inheritance which he daubed at with a handkerchief and rubbed with the back of his hand without being aware of what he a doing. There was always an itch, he said, on the end of his nose.

At least, Lew thought, Edward's smiling now and paying attention to this humorous interlope with the big nose and a big heart." Big commotion up on Brattle," Anthony boomed. "Burglary!

**"In being a thief
And persisting in theft
With cynical daring."**

**from THE BAD ISLAND-EASTER
Robert Frost**

Chapter 2

"That's why I'm here in *your* neighborhood and have
been since this afternoon. Oh, hullo Cat. How's the book
going?" Anthony spoke to Cat as he eyed the dessert table and
rubbed his hands together. "I'd love some of that coffee—mmm,
smells good—and maybe some dessert. Looks good. What is
it?" Cat lifted her head and pointed with her chin to a cup and
saucer on the tray.

"Can you pour your own?" She showed no sign of
moving so Anthony proceeded to the table and picked up the
cup.

"Sure, sure." As he poured, he made a mental note that
once again he must have committed an infractin of Cat's "rules of
modern etiquette and behavior for aging-but-receptive-to-change
male chauvinist pigs." He was never too sure just what her rules
were and he didn't mean to violate them, but he knew he often
did. He was happy to serve himself.

"It's Isobel's fault," Anthony said faintly as he closed his eyes and sipped his coffee. "She spoiled me . . . and my mother and sisters before her. I was the only boy of the five, you know." He was talking to Cat, and she seemed to be ignoring him. "I didn't even know I was being catered to. I thought it was the way things were." He looked at Cat for a response. She could resist no longer, put down her pencil, and gave him full attention, like she would a cute, lovable dog.

"Oh, I can forgive you. You're learning. Besides, I've always suspected a closet equal rights sympathizer lurking under the chauvinism. And, there's some supper in the kitchen, if you want. But tell us first about the burglary; I think you just like to keep us dangling. Where? Who? What was taken?"

"I'll just have some coffee and some of this," he pointed at the torte, "What did you say it is?" he looked up with a little smile, knowing he was teasing.

"Will you stop it! I know you're dying to spill it all out to us!" Cat looked ready to throw the needlepoint pillow she had in her hand at him. "It's Linzer torte," she finally answered his question.

"You know the Wadsworths, don't you? Of course you do. Up on Brattle." Everyone nodded. "Well, they've put together some of their first editions for a permanent exhibition at the Heineken Museum." He glanced at his audience. "I'm sure you know more about the new American Writers' Room for American literary acquisitions than I do." He said that last bit slowly to be sure he got it right, as though he had just memorized it. "They, the Wadsworths, had about fifty books: Longfellow, Whittier, Emerson, Lowell; you know, the good old crowd pleasers, inventoried and ready for their new home, on Friday afternoon. They left them just where they've always been: in their library. The books were separated from the rest of the library in groups, stacks, and boxed ready for the Heineken crew to pick up early this week though no definite time had been set. Then they locked up the house, punched in the alarm code and left for a weekend on the Cape. It's something they often do apparently. Spend the weekend on the Cape, that is. Truro. It's almost at the end of the Cape; about 140 miles from here. That's where their summer cottage is. So you see, it's a fairly long trip especially when you add in the traffic that bottles up on that narrow Section of Route 6."

Before he sat at the other end of the sofa, Anthony put a rather large slice of torte on his saucer. As usual, his cup was too full and spilling it would be so easy, so he took a big gulp of coffee before sitting down and setting his saucer on the arm of the sofa. Carefully, so as not to disturb any of Cat's papers, he settled himself—there wasn't much room left. He picked up the torte with his fingers and took a bite. "Great stuff!" he chewed and beamed.

Edward and Lew watched Anthony from the chess table and Cat put down her work. Basking in their full attention, he took up his story, "They returned late Sunday night--last night-- after heavy weekend traffic tie-ups." He took a swallow, " . . . and it isn't even the season yet. Anyhow, they came in, unloaded, and went to bed. There had been no problem with the alarm system." he paused, "It hadn't been set off. The lights were on the usual timers which they leave set even when they're home." He looked up. "It's a good idea. Do you do that? You should."

He left them hanging with that for a few seconds while he took a bite of torte and drank some of his coffee, carefully placing the cup back into the saucer on the arm of the sofa. "No one even went into the library until today; but when they did, they had a shock." His words infused with drama, his hands opened in a magician's pose, he said, "The books were gone! Poof! Gone!"

"All of them?" Edward had started to perk up. "Was it only the books for the Heineken or others as well?"

Cat's eyes grew wider with each of Anthony's gestures but it wasn't his story commanding her attention; it was the jiggling cup and saucer on the arm of the sofa. She said nothing but if Anthony had been looking at her he would have seen relief as he picked up his cup and drained it.

Across the room, Edward had reacted like a plant growing in time-lapse photography--a shoot unfurling, growing upright and gaining strength in a matter of minutes. Unlike the chess game, Anthony's moves had his undivided attention.

Anthony rubbed his nose with the back of his hand and nodded at Edward, "Yes, all of the books slated for the Museum were gone. They simply couldn't believe it. At first they thought that somehow the Museum crew had already come and taken the books away. Then they realized that was impossible because of the alarms and locks. They, of course, called the Museum to make sure, and they were right. The museum didn't have the books!" He shook his head, "That would've been too simple."

The phone rang. Cat jumped up, glanced at her watch and said, "I'll get it. It's probably Mark. He should have been here by now." On her way to the telephone, she picked up Anthony's empty cup and saucer.

If Anthony thought she was going to refill it, he soon saw he was mistaken. She simply shoved them onto one end of the dessert table. Though he was a little bewildered, he accepted her action and figured he had done something wrong again, but he didn't know what.

Edward turned from Anthony to Lew and back again. "Is anything else missing?" he asked. "They have some valuable antiques: Paul Revere silver and some rare oriental relics from the clipper-ship trade. That's where they made their money, you know. There's an antique gun collection that's considered priceless." He elaborated, ". . . some jeweled pistols from the eighteenth century." And in the same breath, "I wonder if the Frost volumes were taken. They were all dedicated and inscribed by Frost. I would love to have them myself."

"Maybe I should look around here," Anthony chuckled and watched for a reaction from Edward who rewarded him with a big smile. "Our initial inspection of the premises didn't shed much light. We'll go back in the morning after the Wadsworths get a copy of the inventory of the room from their lawyers. Maybe there's a clue there or something that they've overlooked. I hope so." He got up and walked to the chess table.

The chessboard had taken a back seat even though Edward and Lew still sat at it. Edward had started the new game by moving his pawn into sacrificial territory.

"Deviating from the Queen's Gambit again?" Anthony wasn't much of a chess player but he had been reading up and knew some of the classic moves. He stood over Lew and Edward feigning interest, pondering strategy and nodding his head in a knowing fashion. Both Edward and Lew smiled indulgently.

"You'll have to play the loser!" Lew joked as he eyed their unpoliceman-like friend who made up the shorter but more colorful third of the familiar Cambridge trio.

Anthony pouted and walked back over to the dessert table. "I'll take you both on sometime soon!" Then he added, glancing sideways at them, "after I solve this Wadsworth business," giving himself a margin of time. He picked up another piece of Linzer torte and looked for his cup to refill. After looking around the room, he concluded that his cup was the one on the dessert table though he didn't remember putting it there. So he picked it up and refilled it with a little chractristic florish.

**"And could in one burst overwhelm
And dayify the darkest realm . . .**

**From TWO LEADING LIGHTS
Robert Frost**

Chapter 3

"I wonder who would do such a thing?" Lew asked and Edward responded as he threw a quick glance at Anthony and turned his chair to face him.

"I think a fanatic who simply wanted to possess the books, like some of the art treasures that have been stolen, would be a prospect. Or, we know they're worth quite a lot of money but there probably would be a problem selling them; it would have to be to an unscrupulous collector who didn't care if the provenance weren't clear. Most of us who would like to possess them would not steal them from someone who owned and loved them." Edward pulled a little notepad from the chess table drawer.

Lew's jaw dropped in amazement at the change he saw bubbling up in Edward before his eyes. Edward was showing interest in something without a bomb placed under him. Maybe this theft is a good thing, he thought.

"You know," Cat said, "I wouldn't be surprised if the culprit were that replacement of yours in the Department." She stuffed the rest of her torte into her mouth. Three deadpan faces looked as though they didn't know what she was talking about and were afraid to say so.

"The first editions!" she blurted, "Everyone knows Professor Canfield's thesis is that first editions belong, by rights, to scholars and posterity. So maybe he has taken it upon himself to see that they do." She raised her hand to stop Edward who started to say something, and plunged ahead, "And he hasn't taken your place, just moved into your old office. Really, he is so intractable. I hate going to see him. And I can imagine him doing something like this—thinking it would serve the poetic end." She paused, looked sheepishly around and said, "I don't suppose he really did it, though."

She was pouting and Lew thought he saw through the outburst. Canfield had probably not paid the same level of attention to Cat that Edward had. Cat was not ordinarily a gossip nor was she one to put a negative slant on an innocuous comment: like Canfield's about the rights of scholars and posterity, he thought. She was self-centered he had to admit. He asked, "Why? Is he not liked? Uninvolved? Self-centered? Are his credentials in question? Is he just not friendly? Is he stingy with his support?"

When Cat didn't respond, Edward chided her, "Joshua Canfield is a respected and renowned scholar. I know there's been a rumor that I was forced out and it's completely untrue. You, of all people should know it! He wasn't even around when I made my decision to leave---it was time for me to go." He shifted in his chair, "He just looks unapproachable because he doesn't often wear a smile. You can't blame anyone for their looks, can you?"

Lew was still thinking about Cat and watched her while she listened. He smiled to himself as the apt cliché about judging a book by its cover came to mind. That Canfield looked sour and really wasn't, appealed to Lew and he thought, but did not say anything, about Cat's dizzy, completely misleading appearance.

Edward was still defending Canfield, "He has written and published some of the finest and most definitive works on modern poets and their influence and influences. Maybe he is not as gregarious as you might like, but something like this? I don't think so. He is honorable. I'd stake my life on it."

Anthony threw up his hands, palms up, and stared at the ceiling as if to say, what's this all about? He seemed baffled by the turn the conversation had taken, "It's probably too early to check the usual fences." He smiled broadly, "But we'll get that part of the investigation started in the morning."

He went on, "There weren't any fingerprints to speak of. Not that it means anything. The housekeeper dusts and vacuums on Fridays and had waited until after the books were stacked and packed to dust and polish in the library; so if there had been any prints, they would have shown up—unless of course, they were purposefully wiped away." He shrugged and held up his hands again—it was something his friends often saw him do.

"Nothing else was out of place as far as they could tell except in the kitchen. This morning when Mrs. Wadsworth went into the kitchen, the counter was messy with crumbs, dirty knives and plates, sticky pickle juice and mayonnaise. It wasn't chaos; someone just hadn't cleaned up. When she chided Mr. Wadsworth for the mess, he denied even stepping into the kitchen before she did. Mrs. Wadsworth said she had put together a few sandwiches for the trip to the Cape on Friday and was sure she had put things away before leaving but couldn't help thinking that maybe she was starting to be forgetful.

"What kind of a thief stops to fix himself a snack?" muttered Lew.

Anthony pressed on, "They think that only the editions earmarked for the Heineken were taken. The inventory will be checked thoroughly in the morning. It's easy to overlook something in a room as full as that library is."

Edward was making notes and said without looking up, "You missed a great dinner, Anthony--*coq au vin*--Cat outdid herself."

"There's plenty if you'd like some Anthony," said Cat. "I saved a plate for Mark but he won't be coming tonight. That was him on the phone." Cat was shaking her head as she made her way back to her nest in the sofa. "He stopped in at the Government School, a photo opportunity he called it, where there was an impromptu debate going on about. . . " she looked at each of the three individually, " . . . discrimination in tenure for women at the School."

She plunked herself back down on the sofa and rustled around a bit, straightening papers and fretfully putting things together, it looked without purpose, before she said in a much stronger, testy tone, "I wish the University would take a firm stance and stick to the definitions they themselves have mandated and just do what's right. They might as well appear magnanimous and stop this nitpicking. They'll come around in the end, anyway."

No one in the room was going to touch that without a ten-foot pole and a quick egress.

She stopped and looked up from the paper she was crumpling and giggled self-consciously. The three men stared back at her in a room that was as still as the aftermath of a storm.

Edward broke the silence and said with a new enthusiasm, "I've made a few notes and I'll go over to the Wadsworth's in the morning. Maybe there's something I can do. I hope nothing has happened to the Frost set." He picked up his piece of torte, took a bite and smiled a Cheshire-cat smile at the rest of the room.

Anthony said, "Yes, go see them. They probably feel frustrated and violated at the same time and need reassurance that something's being done." he nodded and emphasized, "It's the classic victim syndrome. After you've seen the scene and talked with the Wadsworths you may come up with something we'd have missed. There certainly isn't a clear-cut motive. I mean, they could have taken much more valuable stuff."

Lew looked around the room, eyebrows raised, nodding slowly and considered the scene before him. Too bad for the Wadsworths, he thought, but this riddle is just what the doctor ordered. It was like a shot of adrenaline for Edward. A barely audible sigh of relief passed his lips as he joined in the speculating and questioning. He bumped the chess table again and for the second time that night upset the chessboard. "Let's just start over next week." Edward nodded and Lew relaxed and carefully stored the chessmen. He was glad that game was over and done.

As Sherlock Holmes would say, "a new game is afoot."

**"only someone lived in turning to
fresh tasks
Could so forget his handiwork on
which
He spent himself . . . . "**

**from THE WOOD PILE
Robert Frost**

Chapter 4

"You're up early." Cat poured coffee for herself and
Edward as she glanced at the clock. Eight o'clock. "It's too early
to go to the Wadsworth's. Give them a chance to get up." She
didn't really think he was going to dart over to the Wadsworth's
house, but it was nice to have some triviality to josh him about.
And it was not that the theft was unimportant; it was that he
hadn't paid attention to anything with such focus for a very long
time.

He was, in the twinkling of a theft, a changed person.

The

kitchen smelled like home—fresh coffee and burnt toast. Cat
stood at the sink carefully scraping some of the burnage off. She
scrutinized the slice, turning it over twice before placing it on the
pile in the middle of the table. Raspberry jam and orange
marmelade were ready to camouflage and hide the not perfect

toast. She walked to the window, pulled back the small linen-like curtain and said with a theatrical sigh, "It's another typical New England day. Looks like rain, but it probably won't. It'll just stay dreary all day long." Cat liked to tease Edward with little jabs about New England and its weather. And he usually defended the four seasons with a worn out bit of Twain rhetoric about waiting a minute. Cat was from sunny Southern California and she liked to say so on days like this. Today, Edward didn't hear her or if he did, he didn't acknowledge it in any way. He was busy rifling through the **Boston Globe.**

He looked up for a second when he heard her say, "Anthony's coming up the walk."

Anthony tapped his signature tattoo--tat-ta-rat-tat-tat-tat--on the door to announce himself before he pushed open the door and swamped the small room with his presence. "Morning all," he said filling the quietness and pulling out a chair. He plopped down across from Edward with a thud.

Cat murmured, "M-m-m-m-m," and handed him a cup and plate, which he accepted without question or protest but gave a little sideways glance that mutely asked if he were within acceptable bounds. Picking up the sports section of the paper Edward had discarded, he poured himself a cup of coffee and sniffed it, "Ah-h-h." Then he pulled his handkerchief out of his pocket, pushed his nose around with it and put it back in his pocket. It was an unconscious performance. His nose was red and swollen and itchy. He twitched it a few times.

"Poor Anthony. He's blooming like the spring flowers!" Cat stifled a giggle.

Anthony cast a quick, huffy but indulgent, glance at Cat and then addressed Edward who had finally looked up from the newspaper. "I have to make a stop at the Wadsworth's to check on that inventory. You said you were going to drop in on them, so why don't we walk over together. I only intend to stay long enough to ask a few questions and assure them that we're doing everything we can to find their books. I told them to expect me about nine." He reached for the jam jar and a piece of toast. Like Cat, he turned the toast over a couple of times, then with a shrug piled on some raspberry jam and took a bite. "They'll have the inventory and they're going to check out the room this morning. It would help to know if anything else were obviously missing before going through the whole inventory."

"That makes sense," said Edward looking over his glasses for a moment and then impatiently turning the pages of the paper. "I didn't see anything in the paper about the theft."

The sports page seemed to have Anthony's undivided attention. Edward folded the paper and with a little slap let it land right next to Anthony's coffee.

A little startled, Anthony looked up, thought for a few seconds, and said, "Oh, sorry. Look under 'Local Briefs.' There's a short paragraph. Just says, 'break-in on Brattle Street.' No details--we don't have many, anyhow." He turned back to the Sports page, "The Celtics won last night in overtime. Must have been one great game. Cambridge has produced some great basketball players, you know. That Ewing fellow certainly put New York on the map . He was a Cambridge Rindge and Latin grad you know. Took Cambridge to the top too." He looked up to see Edward and Cat both staring at him with "you're-not-paying-attention-looks" on their faces.

He reached for another piece of toast and garnished it with a spoonful of marmalade before he pulled out his notebook and read aloud: "Why is it that no one discovered the theft until Monday afternoon? Why wasn't the alarm doing *something like* making a noise or beeping or at least registering malfunction? He looked up, "Maybe it was someone who knew the Wadsworths quite well. We need to know who outside the family had a key and knew the alarm code." He scribbled again. "Or maybe the theft was carried out Sunday night after the Wadsworths returned from the Cape while they were right there in the house and had turned off the alarm." He folded the sports section and put it to one side; he had lost that battle--he'd have to catch up with the other sports news later.

"Then it would be a burglary," Cat corrected.

Anthony nodded slowly as though he knew he was going to lose another battle. "I know that," he harumphed, "and besides, it's just a shade off and what difference does it make as long as everyone understands the point?" He sounded annoyed and exasperated, but he ruined his petulant facade by laughing. If you can think of any more questions, I'd like to know.

Cat sometimes argued semantics with Anthony until he was so confused he would throw up his hands in defeat. Cat was sure he liked the jousting and thought that sometimes he made mistakes on purpose just to see how she'd respond. He was always smiling, if that were a clue.

Edward must have been thinking about why the Wadsworths might not have realized on Sunday that they had been robbed when he said, "That house is big and rambling and one wouldn't pass through the library to get to the kitchen or living room or, for that matter, to the upstairs bedrooms. It's easy to see why they didn't go into the room until the next day. They probably were just interested in getting to bed after that tedious drive."

Cat had her coffee in her hand and was on her way out of the kitchen when Edward turned in his chair and said to her, "I'll give Josh Canfield a ring today or maybe walk down to the office. He might have some ideas about what might happen to first editions. I've been meaning to drop in on him for some time anyway." He turned his chair around to the table again before adding, "You should, too, Cat. It's time for him to see your work."

Cat nodded and stopped at the sink instead of going out the door giving Edward a chance to elaborate on going to see Canfield. He looked as though he had more to say, but another short rap on the door postponed any further explanation. It was Lew, standing in the morning light, a sheepish smile on his face.

"Good morning," he said, peering around the doorframe, "I thought I might tag along if you don't mind. I hope the Wadsworths are holding up and if there is anything I can do to help, I'd like to. I've always wanted to tag along on your sleuthing adventures. Now I have time, too, and, you never know, I might surprise you with an astute observation or two." Before he sat down, he picked out a cup from the cupboard and filled it with coffee. He squinted at the pile of toast but let it be. "Any of that torte left?" No answer came from Cat. Her favorite breakfast was leftover dessert. The torte was gone. And within seconds so was Cat.

"Like two kinds of jewels, a vision for thieves"

from BLUEBERRIES
Robert Frost

Chapter 5

Edward called out after Cat, "If you happen to see Canfield, you might mention that I'm going to drop by. I'll call him."

"O.k." came a faint, distant reply. At the same moment, the telephone rang.

Edward reached across the table to the wall phone, picked it up, said hello and listened for a moment, "It's for you, Anthony." He handed the phone to Anthony.

Brows arched in surprise, "For me?" Anthony put the phone to his ear, harumphed into it, and listened a while before responding. "O.k. Get there as soon as you can." Putting the phone back to its place on the wall, he explained, "There's been a bad accident on Memorial Drive and Dicky'll be delayed getting to the Wadsworths. Looks like I'll be there for longer than I thought." Then he assured Lew, "Yes, come along. I'll be glad to have another point of view and another pair of eyes. I'll deputize you both!" he chuckled.

Before Anthony left the station earlier, he told Dicky-- Dicky Cronin, "his man Friday"--that even though it was unorthodox for non-police to accompany the detail to a crime scene, it was not unprecedented, and besides Edward would be seeing the Wadsworths as a friend, "so don't look shocked if you see Edward with me. I don't know for sure that he'll be coming anyway." He told Dicky how Edward had helped put him on the road to solving conundrums in the past just by offering a different perspective.

And now Lew was joining them too.

Oh, well, Dicky would understand. He was good at making people feel comfortable. He had a kind of Jimmy-Stewart-awkward and self-effacing posture, thought Anthony, that makes people smile and relax. Whatever it was, he was grateful for it especially when he himself often presented a less-than-patient facade. He would tell you it wasn't that he was impatient. He was just . . . well, maybe a little impatient. Mostly, he was in a hurry to get things moving. He liked "solved."

The three friends finished their coffee and put their cups in the sink. Edward and Lew watched while Anthony cleared the table, picked up the sponge from the sink and wiped some crumbs off into his hand before tossing the sponge back into the sink with a Celtic's shot. "Think that'll please her? Didn't you think she was overly touchy last night?" It was a rhetorical question and he answered it himself, "Maybe it was because Mark didn't show up or something?" Anthony looked at his watch as he gave his nose a quick rub with the back of his hand, "Let's go, it's almost nine."

They walked out the back door, down the path and the short distance down Brattle to the Wadsworth's. The three of them didn't fit across the narrow brick sidewalk so Anthony briskly led the way, reeling his head back and forth and commenting all the way. "These brick sidewalks are too narrow. Watch that curb! What are the Wadsworths' names again? I hope Dicky's not too late."

A few minutes later they reached the Wadsworth house, walked up the steps and rang the bell. Barbara and James Wadsworth greeted them warmly, showed them into the library, handed Anthony the inventory, and graciously left the room.

The three spent the better part of the morning in the library. Anthony noted facts about times and locks and window access when Jim Wadsworth showed him around the house. As Dicky hadn't shown up, Edward and Lew took over checking the inventory. Anthony was glad to have them along. The inventory was lengthy and sometimes the listings were obscure to him.

"What's a triptych?" Anthony asked and scratched his head as he pondered the inventory. "Sounds like travel arrangements."

Edward pointed to a small, three-sectioned, hinged, painted tablet of three Greek saints that stood on the bookshelf. "This is a triptych; it has three sections. A diptych has only two," he said.

"I see," said Anthony, but Edward wondered if he did.

The labored inventory checking was not a waste of time. During the course of the morning, they found that more than just the proposed bequest was missing. The two antique, ruby-handled pistols, three small, but priceless Fragonard miniatures, two autographed Twain first editions which were not going to the Museum, and a five-book set of Frost poetry, inscribed to the family and autographed, which had been earmarked for the Museum eventually but had not been included with the present donation, were added to the list.

Anthony called Goodspeed's, the Boston bookshop and well-known authority on rare and valuable books. The result was a quick education. "The Twain editions are not in the same class as the others. Collectors," he quoted the expert, "don't consider dog-eared, much used books very collectible--they're valuable to the owner, but not of the same worth as the pristine-condition, first editions are to the collectors. Goodspeed's asked for a list of the stolen books, which I'll have sent to them. They'll be on the lookout." He scribbled in his notebook.

"So," concluded Lew, "the Twain editions don't cut it by those standards, but all the rest do as they were not handled because--and this was a smart thing to do--there were duplicates shelved with the originals for reading and carrying around except for the Twain editions which they did not consider very valuable anyhow."

"Yes, and the Wadsworth grandchildren may have taken the Twain books from the library to read when they were visiting, and then just left them in a bedroom bookcase or some other infrequently used area where kids like to make a reading hide-a-way. I bet they'll be found in just such a place and as they were not part of the collection going to the Museum, we'll worry about them later."   It made sense to Anthony as he related his theory.

"Right" chimed in Edward, "I know that my boys both read from those editions when they were young. The books were made available to anyone, as long as they returned and respected them." He opened and closed a book in his hands. "It's usually the bindings that suffer, but as long as the page is there, the words are too; they don't fade or become weaker with reading." As an after-thought, Edward smiled, "I could even make a case for words getting stronger the more they're read."

As he spoke, Edward walked over to a wall filled with framed photos and studied them for a few minutes. Amid other family and friend photos was one of Dana and Jeanne Wadsworth with the Whitman twins when they were eight or nine years old. They all looked happy and fresh-faced and old-fashioned, standing on the front lawn, arms around each other's shoulders. Jeanne wore a wide-brimmed straw hat. The small fir tree in the picture had grown too—its branches now fanned overhead to more than ten feet.

Images of the twins, Rennie and Teddy, were looming more and more into Edward's thoughts, conversations and nostalgic recollections. Were these intrusions or were they harbingers of brighter days? Edward asked himself. Here, in the photos, they were children. How had they grown up—they were eighteen when he last saw them and though he tried to think of them as grown-ups, in his mind they were the boys in the photo. He vowed to find them and, if necessary, enlist aid to help him search. He wanted them to know he cared and was sorry he had been such a neglectful father, and, if he could, make it up to them. There were sizable legacies through Ann and himself; where else would the benefits go? He knew that Jeanne and Dana were married; he had seen their children tearing about the neighborhood when they visited. The grandchildren were just about the same age now as the twins had been in the photos. It made Edward even more aware of the passage of time.

James thanked them for coming and said, peering around the room as though he was looking at it for the first time, "It's a terrible feeling to know that some stranger has walked around your house, through your private spaces and worse, taken your possessions without a thought about how he might be disturbing your psyche." He paced the library floor as he rambled, glancing around and shaking his head. Then he pointed and said, "There's the display case for the pistols—why didn't they take the whole thing? The case was specially made to keep them in good condition and I oil them and would clean them, but the flannel lining seems to do the trick." He picked up the polished, rosewood case and shook it. Something fell to the floor. He stooped and picked up a small bullet, showing it to his audience. "It's silver, you know. There should be a couple more like it," he shook the box again, "but maybe they're in one of the pistol chambers. I recall something about that now.

Someone suggested they wouldn't tarnish if they were in the chamber. Sounds crazy now. I could be wrong. It was a while ago. One shouldn't leave bullets in guns . . . ever . . . for any reason."

"But people always do," said Anthony also shaking his head.

Barbara nodded and continued as though her husband's words had been hers, "I think the worst part is that we're not sure what's here and what's not. That's why we really appreciate your going over the inventory. I don't think we could do it. I know I would just keep getting more and more upset." She sniffed a little and said, "I never understood before what theft victims meant when they talked about being personally violated. Now I understand all too well."

When she paused, Anthony asked if either of them could think of anyone who had coveted anything in particular. He said, "For example, Edward would like to have those Frost books!" He gave a little chuckle showing he wasn't serious about Edward but wanted them to give it some thought.

Neither James nor Barbara could think of anything that had ever been said in anything more than jest. Friends had made jokes about their having the heirlooms out on display, but no one ever took it seriously. "They're all insured, of course." She paused, "I can't imagine why they didn't take the silver or some of the other obviously valuable things." She stood up, "I'm puzzled, but I'm glad!

They seem not to have ventured upstairs where they could have found my jewelry out on the dressing table and Jim's great-grandfather's gold cufflinks on his dresser." With that she left the room and returned a few minutes later with a pot of coffee and ginger snaps, and everyone sat down to go over the findings--or the "missings" as Barbara put it.

When Anthony asked who else might have keys, James explained, "We've had a combination lock on the front door for at least twenty years--it was the first I'd ever seen on an entryway. Before then, one of us was always losing or misplacing keys. After we had it installed, we never thought about it again. It took a lot of worry out of security and it's easy to use. I'm sure the extra expense of the initial installation has been saved many times over. There is no key to slip through a hole in a pocket and you don't have to find a place to hide it outside. A simple three number code and you're in! The alarm code is also a three number sequence." He shifted his coffee and crossed one ankle over his knee. "Don't tell anyone, but, it's the reverse of the lock code." He poked at the air with his finger and mumbled some numbers. "So, you see, there are no keys!"

They could think of no one except those who had to know, ". . . but there are probably quite a few of them," said Barbara. "There's Elise, the cleaning lady who comes on Fridays and has for at least twenty years and Mr. Cohan, the gardener, who comes when the yard needs doing, and the deliveryman from the Huron Market, who comes on Thursdays and leaves the order in the kitchen. He's nice enough to put away the things that need to be refrigerated." She said there were probably others too. Friends and relatives knew.

Anthony took copious notes and kept looking around as though he expected something to happen in the middle of the room. That Dicky never showed up hadn't helped his disposition. Checking the inventory had taken longer than expected, and Anthony impatiently tapped his foot.

Edward and Lew, however, were enjoying a dip into the past with the Wadsworths as they laughed about some of the escapades of the children. James reminded them of the time the four children had had a dog-bathing sale. "One of them," he said, "I think it was Jeanne, put too much of Barbara's expensive bubble bath into the dog's tub on the front lawn. I heard the commotion and stuck my head out the upstairs window. Huge bubbles were escaping the tub along with the dogs rolling and rubbing in the grass and dirt to rid themselves of the alien scent. I wish I had a video of it." He laughed, "I did run downstairs with my camera though!" He pointed to a photo on the wall of wet dogs and giggling children in a heap on the lawn. It could have been a Norman Rockwell scene.

"Have you heard from them recently?" asked Barbara. "One never knew what to expect when they were around." She was laughing and added, "They were never dull!"

Edward just smiled and shook his head.

With the inventory thoroughly checked, the time-line set, and names and telephone numbers of everyone they could think of who had access to the codes, they prepared to leave the Wadsworths, expressing positive hopes about finding everything.

"It would be prudent," Anthony ventured, "to have the codes to the lock and alarm changed." They agreed.

"We've never, in all the years we've had it, changed the numbers," James told them, "I don't think it ever occurred to me. Did you ever think about it, Barbara?"

"Never," she said. "Why would we? That's why we got the combination lock in the first place--so we wouldn't have to think about it again."

Edward asked to use the phone as the others were getting into their coats. "Hello, Joshua. Edward Whitman here. I'm going to be down that way and thought I might pry you loose for lunch . . . Fine . . . I'll be there before one."

Anthony pouted a little and said, "I was hoping you'd both be my guests for lunch today at a new Italian place near the station that I've tried and I think is very, very good." He rubbed his hands together.

"Another time, Anthony. I'll be in touch with you later. You'll be at the office?" Edward said good-bye and ambled off down Brattle with a noticeable spring in his step.

Lew had plans too. His editor, he said, was trying to hurry his latest book along before his theories were outdated. "Theories" he said, "--economic ones in particular--are always being outdated and recycled and outdated again. I'm challenging Adam Smith's concept of the division of labor and the theory that value comes from productive labor. It's ripening on the vine and I want to get it out there before it ripens and rots!" The editor was pressing him for finished chapters and Lew, being Lew, was obliging.

"Sometimes," he told Anthony, "I wish I hadn't promised to write this book. It will be the last and I'll be glad when it's finished." They both watched the retreating Edward, "Can you believe that's the same man we were pulling out of the doldrums last week?"

Anthony agreed it was a different Edward they saw parading down Brattle Street and he heard Lew say softly, "I just hope it lasts."

A scent of ripeness from over a wall.
And come to leave the routine road
And look for what had made me stall,

from UNHARVESTED
Robert Frost

Chapter 6

I'm sure Cat is wrong about Canfield, Edward thought, as he strolled down Brattle Street. The dull morning had transformed into an A-number-one beautiful New England spring day—which Cat was wrong about and he made a mental note to remind her of it. Tit for tat. Scilla and crocus dotted the almost-green lawns with blue and yellow. Birds chirped in the leafing shrubs and trees. Edward picked up his pace, swinging his arms, and it felt natural when he turned the corner into his old building and walked down the familiar corridor. He knocked on the half-open door.

"Come in." said a voice from within. Joshua Canfield rose from the desk and stretched out his hand, "It's good to see you, Edward. Sit down."

"Just thought I'd see how things were going. I'm not keeping you from any appointments?"

"No. My calendar is not very full. I have a light teaching schedule this term. I seldom see students here. I don't know why. I invite them."

"Maybe if you left the door open?"

"It's always open; and I never lock it. Can't," he shrugged a good-natured shrug, "I don't have a key. I was never given one and never felt the need to ask for one."

"I know. I never used one either." Edward had another thought, "But this is a different time and things have changed. And though I never locked the door, Mr. Carlson locked the building up tight at six o'clock every evening, and if I needed to get back in or forgot something, he was always at the front door within a few minutes after I rang the bell. Mr. Carlson kept an eagle eye on everything." He paused, "I understand he's no longer here."

"He left last year. With all the budget cuts, I guess the administration felt that a full-time janitor was one of the jobs that could be eliminated when Mr. Carlson retired, so he hasn't been replaced. Well, Mr. Nuffield comes in the morning for a few hours to open up and again in the afternoon to close and lock the outside door. And, maybe they were right; I haven't any complaints. My wastebasket still gets emptied. There's seldom anyone here after seven in the evenings anyhow, and I've never wished to get in when I couldn't."

"You know," said Edward squinting as though trying to remember, "I think I still have a couple of keys that might just be the keys to the office and the front door. I'll dig them out and bring them over."

Edward suggested walking into the Square for lunch. Canfield pulled his coat and hat from the coat tree, closed the door, and moved the hand on the door sign clock to, "I'll be back at 3." The two poets walked down the brick path cutting through the Quad teasing with spring and, like a secret garden was about to burst into bloom. They walked silently as though each was adrift in the meter and rhythm that supersaturated the balmy spring air.

They spent almost two hours lunching in a quiet corner of the Harvest Restaurant discussing the poetry contest, the student anthology Canfield was promoting, and the paper he was to present at the Spring Robert Frost Colloquium at the University. "You're coming, of course," said Canfield.

Edward answered, "Yes. Delighted." He really was, but he wondered why Joshua hadn't invited him to be a judge for the poetry contest. He probably will, he thought.

Back in the office, Edward steered the conversation to first editions and the theft at the Wadsworth house. Canfield hadn't heard about it and was shocked and upset by the news. "I hope whoever took them doesn't destroy them," he said and stood up and walked around his desk. His eyes scanned the bookshelves. He reached into a bookcase beside the door, pulled out a book and handed it to Edward. "I suppose I had better find a better place for this. I like to have it at the ready when someone says narrative poetry is dull."

He handed Edward a first edition of Archibald MacLeish's "Conquistador" signed by MacLeish and inscribed to Canfield. He said, "As you well know, original and first editions have a mystique that inspires even the most prosaic of students. It's a shame that the Wadsworths didn't hand them over years ago. The books really shouldn't be in a private collection; don't you agree?" Edward nodded vigorously and tried not to look guilty about already knowing Canfield's posture on first editions. "The museums know so much about preservation techniques they should be empowered to keep them not only for posterity but for use by scholars as well." Edward leafed through the pages and returned it to Canfield who placed "Conquistador" down on his desk and patted it fondly. "But, what good is a book that's never opened? It might as well be a doorstop!" He chuckled.

Canfield spent a few minutes bemoaning the fact that scholarships and endowments were so few and said he wished there were more incentives available to this department. "That's why I think this poetry contest and the anthology are so important. It will draw attention to us and give the University something to point to and declare a product of its faith."

Edward praised Cat and her upcoming volume and Joshua agreed wholeheartedly. He said, "She shows great promise and I think she will take her place among the notables of the decade. I hope she will enter the contest."

As Edward walked home, he thought about Cat's comments of the previous evening. He had seen in Canfield none of the unpleasantness to which Cat had alluded. Canfield seemed eager to see students and had some good ideas for publishing the student anthology. In fact, in his mind's eye, Edward pictured Canfield and could find nothing that was objectionable. He was thoroughly neutral and medium: height, build, grey hair, blue eyes, conservative suit and tie-- unremarkable in all areas except one that didn't show. He far excelled everyone in his field. His treatises on Frost had been published worldwide and he was renowned for his insight and understanding of the poet and his life.

Cat was right, though, about his attitude on first editions and, Edward, after briefly considering that the stolen editions might be lost forever, was inclined to agree with Canfield that the treasures really did belong to posterity and should be kept in a safe environment.

He enjoyed the short walk home and the burgeoning season all around him in purple, yellow and blue hidden for the interminable winter and now sprouting, eager to show off. And, more, he felt a new spring in his step. He wasn't dancing but his pace had picked up and he raised his head to smile at the newly leafing magnolias.

As soon as he entered the house, he looked for his old keys. They weren't on the key rack inside the back door and they weren't in the desk drawer in the study. In a flash of revelation he remembered something that was tugging at his memory: the keys were in one of the boxes now piled in the cellar.

He opened the cellar door, switched on the light and hesitated at the top of the stairs. He didn't like to go into the cellar. There were too many of Ann's things down there. Memories of happier and familial times wafted from the chests and boxes, and spirits lurked in the corners waiting to pounce and deflate his very essence. He remembered the last time he was in the cellar he had felt that if he had lingered, he would be overpowered and he would never be able to summon the fortitude or strength to get back up the stairs.

He steeled himself and told himself not to be so foolish; there was nothing there but boxes . . . memories . . . and maybe some guilt. No demons lurking in the corners. He slowly descended the stairs, walked directly to the most recent additions, and started to search. It wasn't long before he found the address-date books in the top of one box, reached in, rattled around for the keys and pulled them out. He turned them over in his hand and hoped they were the right keys.

Edward mounted the stairs, but before he switched off the light and closed the door to the cellar and the ghosts, he couldn't resist a cursory glance backward, like Orpheus banishing forever his Eurydice into the black hole of Hades. He hoped Ann's spirit was free.

As the door clicked shut, he realized with a start that it was after four o'clock in the afternoon and it was the first time he had thought about Ann all day. That was a record, and he visualized a heavy mantle lifting from his shoulders. It was still there, but it was getting lighter. He wanted to be rid of that inhibiting load. He wanted it to float away and take the malaise with it. The time had come to bury his grief and anger alongside Ann. That's what she would have wanted—he knew that. She had said to him once, and he always remembered it: "Turn the page, start a new chapter; the old will finish itself." After all, he thought, she didn't leave me alone and in despair on purpose or to punish me.

She had been philosophical, too, when the doctors at MGH had given her, at the most, five years longer and maybe she would see sixty. Her last words on the day after her sixty-fifth birthday before she slipped into a sleep from which she would never awaken were, "We fooled them all."

He would always miss his muse, his best friend, confidant, and faithful lover and he was working on forgiving her for leaving him. He knew they had been a self-indulgent couple. The only clouds that had cast shadows onto their comfortable sphere were the heartbreaking ordeals with the twins. During Ann's last years Edward had pushed the twins out of his mind to concentrate on her needs. The drugs had made her fuzzy-minded so he told her only things that would bring a smile to her lips.

Now, when Edward thought about Ann and the twins, it was in an out-of-body tableau; as though he were looking down on a scene from someone else's life, and like the boxes in the basement, he closed the door and turned out the light on them. But he still felt guilty and in a frustrating turmoil. Putting off dealing with the matter and fooling himself into believing that somehow the problem would be solved without action on his part only made the impasse steeper and slipperier. He rued the wasted years. How strange it was that he could see so clearly now what others must have seen all along. He must find and ask the boys for forgiveness.

The front doorbell chimed as he closed the cellar door. It was Lew, and Edward let him in. "I just stopped by for my scarf; I think I left it here the other night." He opened the hall closet, "Yes, I thought so. Here it is. I don't need it today--but I might tomorrow." He hung it loosely around his neck.

"You know," he said, "I was thinking about those antique pistols--how beautiful they are and how fascinating their history must be. I can picture them being brandished by Porthos or Aramis wearing a plumed hat and a long white billowy-sleeved shirt: I challenge you to a duel at dawn!" He swung around in a fencer's stance and pointed at Edward, who laughed too and met him with a lunge. They both doubled up with laughter and sat on the stairs breathing heavily from their little charade. "I can't imagine why the display box was not taken too. It is lovely rosewood, lined with deep red flannel—a perfect repository and sure to keep them safe from scratches and tarnish. Remember how Rennie was so intrigued with them? It was only because Teddy told on him that Rennie didn't leave that birthday party with one of them in his pocket!"

Edward nodded, "I remember. It was a beautiful piece of work—if you can call a weapon beautiful. James told me then that the pistols had been in the family since his great—or maybe another great or two--grandfather used one of them in a duel in France. I think he was making that part up!"

Edward defended: "I don't think Rennie was going to steal it. I think he just wanted to keep it for a while. That sounds like a rationalization. I guess I just don't know. Rennie was always unpredictable." He looked straight at Lew and said, "I do know that my delusory practice of excluding the twins from my conscious thoughts and trying to deny that they even exist has been catching up with me and making up for lost time. They've been popping into my head more and more lately. Talking about them today with the Wadsworths and seeing the photos of some of the good times made me realize that I will have no peace until I've settled my debt. And, too, you know I have no other heirs. He frowned. "Maybe they wouldn't be interested in this old house."

Edward did not look happy but Lew did not stop him or interrupt. It was, after all, just what Edward needed to do— recognize that he had to come to terms with reality and forgive both the twins and himself. "I wasn't a good father. I know that now. I should have been more involved with them day-to-day instead of trying to step in with discipline I didn't know how to administer. But Ann always said it was easier to deal with problems if she didn't have to consider another point of view; mine, she meant. It was hard enough, she said, to sort out an answer appropriate to both boys without having another option, even if it were more reasonable."

Lew offered some solace, "I think you were more liberal dealing with the boys--more understanding than she. Probably you remembered some of the scrapes we got into as boys and tried to walk in their moccasins. Of course, they were so charming and attractive that none of us knew how they were manipulating us. I was taken in more than once."

Edward shook his head, "No. I took the easy way. I see that now." He went on to explain, "Early on, when I bowed out of the disciplinarian role, I gave up, too, trying to teach them good citizenship and loyalty and honor. And, I have felt guilty about not even trying to go after them when Anthony used his powers and traced them to Central America."

Lew spoke softly: "You couldn't have left Ann in her advanced state. She needed you more. Retrospect—especially after so many years—blots out the everyday logistical anxieties that plague one trying to cope with the final days of a loved one. There are doctor appointments, therapy sessions, visiting hours, everything! Stop torturing yourself. It's anybody's guess as to where those boys went then or where they are now. It was no one's fault they had each other, and that's all they ever needed. Remember how they used to tease and taunt classmates? It's strange isn't it, that though love was what drove you and Ann, Teddy and Rennie seemed to skirt the emotions that held families and friends together. Maybe, wherever they are, they're learning."

Lew fiddled with the scarf hanging around his neck and, changing both his tone and the subject, said "How was lunch?"

"Fine, fine." Edward's tone changed too as he said, "Joshua has a lot on his plate right now. He's promoting not only the poetry contest but also an anthology of the contest poetry winners and contributors along with hosting the spring poetry colloquium. He's hoping all this activity will boost the department to the front of the budget committee's minds." He looked absently beyond Lew and said it was strange that Canfield didn't ask him to be a judge for poetry contest. Maybe he hasn't chosen a panel yet."

He fished in his pocket and held up the key ring. "Joshua doesn't have a key to the office and I'm pretty sure that one of these is it and that the other is to the front door of the building. I ought to take them right down to him before I forget or misplace them again," he chuckled.

Lew offered, "I'm on my way to the University now: more medical and retirement papers to sign. I'll be happy to drop them off," Edward handed the keys to Lew who dropped them into his coat pocket. "Thanks," he said, "That's one thing I can cross off my list." Lew was almost out the door when Edward placed a hand on his arm. "You know, Lew, I must make my peace with the twins."

"Yes. I've been hoping you'd get around to that. If you need help in any way, I'm right next door.

". . . I would not come in.
I meant not even if asked;
And I hadn't been.

from COME IN
Robert Frost

Chapter 7

It was early afternoon and Edward sat awkwardly at the small table that usually stood beside the wing chair in the living room. The table wasn't big enough to be used as a desk but he had his notebook and some papers strewn across the small surface anyway. He fretted a bit trying to fit everything into an impossible space, picking things up, squaring papers and then hiding them under others. I should pick up everything, he thought, and take it all into the study. But he didn't do it. He liked being able to look onto the terrace through the French doors, and see spring pushing its way into the yard. There wasn't much yet but he could see green shoots and bits of color not in full bloom. It made him happy to be alive and glad for the end to a long, cold and unproductive winter. Spring beckoned a new beginning all around.

He pulled his notebook onto his lap and with a red pencil started ticking off entries on a list when Cat and Mark breezed into the living room and melted into the old, overstuffed chintz-covered sofa. As he glanced up, he thought, there's more than the book going on with these two. Best not to remark on perceptions, though, because one never knew how these young people would react; and maybe he was wrong.

To Cat he said, "I saw Professor Canfield. I really think you're wrong about him. He told me he'd like to see more of his students in his office. He seemed really eager to help anyone who needs or wants guidance or even just to air ideas. I don't know where you got the impression that he's aloof." He glanced at Cat quickly and added, "I'm sure you've misread or at least have misinterpreted him. I think he's just shy."

Cat listened and squirmed as though trying to settle into a comfortable spot as Edward went on, "I hope you'll take advantage of his expertise; he's a fine poet with a fine mind. And he certainly has taken on a big project with the contest and the anthology which he hopes will generate some overdue recognition for the department and make more scholarship and grant money available." He put down his pencil and notebook, "How's the book coming?"

"We're making progress." Cat impatiently shrugged Mark's arm off her shoulder, got up, pulled a portfolio from her stack of books and papers and placed a few sheets on the table in front of Edward. There wasn't enough space for them either but she just picked up the portfolio, opened it and put it on top of everything else, "Some of the images Mark has caught with his omniscient lens are perfect." Mark's face lit up. "And some just are not what I had in mind." With that Mark's mouth turned down, and he picked up his camera, aimed it at Cat and snapped a few shots.

Mark spoke lightly offering an explanation, "There are only three shots that are giving us trouble and I'm sure we'll get them right in the end." He seemed a little tentative, "Cat could change a few words." He ducked as Cat picked up a pillow and threw it, hitting him in the face. It looked like a playful gesture but Edward thought Cat had put a little too much vigor into it.

"Maybe I could, but I'm not going to." Her voice had a caustic, pedantic tone. "Every word has significance and each word bears a sententious relation to the next. If I start changing, I'll have to change, and change, and change. Oh, forget it!" She turned to Mark, "I don't want to talk about it. You wouldn't understand; you don't understand the poet's mind." She hopped to her feet and offhandedly and lightly said, "Anyone else for a sandwich?" Without waiting for an answer, she hurried through to the kitchen and started banging around.

Mark watched her burst out the door. He turned to Edward with a little shrug. "She's worrying too much. I always know what she wants. I just don't always have the concrete image at hand. And, besides, I see photography as poetry in image and form; to me it even rhymes and has meter." As though he was conducting an orchestra, his hands dipped and swayed as he painted a rhythmic cadence.

Edward nodded in agreement and tried to hide his surprise. He hadn't really ever noticed Mark before or maybe he hadn't ever listened to him. Or, maybe, Edward thought, he's just always been eclipsed by Cat, and, now, after all these months, he's getting more comfortable around here. Whatever the reason, Edward made a quick resolution to be more solicitous of this talented individual who seemed dimmed in the shadow of a cynosure which is not an auspicious space to occupy. It reminded him of the twins' situation. One of them was always clouded in the shade of the other and most of the time, he remembered, Teddy was in the shadow of Rennie's braggadocio.

In a twinkling that didn't seem long enough for her to have done anything at all, Cat burst back into the room as tempestuously as she had left. Unsettled, stormy, Edward liked to joke, was a normal forecast for Cat. She had a tray piled with mugs, a plateful of grilled cheese sandwiches, a jar of dill pickles, and a pot of coffee. She placed the tray squarely on the coffee table and then walked to Edward to peer over his shoulder. Edward noticed that her annoyance—If that was indeed what it had been—had disappeared as Mark paired some of the photos and the verses. Both Cat and Mark beamed when Edward nodded and hummed approval. "You two have done a great deal since I last saw this, it's really coming together. And I like the juxtaposition of the black and white in the snow verse. Yes, I think you've got it. I sound like Henry Higgins!" he chuckled.

Edward moved to sit with them at the coffee table and poured himself coffee while Cat and Mark made short work of the sandwiches. The subject of the theft arose and they all rehashed the Wadsworth's bad luck. Edward told them about the discovery of the losses of the pistols and the Fragonards. He said, "We're hoping the Twain editions will be found in the house. My biggest concern of course, is the Frost set. I hope nothing has happened to it and that it will be found intact and not broken up and sold off individually."

"The real question is," said Mark, "Who would risk stealing things that would either be difficult to sell or that everyone knew about? Like the theft at the Gardner Museum, those paintings can never be displayed anywhere. And I shouldn't think there would be a big market for those old pistols. Still, I suppose a collector, or a fanatic, would pay a good price for something even if the provenance weren't clear. Of course, someone may have requisitioned them. Which is my theory about the Gardner heist. Someone with a lot of money wanted them and someone else knew how to get them. A completed equation."

"Don't forget the first editions. The same kind of reasoning could apply to them." Cat interrupted Mark as though she meant to stop him and his prognostications. She walked over to the photos and verses, eyed them from a different angle, then picked them up and placed them gently in the portfolio, tied it, and put it next to the sofa where Mark's bulging pack was overflowing with papers and an envelope of photos. "What are these? Anything I should see?" she asked, picking up the yellow photo envelope.

"You can if you want. They're just the candids I took at the Government School the other night. They didn't come out too well, but there are a few good ones of some sixties-looking characters with scruffy beards and long hair, though I doubt if they are old enough to be hippies. I thought there would be a really heated discussion and I had hoped to get some earthy emotions on film, but everyone kept a rein on language and feelings—it was a very civilized discussion." He raised his eyebrows to question Edward, "Not like the old days, huh?"

Edward answered with a small smile and a shrug of his shoulders as if to say he didn't understand the question.

Cat thumbed quickly through the pictures without focusing on them, "Some of these are pretty good. I see what you mean about the hippies." She said offhandedly and started to put the photos back into the envelope before turning her attention to Edward, "I know I usually cook on Tuesdays but do you think you could manage with some cold chicken if I leave some broccoli soup ready for the microwave and some biscuits? There's a reception tonight to introduce three new department members. It says 'buffet' on the invitation, so you can imagine what our dinner will be like." She grimaced in anticipation.

Edward nodded, "Fine. Is there enough for Lew and Anthony to join me?" Cat nodded and smiled.

Not long ago he had been trying to think of ways to get away from everyone and today he was eager to join them. He knew everyone had been tip-toeing around him, trying to prod him into some kind of response or action that he had been pig-headed enough not to acknowledge. It was as though he had been suspended in limbo for two years.

Why hadn't he seen it before? There were two things that had always lifted him. One was his poetry. That alone should have saved him. But he hadn't picked up his pen since his retirement. It was a clue he had ignored. And he had always known, that he was at his best when he was engaged intellectually unraveling a mystery whether it was literary, political, economic, or criminal. Those times in the past when he had helped Anthony Argus were times he liked to remember.

He heard Cat say, "Plenty for everyone." Then, "Oh, rats! Murphy's law prevails!" She threw up her hands in disgust. The photos that she had been carefully replacing in the envelope skittered out of her hands while she was talking and scattered over the sofa. "There wasn't even the most remote possibility that those things should have fallen out like that! I replaced the flap and everything." She hurriedly picked up the photos, evened the edges, and replaced them in their envelope. This time she opened Mark's pack pocket, shoved them in, and zippered it closed. "There!"

Edward heard the door close as Cat and Mark left, but he was already rewinding his memory to a time years ago when he and Anthony had been deep in another theft case. At Edward's insistence, Anthony had finally gotten a search warrant for that old warehouse on Franklin Street. He tried to remember what had put him on to it in the first place but couldn't. What he did remember was the excitement pulsing through him when he stood in the background as a squad rapped on the door, made their way in, and found the stolen merchandise still in numbered packing cases. Inspiring! He smiled to himself recalling the incident.

A while ago he wrote a short bit for the *Chronicle* about Cambridge and its anomalies: it's a mix of town and gown that served to unite a diverse population into a cohesive whole. Cambridge is still a small town with small town ties, but there is a global perspective that tempers the otherwise insular *mise en scene* of an old New England town.   And Edward was going to resume his part in it again.

He finished a final gulp of coffee before setting the mug down on the tray to take back into the kitchen. He sat back and thought about how lucky he was to have wonderful friends. They believed in him, and more, he was beginning to believe in himself again.

"The moral is, it hardly need be shown,
All those who try to go it sole alone,
Too proud to be beholden for relief,
Are absolutely sure to come to grief."

from HAEC FABULA DOCET - Moral -
Robert Frost

Chapter 8

Edward's afternoon, while not exactly frittered away, was almost gone and he had not accomplished much of anything. That was going to change.

Too long he had pushed the most important things he meant to accomplish to the back of his mind—almost out of his mind altogether. He was going to pick up his pen again and begin a new page with revelations he hadn't acknowledged before: nothing can take the place of friends or family. He *must*, no *will*, find the twins, initiate a tranquil and harmonious rapprochement, and ask them to forgive him and, also work on forgiving himself: that's what Ann would have wanted. And there was forgiveness due there too. She would have been unhappy with his unwillingness to accept her death. He saw his resolve in big, bold red letters: FIND THE TWINS AND MAKE ATONEMENT

The light was beginning to fade—it was four-thirty already. Edward opened the icebox door and started to take out the cold chicken when the phone rang.

It was Anthony, "Lew and I will be right over," he said in Edward's ear, "and I saw Cat, so I know your fabulous cook has left you on your own tonight. We won't take no for an answer. That new Italian restaurant I told you about was just written up in the *Chronicle* so it won't be my own private cucina for much longer. We'll be there in a minute . . .o.k.?" Anthony left no space between his words.

"I wasn't going to say no. In fact, I was just going to call to invite you and Lew here." replied Edward. "But that sounds better. There's nothing like good rich Italian food to clog up my old arteries." Edward was chuckling. "Where are you? I'll meet you," he listened for a moment, replaced the phone, put the chicken back in the icebox, donned his coat and hat, walked out the door and down the front path, feeling better than he had in ages.

Like most people testing a new endeavor, he hurried to leave the tired routines behind. Those oppressive ghosts had tied him up and tired him out for too long. He felt a buoyancy in his soul lift him right off the ground and his step down the path to meet his friends had an urgent lightness to it. His heels clicked in a poetic rhythm. He liked the sound and hummed with it. He wasn't dancing—but very close to it!

Within seconds Anthony's car pulled up at the end of the walk. The door opened for him to get in.

Edward and Lew greeted each other with, "That was fast!" Edward barely struggled getting into the front seat.

"You know, Lew, I can sit in the back much more easily than you--with those knees of yours," Edward being solicitous was another change. For the past two years, he had just accepted things as they were no matter how his friends had tried to make things easier and more comfortable for him. And, of course, he didn't much think about others' comfort or pain.

"I say, Edward," said Lew, "are you sure you haven't taken some of that sulphur and molasses on the side? I'm still trudging along with feet of clay and you're tap dancing on top of the world!"

"You're right, I do feel a new lease on life. But it's not sulphur and molasses that's responsible. Maybe it's spring. I've been noticing things I've neglected, like that old suit. You were right. I'm going to get rid of it and start wearing newer ones that have just been hanging in the closet. Do you like this one?" He stuck out his arm revealing a grey tweed. "It's as though a vise has been loosened from my brain and I can think clearly. At least I'm beginning. I've made some major decisions." Edward's words had a vitality that had been lacking for so long. "How about you? I think you've lost more weight. Don't you think so, Anthony?"

Anthony said he thought Lew looked just fine. They drove along Mass. Avenue for a few blocks in comfortable silence. Edward pretended not to notice the knowing glances between Lew and Anthony. They didn't know yet that he had vowed never again to slip into what he now viewed as a self-pitying morass. Ann was gone and she would not be back and the university chair was filled with an impressive presence. All he had needed was a sign, something to show him how he had been avoiding life. The complexity and uniqueness of the

Wadsworth theft had been the slit in the clouds. He was at his best when he was focused on and immersed in a perplexing enigma. He was beginning to gain some perspective. He knew he did not have the time for malingering and feeling sorry for himself.

They passed the Police Station and slid into a parking space on the Avenue just around the corner from the restaurant.

The flamboyant owner, Tonio, greeted them with big smiles and flourishes of his expressive hands ushering Anthony to play the genial host by leading the way to a table in a corner close to the window of the little twelve-table bistro tucked in a doorway just off Mass. Avenue. He picked off the "reserved" sign and motioned for Lew and Edward to sit. The waiter, clad in typical Italian restaurant style with white, starched, short jacket and black pants, black, shined shoes and a bright welcome. Umberto, was already at the table to pour wine and Anthony tasted it with the flair of a sommelier. It was perfect; he smacked his lips and closed his eyes. Umberto, happy with the pronouncement of "perfect" poured for everyone. They raised their glasses. Anthony offered a simple toast with a big smile, "To the troyka!"

The antipasto disappeared as Anthony poured more wine for Edward and Lew, being careful to measure his own intake. "I think you'll like the veal. I should have invited Cat. She would really appreciate the gourmet sauces and probably would have duplicated them for us in her magic kitchen." Anthony's fork accented his words.

"She and Mark were obliged to attend a reception for three new members of the department." Edward allowed, "I'm sure she'd rather be here."

The small room overflowed with diners and waiters. The attentive, white-jacketed Umberto hovered at Anthony's elbow, replenishing the wine, clearing the table and replacing crispy Italian bread in the basket. He served the veal fettuccini with an Italian flourish of pride, as though he had cooked it himself. Umberto seemed to take pleasure in serving these good friends who enjoyed good food and each other's company. They were well into their second round of espresso before anyone broached the subject of the Wadsworth theft.

Lew cupped his chin in his hand, "If I were going to go to the trouble of breaking into a house," he paused and said in a more confidential tone, "I would have taken some of the other valuables that were right out in plain sight."

"I agree. Like the Paul Revere silver service," said Edward.

"Or the Ming or Tang, or whatever dynasty it is, vases on the mantel" joined Anthony. "Or the entire pistol collection. There are several others, not jeweled, but valuable. An early Colt." As an aside he added, " I don't know why anyone would want to collect firearms though—I would be happy if all guns and firearms were shipped into outer space—or just destroyed."

"I think motive is the key here," said Lew. "and who would break into a house without a reason—it certainly was not to keep us busy testing motives. Perhaps they didn't know what a treasure trove they broke into and were, perhaps, coming back later after they found a way to carry things away. Maybe they didn't have a car.

Anthony sighed and rolled his eyes, "Motive is always the key. It's just that motive is not always apparent, is it?" He forced a smile across the table and nodded.

Earlier that afternoon when Dicky Cronin returned to the station from his Memorial Drive tie-up Anthony brought Dicky up to date on the morning at the Wadsworth's and told him that while he liked having Lew involved he wasn't sure he had the patience for a beginner and hoped that this investigation was not going to get bogged down with too many fingers in the broth. Right now, enjoying the evening, he felt a little guilty about his remarks and read more offense into his words than he had intended.

"I guess that's obvious to you," Lew apologized, "but it seems to me that the motive is the most important part of any crime and there doesn't seem to be one. I can't imagine a reasonable one for this. What thief would not grab valuables in plain sight?" After a pause he added, "And what kind of a thief would stop to fix a snack?!"

Anthony was quick, "I don't know about the snack, but perhaps the thieves just couldn't carry everything or hadn't come prepared to take heavy items or intended to return or were interrupted and like you said, maybe they didn't have a car available. There are any number of reasons."

Lew said, "The common motives for all crime, I think, are greed, envy and revenge. A greedy thief would not leave valuable stuff no matter how cumbersome it was. I guess envy is reasonable sometimes, but not here, I think. The Wadsworths are well off, but they seem unassuming and share as part of their nature—the Heineken gift, for example. And, I can't imagine, nor could the Wadsworths, any reason for revenge."

Anthony said, "It's important to keep everything in perspective: What we know. What we suspect. And, Lew, you're right. Motive is the key. It's sorting it out that always proves difficult." He played with the espresso cup, swirling the dregs around and sipping off the last of it. "Once you know why, who is usually close behind!"

"I don't mean to contradict," Edward interjected, "but isn't it usually the other way about. If you know who, you know why?

"No, I think it's usually why first, then who comes after. For instance, if only the Frost books had been taken I would say to myself that the thief wanted these books for himself and then I would go to Berkeley Street and arrest you!"

Everyone laughed. "But," said Edward, "what if you found the books at Goodspeeds. Say they had been sold before anyone knew they were missing. You would know the "why"— for monetary gain. But you wouldn't know the "who."

"What it boils down to," ventured Lew, "is that there is no sure formula. Otherwise, of course, you would just follow the recipe and arrest the perpetrator. Right?

Anthony motioned to Umberto for another round of espresso. "You have to separate facts from speculation. What speculations and conclusions are unfounded? And, in this case, we don't know much except that the theft took place and what was stolen. There were a few fingerprints in the kitchen that couldn't be matched. Still, it's early days yet and we know more than we did." He watched Lew to make sure his feelings had mended—if, in fact they had been damaged at all.

Edward said, "When I saw Canfield today, I asked him what he thought about a market for the books. He said he didn't know of one--everyone he knew who might wish they had them, like me, wouldn't employ such methods of obtaining them and then wouldn't give them up if they ever did get their hands on them. He was very concerned that they might be destroyed and lost to future generations. Cat was right about Canfield's posture on first editions. The paintings, we know, of course, would bring a tidy sum. I don't know about the pistols."

"How about the rubies in the handles?" Anthony asked. "When I think of rubies, it's along with diamonds and emeralds and crown jewels. I suppose they could be removed from the handles easily."

Edward thought for a moment, "There are different grades of rubies, just like there are inferior grades of diamonds. I had a chance to handle one of the pistols up close once and though it was impressive and beautiful—I'm not a gemologist, of course—I suspect the rubies were not high grade, but more valuable as part of the pistols." He pushed his chair back and said, "That was an excellent dinner, Anthony, I enjoyed every bite."

At eleven o'clock Umberto whispered to Anthony that Tonio's would be closing soon. Would they like anything more, like another espresso? They all looked at their watches and shook their heads. Anthony gave up his credit card.

A good time was had by all: testing the other deadly sins—sloth, anger, lust, and pride and improvising scenarios that amused each other, but as they couldn't come up with anything realistic or appropriate, they were ready to call it a night. They left Tonio's with full stomachs and light hearts. Tonio, smiling broadly with the compliments from the troyka, ushered them out with hearty handshakes and said he hoped to see them again soon.

Anthony dropped Edward and Lew off, "Keep thinking!"

They heard Anthony's car drive off as they walked the path between their houses, Lew said good night, pausing at Edward's door and placing his hand on his friend's shoulder before continuing down the walk to his own door. Edward called his good night after him just as he had done for more than a half century. He took out his key and mused about his friend as he fitted it into the lock.

It was curious, perhaps poetic, that their names were so alike. Edward Lawrence Whitman and Laurence Edward Woodridge had ties that went back to kindergarten where their teachers had dubbed them the dauntless duo. They were as much like brothers as any brothers ever were. When they were small, they were both blonds with blue eyes and cherubic faces. They were the same height and had the same sturdy build. More, they thought alike and they were able to answer for each other and finish each other's sentences. They were always on the highest rungs of the jungle gym, organizing the great jumps over schoolyard puddles, building the biggest and best equipped snow forts and always the last two back in from recess.

He smiled as he remembered that in the first grade they had been assigned to different rooms. That wasn't in their plans and at recess that first day, they walked away from school. After several frantic hours of searching, they had been found holed up in the playhouse behind the Whitman house, reading in the hammocks and eating cookies. Unfazed by the search and the scolding, they said they weren't going back to school until they were where they belonged: together in the same room.

It took some policy bending and stretching to get them back to school in the same classroom but no one ever doubted that it wasn't the right solution and no one tried to separate them again.

Later they both chose the same university and ended up roommates in the same resident house. They vied for the same seat in crew. In the end, Lew, with his constancy and endurance sat in the stroke seat of the boat and Edward, sturdier and stronger, sat in the six seat. It proved an enviable combination and their boat won the spring race against their archrivals from New Haven three years in a row.

Recently they were reminiscing as they watched the rowers on the Charles River and Lew reminded Edward how uncluttered their lives had been then during those idyllic days when they saw goals clearly and gave their hearts and souls to a cause. "If only one could gain experience without living through it," Lew had said as they stopped on the bridge to watch the swift current hurry on its journey to meet the sea.

Lew, Edward thought, was the only person who really knew him and he was the only person who really knew Lew. Their bonds were strong. Who would have thought that those inseparable five-year-olds would, in their waning years, still be important to each other.

Anthony, he conceded, was a good addition—making up the troyka—and knew them pretty well. But Anthony's bonds were more elastic. They stretched and snapped back with the situation, changing the shape of both questions and answers.

Sometime later during the week, when Cat and Lew talked about how great it was to see Edward acting human again, she said, "I'd like to think it's my book, but I'm pretty sure it's the tangle and intrigue of the Wadsworth theft that wound him up and started him ticking."

Lew, always the diplomat, replied, "I think it's a combination of things." But he, too, felt the heady mystery of the theft figured prominently. It occurred to him that he should start looking about for other mysteries or problems that needed mind-absorbing solutions.

"Funny," Lew said, "that we didn't think of it before, that what Edward needed was a problem with an illusive solution. One that would exercise his 'little grey cells' as another distinguished mystery solver always said."

**"We make ourselves a place apart
Behind light words that tease and
flout . . ."**

**from REVELATION
Robert Frost**

Chapter 9

While the troyka was enjoying Italian *haute cuisine*, across the Square, Cat was not so fortunate. The department reception took place in a room at the faculty club that smelled warmly of furniture polish and faintly of cigars. Smoking was now prohibited in all the university buildings. Cat used to like going to the club. It made her feel mature and cool to be an elite part of academia, and at first she enjoyed the food. After a while she found it started to all taste the same; and now she dreaded it.

Mark got her to admit that the buffet was not as bad as she had expected. "It's just so uninspired and tasteless." She messed around with the fork on her plate and finally put the dish down. "And speaking of uninspired," she said without raising her eyes, "there's Canfield and he's coming this way." Turning to the table she remembered Edward's words in defense of Canfield and silently vowed not to be so opinionated about what she saw as Canfield's unapproachable bearing. She'd give him the opportunity to let him change her mind. It could only help. Maybe she never gave him a chance in the first place. She turned as he approached and greeted him with an outstretched hand and an almost genuine smile.

"Hello, Professor Canfield. We were just wending our way around this awful food to you. Have you met our new colleagues yet?"

"They've been pretty much tied up and I haven't been able to edge my way through to welcome them, but I'm looking forward to it. One of them, Mary McMahon, is a poet. Do you know her? I would think she and you would have a lot in common—you both have that strong sense of feminism and a silver tongue to help the cause along." Canfield smiled shyly and continued, "She has already submitted an entry to the poetry contest. I hope you will, too, Cat."

"Perhaps I shall." She smiled, realizing flattery was winning her over, and instead of balking decided to take advantage of it. "Do you think I could come by with the latest draft of my book? Professor Whitman says it's ready for you to look at." She turned to include Mark. "I'd like you to meet my collaborator and the photographer for my book—our book— Mark Collins. Mark wants me to change some words to fit the pictures," she laughed and rolled her eyes. "I'd really appreciate any input you can give me." Canfield switched his wine glass to his left hand and shook hands with Mark.

"Glad to meet you, Mark." He turned back to Cat, "I would love to see your draft and go over it with you. How about tomorrow afternoon; about three o'clock would be fine, I think." He slapped his pockets and said, "I don't have my book with me right now—must have left it in the office." He frowned. "Why don't you give me a call in the morning to make sure I haven't scheduled something else, too. I sometimes do that." Canfield took a sip of his drink and made no move to leave them.

They stood there awkwardly for a few seconds before Canfield continued with a friendliness and warmth that made Cat feel really guilty, "Cat, I want you to think seriously about submitting an entry to the poetry contest. It's the Committee's plan to publish the entries in an anthology. And I want this anthology to represent the best and to set a precedent for future contests and issues. The first pages will be devoted to the winning poet and the winning work. We've chosen a name for the collection: FROSTING. How do you like it? I thought it was a bit fluffy at first. But, actually, I think it can be carried off with an artistic flair as long as we don't get too glamorous or cutesy." He chuckled and set his drink down so he could reach under his glasses and rub his eyes. "Nothing like this has ever been done here before."

Cat could see Mark's imagination on fast-forward and he asked, "Has the cover format been designed? If it hasn't, I'd like a shot at it." He gave Cat a little jab with his fist. "I already have some images forming in my mind."

Canfield smiled at Mark, the way he might smile at a show-off child, "No, it hasn't. I'd like to see your ideas. Of course, the Committee will have the final say. So far, though, we haven't seen anything we feel is right. We'd like to have a cover design that we can use for subsequent issues. Assuming it will be a successful venture. I think it will be; even though the prizes will be little more than honorary--$500 for first and $250 each for the next three." He added, "We would also be interested in any other thoughts you might have about the anthology. As it will be the first, we don't want to set any precedent we might later regret. And I'm ready to listen."

Cat was amazed. Why had she seen such a different Canfield? Something Edward said jostled her, ". . . respected and renowned scholar and . . . he just looks like a grouch." Had she been so biased by his looks that she couldn't see his real worth? And, even worse, she had practically accused him of stealing the Wadsworth's books? It made her reevaluate her stance. He certainly couldn't have been more cordial.

Everyone finally got to meet their new colleagues and as Cat and Mark were leaving, she saw Canfield and Mary McMahon having an animated conversation with a couple of other department members. They were all laughing and seemed to be enjoying themselves immensely. She remarked to Mark about one of the group, "There's Robert Ambrose, the *New York Times* columnist. He's one of Edward's favorite old students. I wonder what he's doing here?"

"Wasn't he a member of the department before he went to New York? He's probably going to write something about the new members or the old members or the contest or something. It's always good to get mentioned in the *Times*." Like he had been struck by lightening, he said, "Maybe he'll review our book!" He pulled out a pencil and scrap of paper from his jacket pocket. "I'm making a note to see he gets a copy!" They were both smiling when they left the room.

Back at Berkeley Street, Cat said to Mark, "I must have misread or misinterpreted Canfield, just like Edward said. I don't remember him as being so friendly." Mark was settling into the cushions on the sofa, motioning Cat to join him. His dark hair on the beige pillow gave his long face and deep-set dark eyes a religious-icon look. Cat was still on the subject of Canfield. "He's dedicated to the anthology and he really wants to see my work. It sounds as though he's already read some of it, doesn't it? He seems eager to have me submit my work . . . I think I will."

Mark was deep into his own agenda. "Picture this:" he said, his long-fingered hands dramatically sweeping and guiding an image, "A white background with an off-white foreground of a misty figure brushing the whiteness from the intersection of two—also misty—converging paths. You can't tell where the scene is, just that it's light and lonely. FROST- is written in raised block letters across the top of the page, in white, of course, and ING is written across the bottom right in lower case, but raised and white." Cat looked dubious. So he added, "I'm just brainstorming. Or maybe no figure, just the separated words and paths. Or maybe . . . a fence with freshly fallen snow like icing. . . or" he was silent but his mind was working as he blocked out his ideas in the air.

Cat sat down next to him and Mark closed his arm around her. She said, "I have some thinking to do. By myself." She was abrupt with Mark and his bewildered expression said he didn't understand. She softened, "I just want to figure out what I should submit to the contest and have it ready when I meet with Canfield tomorrow."

She hopped up from the sofa and out from under his arm. "How about some Sleepy Time tea, Mark?" I could really use a hot drink. As she put the kettle on she once again fussed to herself about Mark. She liked Mark, but, she tried to keep things on a platonic plane. It wasn't easy. There hadn't been anyone else for some time. She didn't want to mislead Mark simply because she was not involved with anyone at the moment. And she suspected he felt more. Cat eased her conscience by involving herself wholeheartedly in Mark's ruminating about the anthology cover. They sat at the kitchen table for a while discussing the contest and the new colleagues.

After Mark left, Cat felt she had handled the situation quite well. At least he wasn't pouting. How could she get Mark to understand they would never have anything more than a platonic relationship. It was another thing she knew she would have to address straight on—soon. The amount of time she spent feeling guilty when there were so many other important issues that needed her attention was numbing and not productive, she told herself, saying, "not productive" out loud.

She puttered in the kitchen, putting things away and leaving the table set for the morning before she went to her room where she spent an hour or so preparing for her meeting with Canfield.

The next morning she drew back the curtain in her room and the sun streaming in gave her the lift a warm spring day gives to all who have had as much of winter as they can stand.

She felt a fresh, sparkling aura moving with her and she flung out her arms and pirouetted around in her bare feet. It was another beautiful day in a string of several. Almost unheard of in this part of the country where spring can mean icy winter snow or stifling summer heat along with everything in between during the course of one week. The early morning haze was long gone and left the air sweet and bright. She felt like she had put on 3-D glasses; everything seemed intense and clear.

She said a quick "good morning" to Edward sipping his coffee at the kitchen table and reading the morning paper. "It definitely, *definitely*, is a day for lunch outside," so she hurriedly slapped together a sandwich, wrapped it in a bit of plastic wrap, and stuffed it into her bag. It was going to be a good day in every way. She danced out the door, down the path and off to meet the spectacular day she had imagined for herself.

At lunchtime Cat strolled to the Quad, leaned her portfolio against the bench, sat down, and took out the Swiss cheese and lettuce sandwich. It was a little squashed but delicious, she thought, as she took a big bite. She had bought a raspberry soda at the CVS and was looking forward to relaxing in the spring sunshine and enjoying her lunch. She closed her eyes and savored the moment. When she opened her eyes, she was not alone.

"Nice day," said the handsome bearded young man sitting at the other end of the bench. He had been watching her, she thought, because he spoke as soon as she opened her eyes. He looked a little familiar like maybe a Calvin Klein ad she had seen or maybe he just looked like dozens of college men she saw around town. In spite of the youthful bearing, Cat could tell he was not an undergraduate: a graduate student, maybe, and tried to guess his discipline.

"It sure is," she said. It was a wimpy start. She went on, "I hope every day until Memorial Day is like this." He smiled and nodded as she continued, "We are all in better spirits when the barometric pressure is high and today is perfect." She ran her fingers through her short hair, "I love to sit here. It's like a private, quiet room away from the hustle and buzz of the rest of the Square. It's peaceful and green and there are always a few birds to make you think you're in the country. See, there!" As if to prove she was right, a plump robin chirped and strutted across the grass in front of them before he flew into the newly leafing apple tree.

"Yes," he said.

She turned back to her lunch and thought maybe he didn't want to be sociable after all and that was o.k. with her. But he must have been just settling himself more comfortably on his end of the bench. He stretched out his long, blue-jeaned legs and squinted into the tree, "A nest of robins in her hair," he said and leaned back. And so it began.

He and Cat sat there for over an hour. Periodic outbursts of words from one or the other held together the comfortable silence that filled the space between them. Cat looked at her watch and put her lunch wrappings into her carryall before he said, "Maybe I'll see you again?"

"I eat lunch here just about every day--if it's not raining or snowing."

"My name's Ed."

"I'm Catriona--everyone calls me Cat."

She smiled at him, stood up and walked across the Quad and out the Garden Street exit. He sat there fiddling with his backpack for a few minutes before he got up, stretched in the sun, hoisted his backpack onto his shoulder and left by the Brattle Street exit.

Cat was on time for her three o'clock meeting with Professor Canfield. She had made a good selection for her entry to the contest, he said. When she left about an hour later, she was adrift in elysian fields floating well off the ground. He had been more than enthusiastic about her work. He gave her some helpful suggestions about the format and order and said he would like to see it again in a couple weeks' time, after she had a chance to make her changes and let them settle.

Later, she would wish she had spent a little more time with Professor Canfield that afternoon.

**"The flowers were out there with
the thieves
Yet nobody molested them!**

**from LOCKED OUT
Robert Frost**

Chapter 10

The troyka needn't have worried about tracking down the stolen Wadsworth books and first editions. The mystery of their whereabouts was a moot point by Wednesday morning.

Motive was something else—and puzzling—especially in light of the bizarre circumstances surrounding the recovery of the missing volumes.

Dicky Cronin had answered what he thought was a routine crank call at about eight o'clock Tuesday night while his boss was at Tonio's entertaining his friends.

"They're out there again," said Mrs. Oliver, who often called and seemed to enjoy reporting tales of vandalism and pranks. She lived just off Brattle on Lowell Street no more than a few hundred feet from the Wadsworth house. "There's a ruckus in my backyard and someone has scattered rubbish over my front lawn. I wish you would do your job and lock those vandals up! Cambridge has never been the same since the '60's when you people started being so lenient with those Bohemians!"

She means, "hippies," Dicky thought, and almost told her that he was born in 1971 so she couldn't blame him for being too easy with the hippies, but he didn't say anything. Instead, he assured her that he would take care of things and went off to investigate. He took a patrolman and car and wound up spending the next half hour at Mrs. Oliver's picking up newspapers that had been strewn over Mrs. Oliver's front lawn and making sure there was no one hiding in the bushes. It was easier for him to do it than to argue with her about responsibilities. Mrs. Oliver was well known at the Station and Dicky knew that arguing with her was like playing tic-tac-toe with a computer--he couldn't win.

The lights from the cruiser and the front porch gave off plenty of light to see under all the bushes and trees. There was no sign of anyone, though, by the time they arrived, all was quiet and peaceful--except for the explicit directions from Mrs. Oliver, who had metamorphosed, in Dicky's mind, into the Wicked Witch of the West cackling and pointing a long bony finger to the places she thought he had missed. Dicky demurred and looked again under some of the bushes. As he could have told Mrs. Oliver, there was nothing and no one there. "There's only a few small boxes," he said as he hefted one box and thought . . . heavy but not breakable stuff, probably some folders or more newspapers and books. He put the newspapers from the lawn into green trash bags and placed them on the front porch along with the boxes before he left with a promise to come back in the morning, before the city trash collection, to put them out on the curb.

Dicky was the first one at the Station each morning. He started Mr. Coffee and set his agenda before the rest of the day force arrived. At six o'clock each morning, before the city revved up, he ran the bridges: the three-mile course that traced the river up Memorial Drive, across the river, down Storrow Drive then across the River again and back up Memorial Drive to home. Cambridgeport, where he had a small studio apartment, was close to both the station and the river. Not for him the frustrating commutes across town to give a bad start to the day. He mostly left his car—an old green VW beetle— parked in his parking space behind his apartment and walked the half-mile to work each day.

By the time Argus arrived at eight o'clock, Dicky had his schedule set and, as always, open, of course, to changes his boss might deem appropriate. He was at the Station, in the little kitchenette on the second floor, pouring coffee, when he saw his boss breeze past, down the corridor, and heard him fling open the door to his office. Then he heard the window squeaking as it cranked open to let in the sounds of busy Western Avenue below.

"Dicky!?" Argus bellowed as he did each morning. Dicky anticipated the summons and arrived in seconds elbowing his way through the door already slowly closing in deference to the warped floor. He was carefully balancing two cups of coffee and holding a bunch of papers under his arm. Without spilling a drop, he set the cups down. "I don't like spilled coffee or coffee rings on my desk," his boss said as he watched the cups' safe journey, grinned, and picked up his cup.

When Argus took over as Commissioner, he instituted certain routines. One of the first was asking that each of the detectives report informally each morning and bring him up to date, not a written report, just an unceremonious chat over their first cups of coffee.

Dicky started his agenda by saying: "That accident on Mem Drive yesterday morning turned into a nightmare. A couple of fender-benders. I had to spend too much time sorting out wreckage and traffic. Two trucks, neither of which, by law, should have been on the Drive, and one of which got stuck in the underpass at Mass Avenue, collided." He paused to take a big gulp of his coffee, "Fortunately, no one was hurt. And I'm sorry," he said, "I wasn't able to get to the Wadsworths' to help with the inventory." He asked, "How did it go?"

They talked for a while about the theft and its lack of concrete clues. It was Dicky's job, Argus reminded him, to see that lists of the stolen items were distributed to collectors, pawnshops and bookstores now there was a complete list. "I'll take care of it right away," he said and glanced at his watch as he got up from his chair, "I'll be at Mrs. Oliver's over on Lowell Street for a half hour or so, just long enough to put all that rubbish out for pick-up today." He tipped his cup for the last of his coffee and smiling said, "She actually said she was glad about something: that the trash collectors don't come at six a.m. any more! 'They make more noise than a herd of elephants with tin-pan necklaces!' she said." Dicky was laughing. "I told her I'd come by because those boxes are too much for her to be lugging around--she must be a hundred years old and doesn't weigh any more than a hundred pounds. I just left the rubbish on her front porch last night. Some of it was heavy—books, I think." Dicky eyes lit up in horror as he started to put two and two together.

"What rubbish? What books?" Argus was adding things up too.

Dicky quickly recounted the phone call and his trip to Lowell Street the previous evening where he had found a lot of newspapers and rubbish strewn over the lawn along with boxes of heavier items--books, probably--left under some bushes. He didn't doubt that a few young scamps had been there, he said, but he hadn't seen any kids on his way and all was quiet when he arrived at Mrs. Oliver's. He had checked the area and the house to make sure it was secure.

Argus grabbed for the phone and in doing so bumped his coffee cup. As he dialed he watched the coffee slosh back and forth in his cup, willing it to stay inside. "Edward" he said, "meet me at the Oliver house on Lowell Street!" With no more explanation, he put the phone down and raced down the stairs with Dicky close behind.

"They are yours, and be the measure
Of their worth for you to treasure,"

from FLOWER-GATHERING
Robert Frost

Chapter 11

When Anthony and Dicky arrived at Mrs. Oliver's house on Lowell Street, Edward was already there with Lew who had been having his morning coffee in Edward's kitchen when Anthony's startling call came.

Dicky had a copy of the inventory with him and together with Edward and Lew spent a good part of the morning on Mrs. Oliver's huge wooden framed front porch checking off the books on the inventory list and going through the plastic bags and the boxes. Mrs. Oliver scurried around thoroughly enjoying the attention and fuss. It gave her the chance to complain again about today's youth, and she did so at great length. She offered them tea; they declined and hurried her inside out of the cool morning but mostly out of their way.

Anthony was a little subdued and not his usual effervescent self when excused himself from the activities by walking up the street to the Wadsworths' to give them the good news. As he walked along he shuddered to think what might have happened had Dicky Cronin not brought in coffee this morning. It wouldn't have been Dicky's fault; he didn't know enough, at the time, about the theft and missing books, to draw conclusions or connections. That it turned out all right was no consolation because it could have been disastrous. All those valuable books in the rubbish and off to the dump. He shuddered but was thankful he had instituted those morning routines at the station. Certainly the expense of the Mr. Coffee machine and coffee had proved worthy of the initial outlay if only by today's save.

"The Wadsworths are happy and grateful," Anthony reported upon his return, "and even though I tried to tell them the books were not returned as a result of the investigation we had hardly started, they insist we were instrumental." He rubbed his red nose distractedly and continued, "Actually, it's Dicky they should be thanking."

"Trash, indeed," Edward mumbled holding two of the wayward books in his hands. "We've checked them off and they're all here. Can you imagine? First editions left outside! What if it had rained? Even dew could damage the bindings and warp the covers." He turned one of the books over, scrutinized it and placed it in the pile. "I'm just thankful that we have them now. It's a big relief. Do you have a safe place for them?" Edward asked Anthony, whose hands were thrust in his pockets as he paced the porch.

Anthony pulled out his handkerchief and rubbed at his nose again and nodded, "Of course," with a look that said it was a foolish question in the first place, "I'll have them tagged and locked up in the evidence room at the Station. We'll need to go through the books in case there is something there—like a fingerprint. Funny, we don't depend so much on fingerprints anymore but I wish everyone would stop handling the books just in case there are some that can be lifted from the covers. Later the Wadsworths can have the Museum staff pick the books up if that's what they want. Are you sure they're the right ones? That there's no mistake?"

"Positive. See. Here in this one." Edward gingerly opened the book trying to keep his hands on the edges so as not to smudge any prints there might be. "Frost's scrawled handwriting. I'd know it anywhere" he said as he showed the page to Anthony to confirm his words. Anthony looked at it impatiently, to please Edward, and waved it back into Edward's caring hands. "And, we've checked them against the list." Edward's brow wrinkled, "There's no sign of the Fragonards or the pistols?"

Anthony shook his head slowly, "Not a trace. The team will go over the Oliver property and the neighboring yards carefully. I just hope finding them is as easy." He sounded optimistic but he was thinking it would probably be harder than ever to trace the paintings and pistols now that they were separated from the books. "And what kind of crazy thieves would leave valuable books around on a lawn? Nothing is ever easy--to find or to figure out."

Lew stood up and stretched. He was still the handsome one: tall and slim, almost too thin, his once thick, gingery-blond hair seemed a bit faded and sparse but his blue, intense eyes that crinkled and sparkled before his smile caught up were the same as ever. He looked like the storybook Englishman who rode to hounds and sat in the House of Lords.

"This sure doesn't look very valuable. It's just a book," Lew teased. He had one of the Frost first editions in his hand, . . . personally I support the ideology of the transience of material possessions as a hedge against sentimentality. The important thing is the words and composition, and they'll never be lost." He scratched his head. "Maybe as an economist I've bypassed the emotional attachments of things like first editions and keepsakes." He turned the book over a few times, scrutinized it and said, "I'm in complete agreement with Keynes, and Keynes, you know," he was addressing Edward, "shunned tradition and sentimentality as economic stabilizers. As a member of the Bloomsbury Group—they were all creative thinkers—he would say that it was more important that Frost's philosophy prevailed."

"Of course! No one's arguing with that." Edward was quick to pick up the gauntlet. "And it's not sentimentality that makes these editions important. It's history." He went on, lecture style, "The base of culture we depend upon to transmit knowledge to succeeding generations is alive and personal in these books," he thundered. "It's the connection between author and reader that is even more poignant because with first editions the author didn't know whether the impact of his words would warrant notice, let alone subsequent editions. As Canfield said, there's something mystical and magical about first editions that moves even the most prosaic student. And who knows what future generations may divine from them. For instance," he shook his finger at Lew, "if the Franciscans had prized the value of first editions as *history* and not burned the fig-paper tomes as *heresy*, scientists and anthropologists probably would have been able to unravel the mystery of the Mayan civilization. Those tomes would have been the Rosetta Stone of the Mayans, and the glyphs' translations would have given us a defining look into a culture that may well remain a dark puzzle." He shook his head. "Who knows when that riddle will be solved? If ever?"

Anthony had stopped pacing to listen. At first, he wished Lew hadn't teased Edward about such a sensitive subject, but on second thought, he was glad to see some of Edward's former testiness rise up and pursue debate.

"You're right," Lew said, raising his hands to hold back the tide of words, "I concede!" He laughed and then added, getting his last word in, "That was simply misplaced religious zeal—and understanding it doesn't make it any easier to accept."

Anthony, immobile in the center of the porch, hands on hips, stared first at one and then the other and blurted, emphasizing each word, "What on earth are you two going on about now? How can you find so much to say about something so obscure?"

If Lew heard, he didn't acknowledge it and went on talking after a deep breath, "There have been times like that, throughout history, when fanaticism ran rampant and upset not only history and religious superstructure, but the economic base as well. You're absolutely right. And I'm glad these first editions," he pointed to the boxes, "have been found and will take their place in history secure in a safe environment," Lew placed the Frost book with the others. Edward nodded, seconding his words.

Anthony rolled his eyes. "Let's finish up here, and go somewhere for some lunch. We need to take a look at where we stand now in this crazy case. Even though we've recovered most of what went missing there are still the paintings and the pistols to worry about."

It was Anthony's turn to expound and he did, showing his frustration by flinging his hands around and pacing again. "This is just what no one likes to deal with—no apparent motive and no evidence or witnesses." He pulled his handkerchief from his pocket and began swiping at his nose distractedly. "It's hard to see where to start and harder to know where to go. What is the motive? Do we have a random theft? Why did they take the first editions if they were only going to leave them out on Mrs. Oliver's lawn? Was it to give her something to vent her contempt of all things youthful? I don't think so." He was still pacing furiously and jabbing at his poor red nose. "To ruin them? Maybe someone has a bone to pick with academia, but why not ransom them or burn them or throw them in the rubbish themselves? It's a puzzle. It makes me wonder what we're dealing with." Anthony shook his head, slipped his notebook into his pocket, motioned to Dicky to put everything into the squad car, and gave explicit instructions about where they were to be secured at the Station.

"And Dicky," Anthony said, "leave that Frost set apart from the others. It's in the top of one of those boxes. It was not part of the museum gift and I'll take it to the Wadsworths." Then he looked at Edward and said, "Or maybe you'd like to have the pleasure of returning it. Make sure it gets there without further mishap." Then he chuckled, ". . . just don't take it home with you!"

Edward agreed, "I'd like to do that. Return it to the Wadsworth's—not take it home, that is. Well, I would like to take it home; but I won't."

All three watched Dicky fish out the Frost set in its protective cardboard sleeve, give it tp Edward and amble off behind his valuable rubbish looking like a gangly Jimmy Stewart with his arms and legs dangling just a little too far out of his grey tweed suit that could have done with a pressing. "See you back at the station." It looked like an afterthought when Dicky turned and said, "Don't forget, it's Wednesday. You're supposed to be at the Community Center a little early tonight to look over the play-off schedule before they print it up." Argus nodded. Dicky had a nice way of reminding him of his obligations and he appreciated it. Though he often showed impatience with Dicky, he tried to make it clear to Dicky that it wasn't Dicky's fault because to Argus, Dicky was indispensable.

By way of explanation, Anthony said, "I was late last week for my basketball practice with the teen group, and Dicky and some other fellow who just happened to drop by picked up the slack. I told them I'd be early this week and we'd all go for pizza after the practice." Pretending Globetrotters' tricks he bounced his air ball around his back, over his shoulder and through his legs. "I think that's why some of the boys come. We go for pizza at the slightest excuse! Actually, I don't think it's so much the pizza as it is the camaraderie. Sometimes I worry about shortchanging them by squeezing in the time. I'm always glad when we have a little more time together." He smiled. "So I have to get there early today; but there's still plenty of time for lunch."

Ten minutes later the troyka were seated around Lew's kitchen table. They made themselves sandwiches from the containers and jars Lew pulled out from the icebox and cupboards. It was a fairly decent lunch of ham and cheese and tomatoes and lettuce, some Woodpecker's English cider and cranberry juice for Anthony. No one touched the raspberry jam or Nutella.

"I know we've all asked it time and time again, but what could have been the object of that crazy escapade?" They had started speculating on the Wadsworth theft again. Anthony threw out the question. "It certainly wasn't to keep aging crime solvers occupied!" His eyes met Lew's and silently they nodded at each other as if to say that that was exactly what it had seemed. Edward was more alive and animated than he had been for two years.

"At least, finding the books is something positive to report. But the sooner we find a motive, the better," said Anthony between large bites of sandwich. "What about the mystery of the miniatures and the pistols? Where are they? Does someone have them in his own private collection—never to be seen again?" He dabbed at his face with his napkin, swallowed, and continued, "And why, in the first place?" He looked at Edward and Lew, "What do you think?"

"I always wonder about how criminals become criminals, don't you?" Lew was reasoning. "Is there a criminal gene, for instance? Lately genes have been discovered for just about everything else. Maybe the tendency is inherited; you know, three generations of bank robbers because they can't help it; it's in their genes."

Usually Anthony stayed on the sidelines through these kinds of discussions and impatiently waited for Lew and Edward to volley until one or the other dropped the ball, but he had thought about this topic many times. "I've wondered that too. Especially when there's more than one criminal or felon in a family. Is it environment or heredity? I tend to think it's more environment. At least I hope so because we can do something about that. It's why I spend time at the Youth Center."

"I think the propensity to commit crime and the ability to carry it out have to be related; otherwise, Anthony, we wouldn't need you." Edward smiled and made a steeple with his fingers. "And we wouldn't have puzzlers like this one. It has to be meticulously planned."

"Oh, I don't know about that. We often catch petty criminals because they're stupid. Sometimes they practically tell us their addresses and phone numbers!"

"Right. Of course, some criminals aren't really criminals either. Jean Valjean for example was a victim of circumstances. One needs a pair of shoes or a loaf of bread for his family and as a last resort, they steal. They haven't any idea about how to cover up what they've done—they don't know how to act like criminals. The end is the goal."

"What about the something in all of us that ponders the "perfect crime?" How do you explain that? where the goal is the means?" asked Lew.

Edward added his two-bits' worth, "That's entirely different. That's more like a chess game or climbing Mt. Everest—a challenge—to see if it can be done. Sherlock Holmes, remember, prized his skirmishes with Professor Moriarty, the "Napoleon of Crime," because it made him strain his brain. He had to stay three moves ahead of Moriarty's two!"

"Maybe that's why I have such trouble with chess," Anthony admitted, "I like to see where I'm going--to be able to backtrack if I need to. I find it difficult to plan several steps ahead without getting muddled."

"No, no. That's not it. You think as you've been trained. If you'd played chess all your life as we have, you'd know the moves way in advance because you'd have gotten used to them. There are championship games people play over and over. Think of it like learning to peel a potato. The first one ends up marble size. But if you had K.P. in the army, you'd soon become proficient at peeling just the skins off. It's a challenge. Do you see? Well, experience pays off in thinking as well as peeling!"

Anthony was not convinced but it gave him some encouragement about his chess game. "We should get some feedback soon from the feelers Dicky is sending out. Maybe some leads on the pictures and pistols." He was hopeful. Just having the books back in safe hands made him feel the weight of the ballast diminish and the hull rise. He was ready to change tack, tighten up the luffing sail and gain some speed closer to the wind. He liked the metaphor but wasn't sure how to implement it. He couldn't help wishing that the paintings and pistols would be found as easily as the books and as easy as sailing on a summer day.

**"One ought not to have to care
So much as you and I. . .**

**from LONELINESS
Robert Frost**

Chapter 12

Lew's lunch invitation and presentation had allayed the grumpies of the hungry troyka. They finished, said a round of "thank you's" and hurried off separately.

Edward picked up the Frost set and parted for the Wadsworth's with it tucked under his arm.

Anthony headed in the opposite direction back to the station to spend the afternoon with his detectives and some paperwork before he left for the basketball practice.

Lew was left alone at the kitchen table with his thoughts. He had appointments in the Square later in the afternoon, but there was no hurry; he had plenty of time today. There was still a swallow or two in his cider glass so he picked it up and absentmindedly swirled it around and around.

He was thinking about Edward and how he seemed to have changed in just a few days and how, in the first place, he could have slipped so gradually into a vacuous abyss it was undetectable until it was almost too late. He shuddered and he felt responsible. He should have taken steps long ago when he first noticed the malaise, but he hardly saw it; it had been a steady, barely discernable, drip, drip, dripping erosion.

The recovery of the books might lessen the activity surrounding the theft and the on-going problem might not be enough to keep Edward so involved. Intellectual calisthenics was the answer. Edward's brain had been atrophying for almost two years. Lew tapped his foot and mused about other puzzles to exercise that agile brain.

Lew glanced at his watch and finished off the last of the cider in one gulp. Most of the food he had pulled out of the cupboards and icebox was gone, so he swept the crumbs and lettuce ends off the table into the disposal. The whirring of the disposal was comforting; he liked the sound of the water gurgling. One of the bottles of Woodpecker's was about a third full and he started to pour it down the drain. He stopped mid-pour. It was an excuse to sit down again. He took a swallow from the bottle before setting it on the table. Then he fiddled with it, turning it around and around like the thoughts spinning around in his head. His gaze went beyond the kitchen into the long past.

There had been only one time in their lives when he and Edward hadn't lived within a stone's throw of each other. It was when Lew was on the West Coast and Edward stayed in the East—both building careers—that the twins were born. Teddy was named after his father, Edward, and Rennie was named for Lew, Laurence, their father's best friend. At their christening ceremony, Lew proudly accepted the responsibilities of godfather. He and Sarah had flown to Cambridge often to fill in the no-children gap in their own lives and enjoyed taking part in the joyous early years' rites.

After gaining a name for himself on the West Coast with two highly acclaimed books, Lew accepted a professorship in the Economics Department at the University in Cambridge. He never once regretted the decision, he said. California just was not New England where his roots were so deep and strong that even the years away did not alter his Easternness. He, like Edward, had inherited his family home so it was natural that the two friends should continue as they had for so many years, next door to each other and within easy walking distance of the University and the Square. It was comfortable, not exciting, but comfortable. And that was what he looked forward to now—comfort.

The clock in the living room chimed two, bringing him back from his time ramble. He stood up, put the empty cider bottles in the recycle box and picked up his briefcase before walking out the door to keep his afternoon appointments. As he walked, he reviewed his mental list of "things to do." He was so used to his lists that he could call them up like a computer screen, revise them and then save them anew. His mind was a methodical calendar, and he deleted items only after resolving them. He wondered why others didn't do the same; it was so easy and efficient.

One thing he could cross off his list soon was the plan for the disposition of his estate. His first appointment that afternoon was with his lawyer who had worked out all the details, and the document was in its final stage. He just needed to o.k. the draft. It was a good feeling to finish the details on legal papers that had been plaguing his conscience for a while.

A lot of thought had gone into the disposition of his estate, and he and Sarah had discussed it in detail before she died. They had agreed on an endowment to enable a worthy student to study abroad, specifically at the London School of Economics, and lawyers had been working out stipulations to ensure that the endowment would be used as he and Sarah wished. As with everything else, he laid out the course and followed it, but progress had been frustratingly slow. He had started the legal machinations shortly after Sarah's death and here it was years later and just now in final stages. It seemed straightforward to him and he was annoyed that he had carried this item on his mental calendar for so long.

He turned the corner to his lawyer's building in the Square. He would be glad to have his mind free to work on his book—his final book, he thought with relief—and he wanted to get it finished. The two chapters he had left to write were the easiest and the most enjoyable—summing up and resolving.

Though he loved his research and could lose himself in it for weeks at a time, he most enjoyed the resolutions. Sarah used to complain that she might just as well be on the moon for all the attention she got when he was writing: "He's never more alive and excited than when he can match up two obscure historical events and come up with a single premise based on the economics of the times that would explain why something happened," he had overheard her telling Ann once when they were commiserating, in the kitchen, about being academic widows.

"Of course," Lew would defend himself, "there are dissenters—not everyone is in concert with Keynes or Smith either—but these theories are history now and cited as refinements of Smith's theory that when market forces are allowed to operate without state intervention, 'an invisible hand' will guide self-interest for the well-being of everyone." And he furthered Smith's later emphasis upon self-interest, rather than sympathy, as a basic force in human nature—it was a tenet Lew lived by.

Everyone's excitement arises from different stimuli, he would say. Sarah had understood him and his intellectual pursuits completely—not everyone did.

When Sarah died, Lew grieved, as a devoted spouse, and marked off another segment of his life. He didn't look for another relationship to put in its place; it was not a hole that needed to be filled. It had been a merger that transcended death. He, as always, accepted the vicissitudes of life with equanimity and was content and happy writing and teaching classes and playing chess and sometimes, for variety and a little drama or tingle, working out shadowy puzzles.

Though Lew and Edward could often glimpse into one another's minds, in many ways Lew and Edward were not alike. One might conclude that was why they got along so well. Lew was far less likely to be influenced by outside variables. When they were children, it was Edward who worried about consequences and people. He felt remorse easily, even when he wasn't guilty of anything. Lew could shirk off flutterings of guilt by persuading himself that an uncharitable act hadn't been so bad; it was in the eye of the beholder. Maybe, that was why he had such an affinity for Rennie the rascal—who had been named for him—and he wondered: Do names have anything to do with the way a person's character develops? Would Grigori Rasputin have been less scandalous if he had been christened George Roberts? He laughed at the thought.

Lew remembered a time when he and Edward were about ten years old and Katy Johnson had been blamed for a misdeed of theirs. He chuckled remembering now how he and Edward had sneaked out after dark one spring evening and wrapped up the entire school playground in a jumble of white, toilet tissue ribbons----over the swing set and around the jungle gym, around the trees and doorknobs of the buildings. In the morning the whole school was buzzing and giggling. Speculations about "who" were running wild and everyone had settled on Katy. Edward had been so worried that Katy would be expelled or worse, he had insisted they confess. They did, and no one was expelled----just admonished to think more carefully about pranks before they put them into practice. But, as far as Lew was concerned, confessing put a damper on the triumph of the deed.

Lew felt that throughout his life, Edward had teetered on the balance of propriety and artistry. Still, it was Edward's unconventionality and empathy that secured his place in the world of poetry, and he has suffered for both. He brooded too easily. He spaced out of reality and found solace in the poetry he treasured when he didn't want to cope with a problem.

Lew thought of Sherlock Holmes who resorted to morphine when his brain was not engaged in solving some complex and devious puzzle. Edward was a bit like that though Lew knew Edward had never resorted to morphine or any other drug for that matter. His painkiller was detachment.

"And I thought of the door
With no lock to lock."

from THE LOCKLESS DOOR
Robert Frost

Chapter 13

Harvard Square is always a bitch when it rains, Anthony
mumbled to himself as he pushed his nose and pulled at his tie in
the sticky warmth of his designated blue-and-white already
dense with tepid spring humidity. He steered through the one-
ways behind Mass. Avenue in an attempt to get to James Hall
without using his siren. The siren, he always said, only attracted
more attention; and no one ever got out of the way, anyhow--not
here in Cambridge, at least.

Pedestrians were rushing behind and under the giant
green-blue-and-white-ribbed WGBH umbrellas that popped up
like mushrooms whenever it rained. The umbrellas had taken on
a life of their own on an animated spree, dancing over the curbs
and zig-zagging across streets, giving absolutely no
consideration to those inside the dry—but sticky—four-
wheelers. He grumbled, but yielded to the stormy choreography.

He drove onto the sidewalk as he approached James
Hall, parked at a drunken angle and tore from the steamy
Cambridge police car into the building more in an effort to get

out of the rain than from haste to get to the scene. It wasn't an emergency. Emergency meant life or death and the pronouncement in this situation had already been made. Dicky's message had said it looked like murder.

Two uniformed officers met him halfway down the dull corridor of frosted, glass-fronted doors. Each door was embellished with a name in black, block letters. The door marked: Joshua Canfield, Graduate English Department, Robert Frost Chair, was ajar. A wedge of light angled onto the corridor floor from the half-opened door. The commotion from inside spilled out like a verbal game of Yahtzee and made about as much sense and wouldn't until things could be sorted through and put in order. As Commissioner Argus, Anthony pushed open the door and found Dicky Cronin presiding with his notebook out and his pen poised above it.

"Morning Commissioner," said Dicky as Anthony entered the small room filled with forensic techs and their paraphernalia of plastic bags and powders. Dicky blew some dust from the corner of a desk that took up a good part of the room and blocked the window access. After he looked up at the clock, he opened his notebook and wrote: AA on the scene at 10:10.

He wasn't being officious. His boss often asked him when he, Anthony, had arrived or departed from somewhere, and Dicky always had the time jotted down. For Anthony, knowing the time was important. It routed him through the course of a day and rooted his mind in a fixed space. Dicky had joked to the other detectives at the station, "There are a lot of descriptive traits I could pin on our boss, but being a careless detective is not among them. Nor is half-hearted compassion or feigned interest. If he's not interested, you'll know for sure."

Anthony was listening with his practiced ear and looking with his practiced eye as he moved slowly around the desk to the inert form of Joshua Canfield doubled up on the floor where he had apparently toppled from his chair. As he fell, his head must have broken the glass-fronted bookcase that was under the window behind his desk. Splintered glass was scattered about the ancient yellow-brown somewhat polished oak floor.

Dicky said, "The forensic techs have dusted for prints and Doc Appleby is on his way; should be here by now. He's usually pretty good about arriving in good time." He held his watch up close to his face.

Anthony offered: The Square is an absolute mess—as it always is when it rains in Cambridge. You'd think we could do something about it or control it better. Maybe a new routing. . . " he drifted off to the other side of the room and focused on the form on the floor.

"Professor Canfield was found by the janitor," Dicky scanned his notes, "a Mr. Jethro Nuffield. One of Canfield's students had tried to keep an 8:45 a.m. appointment. The student's name is . . . Eric—Eric Emberg," he read from his notebook and turned the page, "Emberg said he had had an appointment with Professor Canfield. He knocked and knocked, tried the doorknob to no avail, but could see through the frosted-glass that a light was on inside . When Professor Canfield didn't respond, Eric. . .Emberg went for the janitor and persuaded him to open the door. He feared the Professor was sick or had fainted or had had a heart attack. They had entered the office together and simultaneously saw Professor Canfield crumpled behind his desk. Nuffield picked up the phone and called the station. As Emberg only entered the room for less than a minute while Mr. Nuffield called us, I let him go off to his lecture. He'll come by later. The door was locked, by the way."

"It looks like the blood from the wound. . ." Dicky pointed to a spot beside the body and was interrupted before he could finish.

"What kind of wound? Bullet? Knife?" asked his boss.

"Bullet—looks like. Anyhow, there are traces of blood that puddled and dried on the floor. See. There just by the left shoulder. There are blood splatterings to the right. It appears the body had been turned over. I only needed to touch his cold hand to know he had been dead for some time and I haven't touched anything else," said Dicky cautiously, ready to defend himself.

Anthony surprised Dicky with no outward reaction because, even though he was attentive to a point, he had lapsed into a time warp. He was looking out the window into the atrium courtyard. It had been more than two years since he had walked into this office that now bore Canfield's name on the door and would soon bear another's. When it had been Edward Whitman's office he had been in and out a million times and it still looked familiar. But something was different; a lot was different. It was like putting on old shoes and finding someone had replaced the comfortable soles and worn-down heels. The feel was wrong.

And what was it, he thought as he pulled his handkerchief from his pocket and blew his nose, what was it that Cat had said about Canfield the other day? That nobody liked him? Well, at least one person didn't like him; that was for sure. Someone had disliked him enough to do this. Why? It was the obvious question, but he knew that he would ponder it many times, possibly even after apprehending the murderer, if murder it was, and it certainly looked like it was. He turned from the window, gave his nose a last push before jamming his handkerchief back into his pocket, pointed a finger at Dicky, and started in: "Where is the janitor—what's his name?"

"Nuffield. He usually leaves at ten, but he stayed around so you could question him. He's waiting in a little room off the end of the hall where he has a desk, a chair and a phone."

"Is this door always locked at night? Who unlocks it in the morning, if it is? When? Whose are the other offices in this wing? Make sure you ask the other occupants if they noticed anything either last night or this morning. . . or any time else." Dicky raised his eyebrows in a question. Impatiently, his boss continued, "You know, anything different at all--like people who don't belong here or changes in routine, or . . . you know, all the pertinent questions you always ask. Who closed up last night? When?" Argus wasn't by any means finished but he halted when he heard a stumbling around behind him. He turned.

"Ah, Appleby. . . "

Dicky scribbled in his notebook: "Appleby arrived— 10:25 a.m." It was Dicky who had taken the call that came into the station from the janitor at a little after nine o'clock, called the Commissioner and Appleby, and he had written and timed everything that had happened since--leaving out only that he had left his coffee and doughnut on his desk back at the station. Corpse or no corpse, he could use that coffee and doughnut right now.

Dr. Appleby knelt down in the small space next to the corpse. He looked like an old-fashioned country doctor with his black bag filled with vials and wooden sticks and plasters.

Appleby's white hair was, it seemed, glued tidily to his globular head and sat in just the right place for the glaciers of the North Pole. His blue eyes crinkled like that jolly old saint traditionally associated with the North Pole, but there the similarities, except for the rotund middle, ended. Dr. Appleby was known for being grumpy, ill-humored and arrogantly presumptive. He harumphed a few times but said nothing before he started his preliminary examination. It was as though someone had shoved the noise and bustle out the window. The silence was broken only by soft rustlings of plastic and the labored breathing of the doctor.

"He's dead," he said without looking up.

Astounding! thought Anthony, but he, like Dicky, said nothing. Anthony could see out of the corner of his eye that Dicky had buried his head in his notebook to scribble down that profound bit of data.

Appleby continued, "Has been for—a guess, mind you— ten to twelve hours. Rigor has had a good start and because there is probably a little heat in the building at night, is in the finishing phases now. The head lacerations appear to have been caused by his head hitting the bookcase and he was rendered unconscious or in a state of shock but not dead—see the blood. Photos taken?" He asked as he peered over his horn-rimmed glasses. Receiving an affirmative nod, he turned the body over.

Dried blood from the forehead lacerations marred the corpse's face, but the expression was one of surprise. His fair eyebrows were arched and his mouth, turned up at the ends in a smile, was slightly open giving him the look of a grotesque, comedy-mask.

"Could it be suicide?" asked Dicky.

"I hardly think so. Did you find a weapon?" He knew they hadn't and smirked a little smile around the room in general. "He was shot at pretty close range—approximately five feet, from the look of it and what I can tell before closer examination. Pretty hard to self inflict at that distance, I would say. Doubly hard without a gun," he sniffed. "You can still smell a faint cordite odor. I'll be able to tell you more after the autopsy. This entrance hole in his suit front shows the location well. No exit wound, so the bullet is still there, in the heart, it looks. Maybe it will tell us something—the bullet, I mean." He wheeled around on one knee, "Who turned him over?" He waited, no one answered so he said, ". . . before I did. How did you know who it was?" Appleby stood up and brushed his hands together as if to say he was finished with that business. "The forensic crew can finish the picking and packaging and scraping."

Dr. Appleby recited for Dicky that Canfield had been a fit man of about forty-five with greying blond hair and a full face with no remarkable outward marks, and that precise measurements would have to wait for the postmortem examination.

Dicky waited for a lull in Appleby's peroration, "No one turned him over. At least, no one since I've been here, and I was the first into the office except for the janitor and a student who only just stepped inside the door for a moment when they used the phone. Nuffield, the janitor, recognized him by his clothes and the fact that no one else would be in this office."

Mr. Nuffield had been cooperative but had nothing of significance to contribute. He said he opened the door to Canfield's office with a master key and used the phone to call the police. That was all. He supposed he could have walked to his closet-office and called from there, but they both, he and the student, thought they should immediately notify the police. "Was I wrong?" he asked.

"No, no, no—you did the right thing." Anthony then asked him what he thought of Canfield, and Nuffield replied, "He was always pleasant and never asked for anything special," he raised his eyebrows in a knowing way, "like some of them. There's one guy who visits here from New York—I think he's a critic or something—and he often wants to use the small conference room on this floor. That's o.k. I don't mind unlocking it for him but when he asked me to dust it and carry in coffee, I thought that was going a little too far." He laughed a little. "I just left the duster on the table. The lounge with the coffee maker is on the second floor so I don't know if he ever goes there or not. I don't go for him. That's not my job." He tapped the old desk he was sitting at with his forefinger stressing his point.

"Professor Canfield was always considerate and thoughtful--he left a box of cigars and a fruitcake for me and the Mrs. at Christmas. No big presentation. Just 'thank you and I hope you'll enjoy these.' Very civil. The other one never even says 'thanks' when I unlock the door for him."

There was little to be gained from the next interview.

Eric Emberg, a nervous, loner type, with steel rimmed glasses and pink cheeks under blond flyaway hair, stopped by after his class. He was fidgety and kept saying, "I can't believe he's dead. Who could have done it?" Once he added, after feeling Anthony's gaze on him, "It wasn't me, I was just trying to keep my appointment. I wish I had just skipped it. I almost did—skip it I mean—I wasn't ready; I mean my work wasn't ready and I felt guilty about that. But," he looked Anthony straight in the eye and said, "that's all I feel guilty about." Anthony nodded and recalled that some people always look guilty, but he noted that Emberg seemed particularly defensive; maybe he was just in shock. Not surprising. Finding anyone dead, let alone murdered, let alone your esteemed and admirable professor and mentor, could send anyone around the corner of reason.

It was another two hours before Anthony drove his car off the sidewalk in front of James Hall. The few students that had gathered initially around the Hall had dispersed. By the time the police commissioner walked back out the door with all the facts he could gather, the rain had stopped and he felt the warm

dampness pressing spring into action. The winter had been long-
-starting with snow in November--and cold and more dreary than
usual. He was glad it was over. He swiped at his itching nose
and lurched through the ever-present traffic of the Square back to
the Station. In his pocket was a prescription for something to
stop his nose from itching and sneezing and running. Appleby
had scribbled it off quickly after Argus had sneezed eight times
in a row and disturbed the doctor's crime-side recitation. Argus
didn't place much stock in medications but he was so sick of his
nose—he often threatened to cut it off—that he was willing to
try anything. He made a mental note to remember to stop at the
drugstore to have the prescription filled.

The next phase of the work was not difficult, just
frustrating and time consuming. There was always that blasted
paperwork to be completed before the real investigation could
begin.

He bellowed for Dicky as he took the stairs two at a time
and pushed the wayward door to his office wide; it started
closing even before he got to his desk, but Dicky slipped through
and stood waiting, notebook ready.

"We need a team of detectives and investigators who are
free enough to take on another case and you don't have to tell me
no one is ever really free. I know that. There are some less tied
up than others though." He steepled his fingers and rested his
chin on them before looking straight at Dicky, "I want you on
this." Dicky smiled and nodded, pleased to be asked. "What
else do we have to contend with?"

Dicky spewed out the list ending with two other thefts, besides the Wadsworth case, and a basketful of petty crimes involving minors. Percentages of these minor infractions were decreasing city-wide. Anthony's philosophy was to give those kids enough attention and time to avert subsequent involvement in more serious crimes; with some success though not enough he admitted. Consequently, he was reluctant to take anyone away from any of the areas deemed key by him or by some of the parent-involvement groups.

"I wish I never had to worry about funding," he sighed as they juggled the detectives' cases around finally coming up with reasonable teams. "But that's life in the public sector," he said and he was willing to put up with all kinds of burdens to keep even one crime from happening.

He scowled at his watch. "And I need more time. You go ahead and post the assignments, I have to make a couple of phone calls." The first was to Lew. "I wanted to talk with you first, before I called Edward." Anthony said after he recounted Canfield's death.

Lew answered on the second ring, "I'm shocked. I do think you should tell Edward right away. He was a friend of Canfield's; I hardly knew him. I think the only time I met him was at Edward's retirement luncheon. Remember? He seemed a nice enough chap. Do you think robbery was the motive?"

"Doesn't appear to be. The office hadn't been vandalized." Anthony sighed, "He didn't deserve such an end. Of course, no one does. I'll call Edward now and break the news. How do you think he'll take it? It isn't like a death in the family, but he was a friend and colleague. I hope it won't set him back. Actually, I could use his help and yours too. Right now, it's anyone's guess about motive. I'll have relatives and colleagues checked into and maybe we'll know more tomorrow."

Lew was quick to respond, "Yes, of course and I'll go next door right now to be there when you call Edward. He usually watches the news at six; do you think there'll be anything about this on the evening news? It's after five now."

Anthony waited a few minutes before dialing to tell Edward that Joshua Canfield had been found dead, murdered, it certainly seemed, in his, Edward's, old office. He gave him the few details he had gathered, which only made the whole thing seem more unreal. Edward's first reaction was speechlessness, he tried but he couldn't get the words out. Finally he sputtered, "How could such a thing happen? Why? I used to do the same thing—stay late, all alone." There was a long pause.

Anthony said, "I'll talk with you later," and as he prepared to hang up, he could hear some background commotion over the phone.

"Lew just came in. Thanks for letting me know before I got the news from the television. Who would want to kill Canfield?" He didn't expect an answer but it was the question he would repeat many times.

"Who knows? The clues about who and why are practically non-existent--as usual. It's early days yet and I haven't given a statement to the press yet."

Anthony was as discouraged now as he had been elated when the books were found. He was back on the pendulum.

"I make a great noise of rustling all day . . "

from GATHERING LEAVES
Robert Frost

Chapter 14

Anthony yawned, stretched, got up from his desk and paced back and forth to relieve his cramped legs. It took him all of yesterday afternoon, far into the evening and practically all of today, but he finally finished the preliminary work necessary before a full-scale investigation into the death of Joshua Canfield could proceed.

He double checked the detectives' assignments and briefed them about who would be working on which case—and they immediately began: checking witnesses and alibis and combing the scene again. Of course there were no witnesses— only those academics who belonged in the building and were not, in fact, there during the crucial time! Still, they had to be questioned; perhaps one of them had something vital to offer: like an unknown person loitering around looking suspicious. That was a laugh. No one ever saw anything.

Once he had been so anxious to get on with an investigation that he hadn't waited for the slowly grinding mills, and the grand jury had refused to give an indictment. Remembering it made him uneasy. But that was a long time ago and it would never happen again. Of course, this case was different as there was nobody to indict, but he wanted to be sure there was no problem with "death by foul play by person or persons unknown." It definitely was murder.

He did everything by the book—the right way; but he was, he knew, impatient, and he hated waiting for someone else. They always took too long to do a job. Dr. Appleby and the forensic crew had not come through with their reports and they all said, "Tomorrow morning." He ran his hands through his thick, wavy, graying-at-the-temples, hair and tossed his worn-down pencil onto his desk like a pitcher who tosses one final ball after the count and knows it won't make any difference.

It was time to stop; time to get out of this cramped space, time to focus on something else, time to give himself space to breathe and leave his anxious thoughts to rest and maybe gain some perspective. He had written a chronology of events since yesterday and supplemented the time line with his thoughts which would never see the light of day because his thoughts, unlike his spoken words, held a sensitivity and foresight he never outwardly acknowledged. Better to let colleagues and friends think him the prosaic plodder he often felt he portrayed. And, too, he was hungry.

As though he had put his foot on the brakes, his whole body and brain came to a screeching halt; he couldn't think anymore. A deep growl rose from somewhere. It had to be him, but he didn't feel the rumble even though the noise was loud and cavernous. He shook his wrist; his watch must be wrong. It couldn't be after seven. No wonder he was hungry. He had arrived at eight in the morning, early for him, and here it was almost twelve hours later. Where had the day gone? True, he had finished the paperwork, started the ball rolling, and taken care of some other paper work to clear his desk and leave him free for this investigation; well, almost free; he still had the Wadsworth theft to consider. Again, he hoped the thieves would leave the pistols and the Fragonards in a nice easy-to-find place, like the books, but even if they did not, he was glad to have the books back. It was a crazy escapade from the outset. He shook his head as though it would help him to understand. He couldn't take the whole thing too seriously and had an intuition about the solution being closer than it appeared. He liked those intuitions, but they didn't always pan out.

As he straightened and squared his papers, visions of dinner carouseled in his head. It was times like these that he longed for Isobel who was always ready to listen and always ready with a good meal, no matter when he finally came home. It must have been hard to keep things hot and fresh, but she did it and she always sat with him until he finished his meal and his meanderings. Then they would have coffee and he would shut off police business and listen to her day or plan a trip to Italy or Hawaii or some other exotic place. That's what he missed most: a receptive ear eager to listen and join in the planning, even though they both knew "not this year" was realistic.

Now that he was alone in life like his two good friends, Lew and Edward, it didn't matter when he finished work or whether he went home or out to grab a bite. Maybe he'd stop, as he often had, at one of the little Italian or Portuguese restaurants that peppered the crowded streets of East Cambridge.

He could almost smell a delicious stew at the Terre, one of his favorite places, where locals gathered to argue in loud voices about the state of the old country, the state of the new country, the state of the nation and the state of the neighborhood. And though the other patrons thought of their police commissioner friend as being in the thick of things, he seldom ventured an opinion. Instead, he planted seeds and watched some of them grow and others fall fallow by the wayside. Paolo, the cook, for instance, had just taken college entrance exams in the hope of pursuing a career in police work. Anthony liked to think he might have been instrumental in one's finding one's way.

The Terre was just around the corner from the small house where he and Isobel had been happy and was still his home. He could remember the day clearly, when Isobel told him that the house was theirs. It had been with mixed feelings that he called it home. He had pictured Isobel and himself in a quiet suburban community with a little house and garden, fruit trees and children. He had grown up in the city and a house in East Cambridge did not fit his dreams. But, after all those years and still no children, Anthony accepted the city as the best place for him and it certainly had been the best place for Isobel who had filled the void with community service and yoga and art classes at the adult center.

The redbrick, semi-detached townhouse had been left to Isobel by her father who had inherited it from her grandfather, who built it when property close to the Court House had been practically given away. It was just a short walk to the Court

House where her grandfather had gone each day. He, too, had been a policeman and had been assigned to the Court House in his later years. He died, peacefully, waiting on the bench of Courtroom Two where he had spent years escorting good and bad alike to the chambers of justice. Not an auspicious augury and Anthony shuddered.

It was funny, he thought, even though he and Isobel had lived together in the small house for twenty-five years, he still felt like a newcomer to East Cambridge. He had been accepted as Isobel's husband, but for years he felt like an interloper in a plot where the protocol had been set in the last century and had never changed with the times. It bothered him until he realized it was just a ruse to let him know that precedent was more important that presence here in this pleasantly static enclave. So he played by the rules and accepted his wins and losses as part of the price for community stability.

After Isobel died, a proprietary interest in Anthony had been written into the scenario. The greengrocer who saved him beefsteak tomatoes, often called out with a wink and a nod telling him to stop by after work—he had something special. The butcher put away the best cuts of steaks, and the fish monger knew Anthony preferred red snapper and fresh bluefish. There was a bakery next door, and he still had a milkman who rattled bottles every other morning. It was home now and he was comfortable with it. He usually looked forward to getting home and relaxing with a book and some Verdi after a day at the station, but tonight he felt restless and wanted to talk. He needed an accepting ear. The Terre was where he listened.

He called Edward.

As he dialed, he thumbed through the papers he had been working on. They were all in order and he placed them under a paperweight—it was a piece of petrified wood from the first glorious trip he and Isobel had taken across the United States. He put it down and stepped over his ever-present filing system on the floor, gave his nose a swipe with his handkerchief—the itch was always there—and listened to the phone ring on the other end of the line as he wriggled into his jacket. He felt for the prescription Dr. Appleby had written for him still in his pocket. Maybe this new medication would help. It certainly couldn't hurt.

Edward picked up the phone immediately, as though he had been waiting for it to ring, thought Anthony.

"Edward! Can I come by? I can pick up a pizza. No. I love leftovers. Especially Cat's. Ten minutes then," and he was on his way. But, first, he called in the prescription to the drug store across the street and it was waiting for him by the time he arrived. The druggist assured him that this medication worked. "If it doesn't I'll give you your money back," he said as he handed the small plastic vial to Anthony.

Anthony nodded as though he believed every word and shoved it into his pocket.

Ten minutes later he walked up the back path to Edward's kitchen door, tapped his signature rat-ta-rat-tat-tat-tat and entered. Edward was already seated and halfway through a piece of apple pie. "Sorry, I couldn't wait. Actually, I had already started when you called. Yours is in the microwave."

Anthony sat down with a thud and straightened out the silverware and napkin that Edward put out for him. The microwave beeped. Anthony got up and pulled out a plateful of lasagna and sat down again at the old-fashioned wooden kitchen table.

Being careful to not overstep the proprietary bounds of his job he outlined the essentials of the Canfield murder—the facts that would end up being published in the papers—there really wasn't much more. He stopped talking long enough to breathe in the spicy aroma of Cat's leftover lasagna before he attacked it.

It was a while before he spoke again. "This is delicious. Thanks a lot. I spent all day cooped up in that grubby little office. With interruption after interruption, it took me the whole day, to just get a little paper off my desk." Anthony, shook his head and pushed his nose again. Then he remembered and he pulled the new vial out of his pocket, opened it and shook a pill out into his hand. He rose, got a glass of water and swallowed the pill. Edward smiled and nodded confirming that he hoped the pill worked, too.

"I know the feeling of being overwhelmed by trivialities," Edward went on.

"Do you? I thought you never felt that way. You never look frustrated or overwhelmed. I never seem to have enough time. I guess everyone feels that way," he looked up and smiled big, then frowned. "You know, it was eerie," he continued, "being in your old office. It doesn't look very different but it felt very different. It was like an alien's rendition of a known space—like in those movies where a duplicate world is created to fool some unsuspecting Earthling. Do you know what I mean?"

Edward pushed his empty plate from in front of him. He nodded absently but said, "Ann's apple pie was never as good as Cat's. She fussed around the kitchen a lot but the end result was usually just short of really good, either that or Cat should open a restaurant." It was like he was thinking out loud and Anthony was surprised. Edward seldom spoke of Ann, and never before that Anthony could remember, intimated that she had been less than perfect in any way.

"But, yes, I know what you mean about the my old office. I was there a short while ago. Remember? I thought he might have some insight on the fate of the Frost editions. Of course, it felt strange to me but I think it was because the office wasn't mine anymore and my memory, or my ego, still thought it should be. I told you about meeting with him. He was no help." He made a flicking-off motion with his hand. "We had lunch and talked about the conference and the poetry anthology which he was excited about and felt it would be a milestone in the Department. He wanted to see it become a yearly or bi-yearly competition. It's strange. I thought then it was peculiar that he hadn't asked me to be one of the judges. In the mail this morning there was a note from him—I can't tell you how strange it is to read something from someone who is dead—asking for my participation."

Edward slowly moved his head back and forth, lips pursed. "I can't believe he's gone and I can't imagine who would do such a thing or why. When I told him about the theft, he told me his thesis: that world-changing masterpieces should belong to everyone—and I'm inclined to agree. Though I don't believe it could possibly be a motive, Cat was right about his theory on first editions and how they should belong to posterity and the scholars."

"What was it Cat said . . . I've been trying to remember? Something about Canfield not being liked. Do you remember her saying something like that?" asked Anthony.

"That was just Cat being loyal to me. I left the University because it was time to go and not because I was forced to leave by Joshua or anyone else. She thinks Joshua isn't—wasn't—available enough to the students. I think she was wrong. Maybe he hadn't paid enough attention to her but he told me he would welcome all who came by. It was his idea to turn the poetry contest into a collection of student works. That's an unlikely undertaking for anyone not interested in his students. I wonder what will happen to the contest now and who will take it on," Edward said. They were both silent. Edward thinking and Anthony eating.

Anthony's rather forlorn demeanor changed with the infusion of good food. He was hungrier for both food and company than he had realized. His brain was working again and he tapped his fork, drawing Edward's attention, "As you are so close to the situation: you knew Canfield, you know the University, the English Department and the Robert Frost Chair arrangements—things that are foreign to me—I'd like to ask you to be my unofficial consultant again." Anthony could see Edward was pleased to have been asked.

"Yes, of course," confirmed Edward. "I'm happy to help in any way you see fit. This terrible murder will make everyone else in the Department uneasy and cautious. Perhaps I can glean some information by going down and talking with them. I'll do it tomorrow."

After a few minutes of thoughtful silence, Edward asked the details of the crime again. Anthony was glad for the chance to recap. He hoped they would find something to start on; some small point overlooked. Often, in the past, neglected minutiae marked the course to resolution. After Anthony related what he knew they agreed that this was a well-planned act by someone who was careful and organized.

Anthony peered across the table and over the dishes, his chin thrust forward. "I don't think it would have been easy for anyone to hang around the building after hours. There aren't a lot of closets or restrooms or staircases, and almost everyone leaves around five o'clock, according to the janitor. I suppose someone could have hidden in one of the vacant offices until everyone else left. The janitor said everyone locks his own door--if one bothers at all. One can get out of the building easily, but no one can get back in without a key after six o'clock when he locks the front door. By then it's usually deserted. They could ring the bell, but if it were after eight when the janitor leaves, no one would answer it unless, of course, someone was still there and was expecting someone, ergo opened the door for someone himself."

Anthony continued, as though he had a lot of words to get out. "And Canfield's door was locked. His morning appointment couldn't get in and had to get the janitor to open the door. Canfield must have been working late, as he often did, so the janitor says, and someone surprised him. Or maybe he had an appointment and it wasn't a surprise." He paused. "But his appointment book was there on his desk with no entry after 4:15. It could be that someone called him at the last minute and he didn't have to write it down to remember it. That could be it. Then, whoever it was, arrived later—say after eight o'clock. It doesn't appear to have been vandals; nothing was trashed."

Edward interrupted, "Then Canfield would have had to let him, or her, in. But come to think about it, it could have been someone who has an office in the building and has his own key."

"Or," Anthony went on, "someone else who has a reason to have a key. Like the janitor or the head of the department whose office is in the building next door."

"I had a key myself until recently," said Edward.

"Had?"

"When I went to see Joshua, he told me didn't have a key to the office or to the front door. I was cautioning him that not locking his door was not a good idea these days. I never locked up, of course." I was sure I could find my old keys and I supposed the locks hadn't been changed.

"And did you find them and give them to him?"

"I did. I remember it clearly because it was the day I made a vow to put my life in order." He sat up straighter and his voice took on a more determined tone. "I went down into the dreadful basement and after a short search, I found the keys in a box that I brought home from the office two years ago. Everything else in the basement seemed a shamble like my life since Ann died." He turned the pie plate and cut off another small piece of pie. "There's no excuse for that, you know."

He looked up to meet Anthony's eyes, "Ann is dead and I cannot change that--so I had better change what I can. I know that you and Lew have been putting up with me trying to jolly me out of my morbid moods and I appreciate it. Now I see a new path. And I am going to take it." Edward brushed his hands together as though that took care of that. "Anyhow, I did find my keys. So Canfield did have a set of keys and could have locked his own office. But someone else must have relocked it in that case. You said it was locked in the morning, didn't you?"

"Right."

"And no one has found any keys yet? Not in his desk?"

"Right."

"That means that if Canfield had locked his door—but why would he—then he must have opened it for the murderer. But, if it were unlocked when the murderer entered, then the murderer must have locked up when he left—which means that he must have taken the keys and must still have them. But, why lock the door?" Anthony was trying to sort it out. "Maybe to delay discovery of the body. But no one would have found it until the morning—as did happen."

"But who says that anyone acted reasonably or rationally?" Anthony went on, "I suppose there are a few sane calculating killers, but for someone to kill someone else is itself a strong case for suspecting insanity or at least instability. And there has to be a very strong motive for premeditated murder. Almost always it's money. Of course passion and rage are right up there in the top emotions. We're investigating all the angles but I don't think there's much there. Canfield's wife is a professor in Michigan. They had a commuters' marriage, which seemed successful. She has been helpful and, of course, devastated and wants to know just what happened. I hope we can tell her something that will ease her mind. There's very little money, except modest insurance and his retirement fund, and, of course, his royalties.

"I'm sure there are other wayward keys out there, like yours. It certainly looks as though someone entered the building after hours. The janitor made his last rounds--checking washrooms and trying doors—somewhere around eight o'clock. He usually leaves at eight—six o'clock to eight o'clock in the evening. Then he comes again at eight in the morning and stays until ten, only four hours a day altogether. He says that Canfield had his head buried in a pile of papers when he went by on his way out at eight. They exchanged "good nights" and he left Canfield in the building alone, as he often does. Canfield said he wouldn't be too long. So, if he had an appointment, it would have to have been after eight or the janitor would have seen the visitor.

"That's the last we have until the next morning at around nine or a little before when the student who had an appointment with Canfield at 8:45 couldn't get in to see him. He thought it was strange that the door was locked. He said he probably

would not have kept trying but he could see through the glass
that there was a light on inside so he knocked and rattled the
knob for a while. Got no response. He went off to find the
janitor and asked him to open the door as he thought Canfield
might have been listening to an iPod and didn't hear him at the
door, or worse, had a heart attack."

Edward spoke up, "I doubt if Canfield even knew what a
iPod is. I wouldn't if it weren't for Cat dancing around to a secret
unseen and unheard piper. Well, I don't hear the piper, anyway.
She does."

"Probably just as well," they said almost together and
laughed.

"Keeping to the point," Anthony pushed his empty plate
away, "Nuffield, the janitor, was persuaded to unlock the door.
I think the student was afraid of being late for an appointment.
Behind the desk, toppled onto the floor, was Canfield. The
janitor called the station from Canfield's office—the student was
still there—then went outside to the corridor, closing the door
behind him. The call came through while I was on my way in
from home. I was late because I had to stop at the courthouse to
check on a summons, so Dicky went over to secure the premises,
to be sure no one had entered or sullied the evidence at least until
the forensics had their chance. He called forensics and Doc
Appleby from the station. I arrived just after ten. And that's it.
Absolutely no clue as to a motive—not robbery, at least."

They sat in silence for a few minutes. Anthony stood up
to put his plate into the sink. "Boy, that was good and just what I
needed. Thanks. And thanks for listening." He was reaching for

the pie plate when Cat and Mark opened the back door and breezed into the kitchen.

Cat started speaking as she surveyed the scene, "I hope you finished everything! Tomorrow I make my famous veal—care to join us Commissioner? Will Lew be coming?" she looked toward Edward, "It's not your regular chess night but chess seems to have taken a back seat anyhow. How's the detective work going?" Though it sounded like Cat, she seemed a little out of sorts rushing around putting things away and into the dishwasher. Mark lurked in the background leaning against the wall and shifting from one foot to the other.

"Did you miss me?" She looked at Edward for an answer. "No? You didn't even know I was gone?"

"I knew you were gone and I got your message that you were going to your cousin's in New Hampshire for a couple of days. And, yes, I missed you."

Neither Edward nor Anthony said anything about Canfield, as though they were trying the think about how to broach the bad news. They both looked uncomfortable.

"Mandy was in town for the day so I went back with her. Mark came up today to give me a ride back as well as to sneak in a few photos. It's just over the border, you know. It was just what I needed. Mandy's so real and down to earth. And we got some good photos, too. Mark seconded her words with a nod.

"Want pie, Mark?" she asked then added, "I'll put on water for tea."

Mark made his way to the table, pulled out a chair and sat down. He said, as he tipped the chair onto the two back legs and teetered, "I think we've taken the last shots for the book. It was a good idea to get away from phones and dark rooms and just concentrate on images." The half-empty pie plate was in front of him, he spun it to face him. "And, I thought we accomplished a lot." There was a smile on his face, but not as big as it might have been. "It would have been nice if we could have stayed for another day—to enjoy some of the springtime country air and maybe take a little hike."

"That's great news. We should all celebrate. Tomorrow. We'll have Champagne! I'll call Lew. I'm sure he'd like to come. Anthony, you'll come too? You can't beat Cat's veal," Edward said as he watched Cat take out the tea and place cups on the counter with a little thud.

"Before we celebrate," she said, "we'd better wait until the pictures are developed."

"O.k.," Edward retreated a little, "we'll save the Champagne and have a nice Chardonnay instead." Edward skirted further discussion and made a decision by turning to Cat and said, "You know about Professor Canfield?

"What about him?"

"That he was found dead in his office yesterday morning?"

Her eyes opened wide under raised eyebrows and her jaw dropped before she said, "What!? No! When? How would we know? Mandy doesn't have a telly and she doesn't get the paper either! Was it in the papers? When? Did he have a heart attack? A stroke? He's not old enough, though I guess age is not the determining factor." She pulled out a chair and sat down.

"When exactly did this happen?" Her brow furrowed and she turned from Edward to Anthony trying to read beyond the words.

"It was yesterday. Or at least, discovered yesterday morning."

"Oh. Was it suicide? What a waste. I never liked him, but I didn't think he would do anything like that; I mean, he seemed stable enough. I saw him a few days ago and he was in good spirits; in fact he was ebullient. Did he leave a note-- maybe he was terminally ill or something?"

"There was no note. It wasn't suicide, he was shot—no gun has been found. So he didn't shoot himself." Edward forced himself to speak without the emotion and bewilderment that had been plaguing him.

"What?" Cat's hands flew to her face and she held it as though it would fall apart if she didn't. "I heard you. I just can't believe what you said. You mean that someone. . . killed him? Murdered him? Who would do that?"

"You said you didn't like him. I suppose there were others who felt the same or even more strongly. There must have been someone, but I find it hard to believe." said Edward. "Though you don't agree, I saw him as an involved teacher and mentor."

Very quietly she said, looking Edward in the eye, "You were right. I think he was more shy than aloof. When we saw him at the reception for the new members, he was more than friendly; " she looked at Mark who nodded, "he made me feel that he really wanted *my work* in the poetry anthology. I had a good appointment with him the next day; he was very helpful. I wish I had been nicer. Was it robbery? Maybe there's a spate of literary thefts going on; like the Wadsworth's. He had an Archibald MacLeish first edition and probably others right there in his office."

"How did you know about that?" asked Edward. "I only know because we were talking about first editions when the Wadsworth collection went missing and he told me he kept the MacLeish right there where he could show it to students. We must look for it. But, that's not much of a motive."

"No, it's not. The book is right near the door and obvious. I remarked on it and he just said something like he had known MacLeish quite well and had been given the book ages ago," Cat said.

Anthony went over the crime scene again for Cat and Mark—at least that part that the newspapers would have in the morning—there wasn't much more, he said. He had held the press off until this afternoon, prepared a statement for them, but had not answered questions, and put them off by saying he would keep them informed of new developments. His hope was that they wouldn't sensationalize the murder in the press thereby forcing unfounded conclusions that would surely interfere with the investigation. He knew it was too much to expect.

After Anthony and Mark left, Edward made Cat stop puttering around the kitchen and sit down with him. "What's wrong, Cat? I can see something's bothering you. Is it this terrible news? Anything I can help with? We could talk about it." Edward ventured.

"I don't know," she blurted. Then as though she had settled on a topic said, "I know I'm hard to work with. I'm not sure if it's Mark or his suggestions for the book or what. That's why I went away. I needed a break from him." She started to gather up the rest of the silverware and cups and put them in a neat little assemblage on the corner of the table. "All I do know is that every time I see him, I feel like I have to make an excuse for something. And that's silly, because he really is quite sensitive to my way of working and getting things done." She paused, "I guess it really is that I don't want him to think there is more to our relationship than there is." She stirred the dregs of her tea and looked tentative.

"Is that all?" asked Edward.

"Well," she hesitated and then as though she had made a decision said, "Mark and I have a long-standing, working relationship; nothing more. Mark has been around for so long. He's like an old, worn and faded, stretched out sweater with holes I know about but is the kind of comfortable and reliable that I depend on. I don't think he understands that there isn't room for romance, so I feel guilty that I might have led him on. I like him, but not in that way."

She squirmed in her chair.

Edward said, "Mark has been a good friend and he is a wonderful photographer. I've gotten used to having him around, too. At the least, you could talk with him about it so he can understand. He looked like a wounded puppy tonight."

She finished stacking the dishes. "I know I should just tell him clearly, but the book is so close to finished that I don't want him to be upset and not do his best work. That makes me feel more guilty and deceitful. So, I guess I've been grouchy with everyone when I should have told myself to shape up and do the right thing. I'll straighten it out tomorrow." She pushed her chair back, picked up the candidates for the dishwasher from the corner of the table. "What a muddle! But now I feel better. Thanks." Cat sat up straight, a little smile crept over her face and she sighed, but she didn't let Edward in on the fact that she had, indeed, met someone who had started her thinking about relationships.

". . . Someone had better be prepared for
     rage.
There would be more than ocean-water
broken
Before God's last Put out the Light was
spoken."

from ONCE BY THE PACIFIC
Robert Frost

Chapter 15

I am making this entry in my journal to support, not excuse, what I have done; yet at this moment, I cannot conceive the train of thought that led me to taking the life of poor Canfield. It seemed to make sense at the time. And, though I don't intend to confess, I don't want anyone else to suffer for my actions in the future. To make a public confession now would mean I have done this terrible thing for naught.

I'll think of something.

On another plane, I am excited about the new feelings engulfing me. The exhilaration is amazing. I feel like a different person. New! I am!

But then I envision the guilt being etched upon me like a scarlet letter—a cicatrix labeling me a monster. I can feel eyes peeling off the layers to reveal the ugly mark. It shows. I know it shows!

No, of course it doesn't!

I won't be able to deny it if anyone asks.

But no one will ask.

No one would ever guess that I would be responsible for such a thing. Would they? I don't think so.

I am sorry about poor Canfield. I say "poor" because Canfield, I think, was a grey person. Nobody will really miss him. He was a benign spirit. That he caused no harm is not a reason for being. At least, I don't think so. I wish I could say that he was really a despicable character, like Dostoyevsky's contemptible pawnbroker, and I have done a service to mankind.

No. I don't think so. There is no justification for what I have done. None! No matter what I thought then. I am disgusted.

I don't understand this ambivalence.

I don't know if I can continue this charade—the guilt will undo me.

On the other hand, it was so easy. I didn't have to plan anything at all. Everything seemed to fall into place and I don't think I left any "clues." Which only proves that spontaneity can work as well as labored planning—if one is careful not to lose sight of the desired end result. I was only there for a few minutes and didn't touch a thing. There are moments when it is all I can do not to brag just a little and dangle a clue, a scent for that itchy nose to follow.

Everyone, I'm sure, has tried to plan the perfect, undetectable crime. Maybe this is the mark I'll leave on the world!

It's interesting to me how the original motive has faded with the execution of the deed, and I wonder if criminals lose sight of their goals or waiver when fascination rears its curious head.

Sometimes I surprise myself with my commonness.

So, there it is. No one will deny that love and hate force unspeakable deeds on us all. Most crimes are committed in passion of one sort or another. My idea was singularly novel, therefore, undetectable—with no tangible motive. Can I get away with it?

How long do I need to, I wonder? How long and how intense will the suffering be? Not too long, I think. I shall continue to try not to think about it—especially when I am with people—lest I give off vibrations or telepathy or glance that could give me away. No one, though, will ever suspect me or divine the motive.

May God forgive me.

**"So people and things don't pair anymore
With what they used to pair with before."**

**from THE DOOR IN THE DARK
Robert Frost**

Chapter 16

"For Chri' sakes, Teddy, what did you do with it? How could you lose a thing like that? It's not like a glove or a hat! Stop and think. When do you remember last having it in your hands. I don't think I've seen it since we took it. You had it." There was a lot of I-blame-you-you-jerk, in his words.

Teddy slowly shook his head back and forth trying to remember something that wasn't there. He looked sheepishly across the table at his brother who was angrily stirring a cup of coffee and spilling it all over the tabletop. "I don't know. I don't think—no, I know—I didn't do anything with it. How could one be lost and not the other?" He scowled and shook his head, "I wish we hadn't taken the stuff in the first place. It's too much responsibility."

Rennie's angry whisper came spitting out, "What do you mean? Responsibility? What responsibility? We're not responsible for anything and even if we were, what do we care what happens to the things?" His brother grimaced, squeezing his eyes shut, and pulling back nearly tipping his chair over as

Rennie's irascible current, sparked like a short circuit, delivering a blow to his face. "We're not going to benefit by them. No one's ever going to benefit by them, anyway." He calmed down. "No one ever has. They were just possessions that someone kept long enough to be labeled rare and valuable. And no one has the right to own or possess history. It belongs to us as well as to them."

Rennie was presenting his usual, reasonable sounding justification but his brother's attitude was a not-convinced, less usual one—his lips were pursed and his head, almost imperceptibly, moved back and forth. More and more, recently, Rennie had failed to draw Teddy into his persuasive arguments the way he used to.

Teddy threw up his hands, "You're wrong. And nothing belongs to us. We've never taken care of anything—nothing, ever. Never considered obligations or the future or anything else that took accountability. Look at us." The coffee, rocking on the table, spilled some more. "No one with any sense would entrust anything to us. And we wouldn't do right by it if they did. Let's not kid ourselves."

Rennie looked disgusted but said more calmly, "Look," he opened his hands, palms up, "nobody knows and nobody will ever know, or care, once everything is back where it belongs." He finally drank some of the well-stirred coffee.

They were sitting at the University Center Au Bon Pain at an open-air table. Bicycles stood locked together like lovers in one corner of the outside coffee shop. The early crush of habitual morning coffee drinkers had abated and there were several tables still free in the sunshine. The sun through the newly leafing maples cast mottled shadows on the patrons and their morning rituals. No one paid a bit of attention to anyone else. It was too early for the chess players and everyone else was deep into either *The Times* or *The Globe*.

The brothers quibbled, keeping their voices low, and tried to fathom what could have happened to the other ruby-handled pistol. They still had one, but they couldn't find the other and neither of them had an answer nor could remember doing anything with it.

"And another thing," Teddy said, "Why don't we drop this juvenile charade of sneaking around pretending we're not here, go to Berkeley Street and beg forgiveness. I'm willing to admit my mistakes and pay for them. We never did anything really bad until this."

Rennie's anger showed in his petulant voice, "You don't call that brawl and breaking up that bar in Mexico really bad? And then running away? The only reason we aren't rotting away in some rat-hole of a jail in Mexico and believe me, no one would ever have heard from us again, was all the confusion about who was who and who was where!" Rennie's mood was changing and he laughed at the stupidity of those who tried to outsmart them. "It's a good thing we were planning to leave anyhow." He slapped his thigh.

"They're worse than we are. We only took from them what they had stolen from us," Teddy countered.

"Who busted up the bar, then?" He went back to stirring and thinking. He changed the subject abruptly. "Maybe you're right. But it's not like we haven't tried. We should have gone directly home in the first place—as soon as we got here—like we planned. That's why we came! We were ready then. If he had been home maybe everything would be different. And" to emphasize that nothing was his fault, he said, "you were the one that got cold feet every time we started to go home."

"Not cold feet. I just didn't want us to knock on the door and present ourselves like a couple of tramps. I still think it would be best to neaten ourselves up and go home." Teddy's lips twitched.

Rennie had a lot to say about that, "But to just walk up to the door and say we're here? Beg his forgiveness and his mercy? He never had much and I doubt if he has now. I wonder if he has forgiven us for leaving in the first place? I doubt he'd call for the fatted calf. Personally, I think he was glad to see us go."

"Who wouldn't be glad to have a couple of troublemakers out of their hair. Even Mom was getting tired of defending us all the time. She would have helped, that one last time though, if we had asked. "All we needed was a couple of thousand and that pot-head would have left us alone. I never liked to smoke the stuff anyway. So, in that way, we have changed. I wouldn't do anything just for the sake of showing off anymore."

Teddy spoke softly and continued, "I wish she were still around. That article just said the Art Association had a hard time filling her shoes—didn't say how long they had been looking. That could mean she just left."

"She's dead. At least ten or twelve years ago—maybe more. Don't set yourself up for any more disappointments. She's not going to be able to help us." Rennie was sure.

Teddy said with a lop-sided smile, "I wish we had had the chance to say goodbye. She never understood us either, but she thought she did. I just would rather remember her differently than when we left. I can still see her at the kitchen table, holding back tears and saying, 'Then go, you'll do what you want to do anyhow." Teddy flicked a crumb off the table,

"He didn't have to be so hard on us all the time and then cover for us as though he was ashamed of us—maybe he was. We couldn't help it if we didn't have his 'poetic' genes!" He spit out "poetic" like a smoker spits a bit of tobacco from his tongue.

"I think he was just trying to make us behave and didn't know how to discipline us. He knew he didn't scare us even when he was really mad and threatening. He always backed down." Teddy glanced around at the other tables before saying, "I hope I'll be better at it. And I'm tired. I want to stay put for a while. I'm ready to put up with some rules and regulations if that's what it takes. I'm tired of not having a relationship with anyone other than you." He watched for a reaction. He couldn't hide much from Rennie but he hadn't told him about meeting Cat. It was nice to have someone to talk with who didn't know anything about him or his background. He didn't want to ruin it by introducing Rennie into the mix. So he kept quiet about his lunchtime meetings.

When there was no outburst, he continued, "I wish we could undo it. The Wadsworths were always nice to us. I used to like to go there. I wonder where Jeanne and Dana are—what they've done with their lives. They were the only ones who tolerated us and I suppose that was because they didn't care if we liked them or not. They were independent in a different way—everyone liked them."

He took a sip of his coffee, made a face, and poured in another sugar packet. "It was really dumb going into the house in the first place and even dumber leaving those books under the bushes for even one night. They could have been ruined or," and he laughed in spite of the serious tone he had adopted, "stolen." It seemed an ironic twist. "I thought Mrs. Oliver was going to catch us!"

"Don't go ballistic. It was just a prank," said Rennie with a disgusted tone. He argued that they hadn't meant harm to come to anything and the books were back now. "Look at it this way, we did what we had to: made all that noise, Mrs. Oliver complained and called the police; now the books are back where they belong. They might have gotten ruined otherwise. That's what the paper said. So, at least, in that case, we did the responsible thing."

"Once again, Rennie, you've managed to turn things upside-down and practically justify taking the stuff in the first place." Teddy had let his voice get a little louder and looked around before he continued more softly, but no one had skipped a beat in his own agenda of catching up on the news of the day, or maybe the crossword. "It was wrong; we should have been contented with the sandwiches."

"And," Rennie went on as if Teddy had never even spoken, "if they hadn't been so neatly stacked in the library we probably wouldn't have thought of taking them at all. Intent," he stressed it as though it were a key word, "they always talk about intent being an integral part of guilt. We didn't intend to steal those things or cause any harm." Like he had stumbled on a great truth, it fired him up. "In fact, if it hadn't been so easy to get in, we probably wouldn't be having this conversation. It was like an invitation. You'd think they'd have changed the code in all these years. The reason I remembered the code, 4-6-9, is that's the number of letters in Dana, Jeanne and Wadsworth-- that's why they chose them. Remember?"

Teddy stared at Rennie. "Of course! Why didn't I think of that before! It was their fault for not changing the code and then, worst of all, they just left their valuables where we could take them easily!"

Rennie was still stirring his coffee and pouring sugar like a mechanical toy that was stuck and couldn't go on to the next mode in the cycle. If Teddy's words made an impression, he didn't let on, "We just have to think of a way to return the paintings and the pistols--if we can find the other one. It has to be in our room somewhere. Where else would it be? Try to remember." He took the wooden stirrer out of his cup and shot it into the wastepaper basket about 10 feet away. He was pleased with his shot and made a little fist in the air.

"Are you sure you took them both out of that special box at the Wadsworth's? Why didn't you just leave them in the box?" Teddy was now the interrogator.

"Too awkward and too big. I just wrapped them in my scarf and put them in your pack so they would take up less room. They really are beautiful--all polished and shiny. I've always had a secret desire to have them."

"It wasn't so secret. You tried before. Remember? You can't ever keep them. You know that, don't you? What would you do with them? Hide them in a closet? It's not like you could display them." Teddy fiddled with his pack, zipping and unzipping the flap. "Why didn't you put them in your own pack?"

"No room. It was loaded with sandwiches and cans of Spaghettios."

"I only took them out once. I had forgotten they were there" Teddy was remembering out loud, "and I put them right back. I didn't even take them both out--only one. I was in the Quad and I thought I saw Uncle Lew across the path. I was in a hurry to get out of there, but I know I put it back, and the pack has been in the closet ever since, until today. We should have left them with the books on Mrs. Oliver's lawn." He did not look happy.

"Was it Uncle Lew?" asked Rennie.

"Huh?" he refocused, "Oh, I don't know—I don't think so. This guy looked thinner and much older. Still, I suppose he has changed a lot. Maybe I wouldn't recognize him anyway. I didn't hang around to find out.

"I'll go back to the same bench (he did not say he had been there several times already, but was not looking for the pistol) and search under and behind and in the bushes but if it did fall out I don't see how it would still be there.'

"Just go look. And try to remember. You must have taken them out at another time." Rennie picked up a newspaper from the next table, scanned it and folded it purposefully under his arm.

"This is what we do. I'll wrap the paintings in newspaper and leave them in the coatroom at the Museum. Then everything will have been returned--except the pistols. I don't think we should return one without the other. Do you? We'll return them--as soon as we find the other. It ought to be in some really dramatic way. I'll have to think about it." He gulped down some coffee and reconsidered, "In fact, we need a little cash. Take the one we still have down to that pawnshop on Mass. Ave. Make up a name and address and try to look nondescript—see if you can get a hundred or so for it." Rennie spoke as though he were asking his brother to go to the store for a package of gum. He hesitated for a minute as he saw protest mounting his brother's face. "Don't worry," he said, "it'll be safe at the pawnshop. We can get it back." Teddy didn't look convinced, so Rennie said, "Never mind--I'll do it."

"May something always go unharvested!
May much stay out of our stated plan. . .

from UNHARVESTED
Robert Frost

Chapter 17

The shop with its medieval three golden balls over the door was a step back into another time when it was common to pawn possessions. A plate-glass, front window jam packed with musical instruments, watches, and jewelry was shielded with a heavy, iron-mesh lock-up. The owner of Cash-for-Stash, was not in his small, dark and dusty, old-fashioned shop when a young man came in with a beautiful antique pistol. Herman's brother-in-law, Ben, was at the counter, helping out as he often did. Retired for a dozen or so years, he had nothing better to do and he enjoyed meeting and talking with the characters who came in to exchange their treasures for a pittance of their true value and often the value could not be measured in dollar bills.

Herman Schuyler's appointment with the loan officer at the bank made him late returning to the shop at just after five o'clock closing time. Otherwise, he would have phoned the police earlier, he said. It was funny because he had posted the description of the pistols and paintings by the cash register, but his brother-in-law didn't see it

Small wonder. The inside of the shop was as dark and dingy as the outside promised and every inch of space was cluttered with dusty treasures that looked as though they had been forgotten long ago. Mr. Schuyler explained that yesterday he and Ben were so elated with his getting the equity loan on his house that as soon as he came in they closed up shop and they celebrated down the street at the Plow and Stars with a few quaffs. It wasn't until he saw the pistol in the morning that he phoned Ben and asked about it. Then he wasted no time calling the police station.

Anthony responded in a flash and sent the pistol to the lab for tests. "Of course, there were no discernible prints and the forensics are sure this pistol hadn't been fired in at least a hundred years, though it could have been. They removed a silver bullet from the firing chamber. It was one specially made for the pistol just like Jim Wadsworth said. The pistol was clean and the action was free and responsive."

"And something else," Anthony said giving Dicky his "this-is-big" look, "The analyses from the Canfield case have come back: the bullet that was removed from Canfield is 35-caliber and is what this gun uses."

Dicky could tell something else important or outrageous, probably both, was coming next. He waited silently and attentively while Anthony finished.

"It looks as though the Wadsworth burglary and the Canfield murder are linked." He paused, eyebrows raised, "The pistol might be the murder weapon. The post=mortem report doesn't say the bullet was silver, but I'll bet it is."

There it is, thought Dicky, "I had a feeling there was a tie-in, too. Maybe it was the Frost first editions and the Frost chair or maybe it was just the proximity of the scenes. Now it seems more certain."

"Yes," then rhetorically Anthony said, "how many silver bullets are lying around gathering dust these days?"

The traffic outside the open window honked and squealed insinuating the outside world onto their turf. Anthony put his hands to his head and covered his ears for a moment. Dicky always felt Anthony was really talking to himself and that Dicky just happened to be there. He let the words flow over him, absorbing what he could, and knowing that explanations would be forthcoming. Right now he was wondering how a pistol that hadn't been fired in over a hundred years could eject a bullet without a trace. So he wasn't as sure of the connection as his boss.

"There were two pistols—remember?" Argus stopped mid-pace to look at Dicky and spoke as though he had read Dicky's mind. "And one, of course, is still missing, and if one of them could have been fired, the other probably could too."

Dicky was embarrassed, like he was betraying his boss with counter-thoughts, even though he knew Anthony couldn't read his mind. Anthony didn't notice. He said he thought that maybe this was the break they had been hoping for. But after the interview with Schuyler and his brother-in-law, he was almost as discouraged as he had been before. Mr. Schuyler's brother-in-law wore thick glasses that looked like the bottoms of old coke bottles and he had difficulty telling Anthony from Dicky in the dim shop.

He said, "He was about your height and size and he had on grayish clothes. He might have had a beard or maybe just needed a shave. In any case, he was fair--light haired. The shop is so dark I couldn't really tell. If I had known I was going to have to give a description," he was apologetic, "I would have asked him to step closer to the window."

Not a stellar description, but better than nothing, thought Anthony, and at least now they knew there were people involved and not poltergeists, as he had said he suspected when it seemed like the crime was a black hole falling in on itself.

That theft was the craziest thing he had ever run into and they still had no clue about who would attempt such a foolhardy stunt, or why. True, most of the stolen articles were back where they belonged but that didn't make it any less puzzling, more so, in fact, and Anthony was annoyed that the pieces weren't fitting together and forming at least a part of the illusive picture.

It discouraged him, too, that Edward and Lew had not been as helpful as he had hoped. He mumbled aloud to Dicky after they left the pawnshop, "This is their kind of thing-- psychological and weighty." He focused on Dicky, "You know, Dicky, those two minds have unraveled literary and economic tangles that we," he pointed at himself and Dicky, "couldn't even begin to fathom. In the old days Edward could always, after listening to me present a befuddling case, come up with a few astute observations and a few questions and start me on the path to solution. The other day Lew naively said: motive was key. Of course motive is the key!"

He was flinging his hands around and his voice grew louder. People walking up the long stone flight of steps to City Hall turned to look at Anthony and Dicky as they walked back to the station from the pawnshop. Dicky gave him a little nudge with his elbow. Anthony, surprised, looked around, jammed his hands into his pockets and lowered his voice.

He was practically whispering now, "No one commits any kind of crime for itself; there's always a motive: like money or position or control, or revenge or spite or greed. But this appears to have been a random act or did until we made that connection with the gun." He made a little gesture as though he had a gun in his hand and pointed it at Dicky. "You know, of course, that there is no such thing as random," he challenged Dicky and then explained, "You have to plan random. Isn't that a kick? Random is an oxymoron." He was nodding and threw a quick glance at Dicky, "There are whole institutes where professors study and argue about randomness and chaos—related studies." He kicked a pebble off the sidewalk and scuffed along as though it was unbelievable to him too.

Dicky didn't understand what was going on in Anthony's mind; but then, he seldom did. It was always a bunch of fractured thoughts to Dicky, but somehow those thoughts got rearranged and started to make sense as they were lined up and shifted around. Surely, the pistol would lead somewhere and, as he said before, it could be the break they were looking for.

Anthony was rambling. Their walking was a rambling kind of step too, except that it was getting them back to the station. Maybe his meandering talk was going to get them somewhere, too. They turned down the one-way street that led to the back door of the station.

Handsome Harry, who said he was ninety-seven years old shuffled into their path. His attire was, as always, coordinated--red high-tops and a red sweatshirt. He was carrying a green backpack in his hand instead of wearing it on his back. He was mumbling through a growth of beard.

"Here, get yourself a shave and a haircut, Harry," Anthony shoved a bill into Harry's hand without breaking his stride or his chain of thought.

They rehashed all kinds of theories and nothing seemed to fit. They agreed that theft is not the motive for either crime— definitely. Anthony posited, "Unless the thieves took something we don't know about and with those inventories, I just don't think that's possible. And, now it is very likely that the crimes of he theft and the murder are linked in some obscure way. How? is the big question. They seem to have no straight-forward connection." He sighed, and Dicky listened attentively, his face still screwed up in a frown of sorts. "Unless, of course, someone intended to steal the pistols to commit the murder!"

He went on, "The Wadsworths had never even met Canfield. True, some of the stolen editions were of great interest to Canfield, but they were all found at Mrs. Oliver's and Canfield didn't even know about the theft until Edward told him. Right? Right. Nothing seemed to be missing from Canfield's office.

Not even his first editions. For a while they thought that Edward's old keys were missing but, it's possible that Edward's old keys were not even the right keys and Canfield just tossed them—then not even keys would be missing. Then again, if they were the right keys, why would the murderer take them. Was he coming back? Was that why he locked the door?" Dicky shook his head. It didn't make sense to him either. "Maybe that was it! The murderer was coming back later. But why? There's nothing of monetary value, not even a computer. And the first editions could easily have been taken at the time. I just don't get it!"

Anthony wasn't finished. They turned into the 1940's-style concrete building and scaled the stairs to the second floor, "Maybe it was professional jealousy? Who would be jealous of Canfield? Or who would gain by his demise? No one. Cat said Canfield's students didn't like him but that's not a motive for murder. Someone would have to benefit by his death. And, we haven't found anyone yet who would."

It was a muddle and Anthony said, "I know what those poor gerbils on the treadmill must feel like expending all that energy and never getting anywhere. The difference, of course, is that the gerbils don't know any better. I should."

"Edward said we must look at it from a different perspective." Dicky was trying to help, "That what we're seeing is not the true picture or at least it could be something more obscure. Like one of those psychological depictions where you see two champagne glasses that can also be seen as two profiles. It all depends on how you look at it. What you focus on. What you expect to see. We have pieces to the puzzle but the pieces do not seem to fit into the spaces. Nothing fits or lines up."

Anthony nodded, "Exactly!"

They walked into Anthony's office, closed the door and sat opposite each other; with Anthony behind his desk. The phone blinked and Anthony blinked too, waiting for it to stop. It did. He felt uneasy about not answering. It was an inside line, he reasoned to himself, so they'll call back. He didn't want interruptions.

"The other night do you know what the three of us did, Dicky? No, of course you don't. Well, I'll tell you and you may think we're crazy." Anthony's handkerchief was out and swiping at his poor, red nose; then he pulled out the prescription Appleby gave him, shook a little yellow pill out and popped it into his mouth. He reached for his coffee cup from this morning and swallowed the bit of cold coffee from the bottom of the cup. "We tried substituting motives and suspects like that game, **CLUE**. But, as there were no suspects at all and no obvious motive, we just put everyone we could think of who knew Canfield into the scenario, including me, Edward, Lew, Cat and that other old student of Edward's, Ambrose." Anthony was chuckling now. "If I had to choose someone based on our game, it would be Robert Ambrose. He's the only one that I can see who would benefit at all. He's probably going to be the next Robert Frost Fellow, if rumors at the University are right."

"But this is no game. There is a murderer out there somewhere. We'd better come up with something before there's another crime or another murder." Anthony finally ended the diatribe.

Dicky had been quiet throughout and now ventured a thought that had been flitting back and forth in his brain. "I think a good bet is that the theft was staged just to get the pistols."

Anthony looked as if he were trying that on for size. He was nodding his head again.

Dicky went on, "That would mean that the murder had been well planned. Taking the books and paintings was only a cover. Or maybe the books were just afterthoughts that might bring in some easy cash and when they tried to cart them away ran into trouble. I mean, I know they're valuable but they would be cumbersome to lug around trying to peddle or pawn. They could have taken the paintings and pistols with a plan in mind and then had second thoughts about the books and left them in Mrs. Oliver's yard. At least this thief or thieves have consciences. They could have trashed the books and no one would ever have known.

"Or maybe they were coming back for them and just didn't get there until it was too late. It could be that the thieves were not the ones who strew the papers over Mrs. Oliver's lawn or maybe these thieves with consciences didn't want to see the books ruined and knew that Mrs. Oliver would notice immediately and take measures. Or maybe they were interrupted in the first place and had to leave the books wherever they could and get themselves away in a hurry. Remember, the Wadsworths had arrived from the Cape at about ten or ten-thirty tired after the traffic and driving. But it was late enough for anyone to think they might not be returning that evening."

Dicky paused, drummed his fingers on the desk and then went on, "I fail to see any other connection though with the murder of Canfield, besides the possibility of the pistols. And as I said, that could have been the real reason for the theft. Why do you suppose that one of them has turned up but not the other? It could be that the other pistol, the one that is still missing, is the one that was used to shoot Canfield and the murderer has another use for it before pawning it too, or that it has already been disposed of. Do you think there's more than one person involved? I do." Dicky said he felt like a gerbil, too.

Anthony, revitalized by the energetic monologue from Dicky, said thoughtfully, "I don't know, Dicky. Usually murderers are lone wolves. But thieves are often collaborators because they need someone to drive the get-away-car or hold the flashlight or keep watch or to help carry away the loot. That makes a connection difficult to understand and if one of the pistols taken from the Wadsworth's was used to kill Canfield, there certainly is a connection between the two crimes. And it would appear that there must have been a method to the random appearing madness of the theft. And I would have to think there is more than one thief and because we think the theft and murder are linked, more than one to be charged with murderer."

**"But at last came a knock
And I thought of a door
With no lock to lock."**

**From THE LOCKLESS DOOR
Robert Frost**

Chapter 18

It was chess night but it wasn't Monday. Not often but every once in a while something came up that turned Wednesday into chess night. Both Edward and Lew had been struggling with a spring cold so each had cautiously approached the other only to find one another sneezing and coughing. Cat settled it by declaring Wednesday chess night this week. That ended it. And they both were better by Wednesday.

Lew still looked ashen and a little wobbly. But he made his usual stop at the Blacksmith Shop on his way home from the Square. He carefully held the Sacher Torte upright so the icing would not be squashed and end up stuck to the side of the box. It looked beautiful when it was put into the box and he wanted to keep it picture perfect. It was his way; anything less than perfect, he considered a compromise. So he carried it carefully holding it upright instead of dangling it from the end of the string loop handle. He conjured up Cat's appreciative smile and knew she would be pleased with the rich, chocolaty confection. His feet led him along his usual shortcut through the Quad. As was his usual habit, he looked forward to taking a few minutes for a little rest, to sit in contemplative silence before finishing his walk home.

It had been rainy and cold for the preceding four days-- so the balmy sixty-five degrees and sunshine brought everyone out to spend some of the winter dues. He spied a free bench up ahead just off the path and sat down, carefully setting the torte beside him. He tilted his handsome face towards the late afternoon sun and went over in his mind his list of things to do. He had crossed off several items today and kept appointments with his doctor and his lawyer. One more visit to his publisher and that would be finished too.

It annoyed him that he tired more quickly and easily than he used to. He sighed. A quiet hush settled around him as he thought how nice it was to sit and relax with philosophical ponderings, thoughts that didn't have to be acted upon. It was a favorite pastime: Does the concert pianist play well because he loves it or does he love it because he plays so well? Sometimes Lew wondered if he became an economist because he liked orderly progressions or if he liked the orderly progressions because he was an economist. Some people, he thought, write such tripe, but I just think about it and don't clutter pages with words and thoughts that don't merit notice. He didn't really believe that though. He'd tell anyone who would listen that he would have liked to have lived during the Golden Age of the Greeks when logic and metaphysics were revered. He often quoted the ancient Greeks' thesis that great strides in civilization only came with leisure when philosophers could pursue exchanges of ideas and discuss means and goals unencumbered by the pressures of time and earning a living. He chuckled a little to himself and half dozed in the soft spring ambience. Spring is a lovely time—maybe his favorite season; how many more would he be able to enjoy? He unfolded his long legs, got up and resumed his trajectory across the Quad with the torte safely upright. He looked at his watch. There was time for a little reading and maybe a short nap before he went to Edward's for dinner.

Later that evening, Edward praised Cat, "Dinner was right up to your standards." He thumped his middle a little and pushed himself away from the table. "I like all that fancy stuff, but I like meatloaf and baked potatoes best!"

Cat rolled her eyes, "Plebian! And look at you. You've gained some weight. The buttons on that vest are popping." She glanced at Lew and said, "I think you've lost some weight though. How about another helping?"

Lew shook his head. "These old wintery clothes stretch out, get baggy, and make one think they've shed pounds because everything feels looser. Deceiving!"

They all made one clearing-the-dishes-from-the-table-trip to the kitchen then settled in the living room with coffee and Sacher torte. Cat o-o-o-ed. Lew felt he had made a good choice—it certainly looked and smelled delicious. As she started slicing into the torte, Lew took out the chessmen. He placed the ebony and ivory chessmen on the inlaid ash and cherry board slowly and carefully. The rich patina from years of use shone in the lamplight and he fondled each satiny piece as he set it in its place. It was ritual he enjoyed.

The front doorbell sounded and a whoosh breezed through the door ushering in Anthony and Mark. Mark looked as though he would rather be almost anywhere else. He edged to the side, trying to get away from Anthony who was treating him like a wayward child, holding him by the collar.

"Found this young man lurking outside and decided to bring him in with me!" Anthony joked. He released Mark then he changed to a more serious tone, "Don't you think you should lock the front door after dark? I know you lock it later, but it's easy to forget and there has been so much going on lately that I think I would prefer that you err on the conservative side."

"Then someone would have to get up to let you in," said Cat watching Mark toss his parka onto the floor beside the sofa and sink into one end of it. It was where Cat usually sat, but she was sitting, instead, on a straight-backed Windsor artfully balancing her dessert on one knee. "Besides, I always remember to lock up."

Anthony headed straight to the Sacher torte. "Well, it's just a thought. Anyone could walk right in and up the stairs and we would never know it, especially when there is a lively conversation going on. And I'll bet," he looked at Lew, "you don't lock up when you come over here either. You know, the combination lock the Wadsworths have is a good solution. You wouldn't have to carry a key or hide it in the planter or flowerpot or on a hook on the underside of the house."

No one responded and he looked as though he didn't expect it. It was just one of his pronouncements that he said he wished they would heed. He seemed to be giving his full attention to the Sacher torte and looked around for a plate—they were stacked on the other side of the coffee pot—he reached for one. "I had a late lunch at Tonio's so if you were going to offer me supper, I'll decline it tonight." He sniffed. "Smells good, though. You don't have to twist my arm to get me to have some of this. O.K.?" He paused, "I can get it myself." He gave his nose a rub with the back of his hand and waited on himself. He smiled as he sliced a piece of torte with precision and poured himself coffee before picking up a fork and a napkin and making his way to the sofa. "I've got some news!"

Mark looked at his watch and said, "Well, I'd like some of whatever it is that smells so good, I didn't even have time for lunch today. "I'm starving!" Mark who was as tall and thin as an El Greco painting, was always hungry. A bunch of cameras dangling from around his neck pushed his head forward so he looked as though he was stalking someone and should have a big magnifying glass in his hand. Cat often said she thought he probably went to sleep mumbling F-ll . . . 25 feet . . . 200 ASA.

"You know where everything is and please forgive me if I don't get up to get it for you." There was a slight edge to Cat's voice. She softened, "Actually, I left a plate ready for you on the counter by the microwave, but I don't think it's even cold yet— we just finished." Cat took another bite of Sacher torte and smiled a saccharine half-smile at the room in general. Lew eyed Cat from the chessboard and thought she treated Mark like a pesky younger brother who needed help finding his own left foot. He wouldn't have liked it if he had been Mark, especially if he cared about Cat the way it seemed Mark did.

Edward, too, glanced across the room at her and she evened out her smile.

Unaware of the drama going on around him, Anthony sank into the other end of the sofa and dug into his dessert. The chessmen in place, Lew watched, an indulgent smile crossing his face, wondering to himself how this bull-in-a-china-shop character ever managed to get through coffee and dessert on his lap.

An exasperated sigh preceded Cat's next words, "What's the news?"

As though on cue, Anthony's napkin slipped between the cushion and arm of the sofa. He carefully stuck his hand down into the crevice to retrieve it keeping his plate balanced on his knee. He looked up and grinned. "What's this? A bonus?" He pulled out the napkin, opened it, dropped it on his lap and secured it in place by setting his dessert plate on top of it, then he focused on something else he had pulled out with the napkin. He turned two photos around and looked first at one, then the other.

Edward looked over. "What is it? Some of Mark's photos?"

Anthony inspected the photos and handed them to Lew who gave them a cursory glance before he started to hand them on to Cat. They were almost out of his hand when he said, "Wait a minute. Look here Edward." He took the photos back from Cat and handed them to Edward.

"Why. . . yes. I think you're right," Edward's eyes lit up. "Where's Mark?"

Mark came in from the kitchen with a heaped plate and was preparing to sit on the sofa. "What is it? Everyone looks like they're waiting for something to happen. What do you have there? Looks like some of my Government School pictures."

Cat said, "They must have slid between the cushions when I dropped them the other night and they skittered all over the place. I didn't count them when I put them back, but I thought they were all there. Let's see." She looked and did a double take. It looked to her like Ed-of-the-bench-at-lunchtime. She took a breath as if about to speak, decided against it, and just handed the photos to Edward.

"When you took these pictures, did you interview the subjects? I mean did you take names or anything?" Edward was obviously anxious and he stood up to show Mark the photo in question.

"No," said Mark picking up his fork, "I usually try to get names just in case I want to use them, but that night was such a crush and, as you know, it is not easy to get around the open space on the first floor where they often hold those impromptu gatherings. Some of these were taken with a telephoto lens from across the atrium. Why?" He turned back to his plate.

Lew spoke up, "These two might be the twins."

Fork midway, Mark stopped, "Really? Let me see. Oh, I remember them because they did look alike and I thought they would be photogenic. They are, aren't they? I have the negatives if that's of any help. But I didn't take their names." He started eating again.

Edward stood up and started pacing the room as if to keep up with his racing mind. "Is there a way to find out who was there? Maybe someone at the School knows? Did you have to register to get in that evening? Of course not." He answered his own question. "I do think it is Teddy and Rennie."

Lew nodded.

Anthony joined in, "Are you sure? Let me see. I never really knew them well; they were always at school or studying when I was around." He spent a few minutes studying the photos. "You know, I think I've seen these two around Central Square. They made an impression on me at the time because they look alike. There's a new age shop or something like that where they sell crystals and have geodes in the windows that I go by often and I think I've seen them there. Or at least it looked like them . . . or one of them." He leaned his head to one side. "Of course, they look like dozens I've seen about the Square. If I can take this picture, I'll have a go at it and ask around. We certainly should be able to locate them." He stopped and considered the pictures again. "And, you know, this looks like the fellow who has come to the gym and helped with my teenage basketball players." He looked at Edward, "They called him Ed. Dicky would know, I'll ask him."

Cat picked up the photo and quietly studied it this time. Then she walked over to the bookcase shelf, reached up, and pulled out an old photo album and started thumbing through it. Close to the end of the album was a snapshot that she stared at for a minute or two. She passed the album to Edward. "This must be about the last one taken here," she said. The photo was of two handsome teenagers with blond hair and blue eyes smiling at whoever looked. It was like those paintings where the eyes follow you around the room. Neither had a beard but there was a remarkable resemblance to the newly found photos.

"Yes, that's how I remember them. You can see that the beards have changed their looks a little; they look so much older; actually they are. Anything over ten years is a long time when you're young. A world of changes can span a decade."

Cat continued staring at the photo and Mark, still watching from across the room, asked softly, "What is it, Cat?"

"Nothing." She shook her head as if trying to dislodge a filmy bit of cobweb. "It just seems strange that after all these years, they might really be here. I think of them as enchanted spirits wandering about unable to alight."

Lew thought there was more to it. And he wondered what it was.

"Live and let live,
believe and let believe."

from A MASQUE OF MERCY
Robert Frost

Chapter 19

Edward stood by the bookcase holding the photos and the album Cat had handed him. He was adrift in a fold of time as a flurry of images floated through his mind: the twins as babies, toddlers, children, teenagers. "Maybe they feel they have no home." He said quietly and turned the photo album page. A flickering smile came to his lips. "They always preferred longer hair. It was the style," he sighed. "So much time has passed they wouldn't be the same boys who left those many years ago. No doubt they've matured and made some compromises with society. I hope so, at least. But even if they haven't, I want them home." Edward put the album aside, took off his glasses, rubbed them with his napkin and replaced them, giving himself time to gather a few wisps of thought.

He had been hurt when they left but also relieved. They were so difficult; there was always a minefield of crises to tiptoe through or around. It was painful to think that so much time had passed with not a word from them. Had they been so busy that they couldn't have dropped a line to let us know how they were? Did they think we wouldn't worry? Did they think we wouldn't care? Did they think about their mother?   Do they even know she died?

Finally he stopped polishing, replaced his glasses and said, "I've been wishing for a chance to set things straight; maybe this is it." He slowly picked up the album again and turned another page. "Look. Here's one with the Wadsworth children," he turned pages, muttering asides and chuckling. Everyone in the room quietly waited in limbo, not wishing to interrupt or jar Edward. He seemed to be somewhere else anyhow.

He was reviewing the past years like a this-is-your-life show. It wasn't their fault he hadn't known how to be a father. If he had been a better disciplinarian things might have been different; or just if he had been a better father. He never knew how to reconcile the difference between expectation and performance. Not that the twins were dull. They were both artistic, like their mother, and he had always expected—and wanted—them to be more scholarly. The guilt came from expecting them to be more like him—and being disappointed when they weren't. He knew that now.

A serene quiet had descended over the room, and after several silent minutes, Edward said, "I've thought a great deal about the whole situation and I've been doing some personal reckoning, too. I must find them and now it appears that it's going to be possible." Edward put the album down, walked to the lamp beside the fireplace and watched it light up the watercolor over the mantle as he turned it on. "I feel this is my second chance to show them compassion, understanding, and anything else that will help them to forgive me, and I'm not going to miss it."

Anthony fidgeted and said, "I know it will all work out." He waited, patiently for him, for the proper break to tell them the news he was bursting with, but Cat stole his opportunity. So he quietly fussed and ate some more torte, listening to Cat. Lew was in his place at the chessboard. Edward was pacing about.

Cat was turning the pages of the album as she spoke. "I've always wished I had known them. I often feel a presence— maybe one, or the other, or both—in the house when I'm alone and thinking."

Lew, nodding, said, "It's more likely to be Ann's aura than it is to be the twins. Though I adored them both, neither had that quality of instilling confidence or inspiring greater deeds. What they did know was how to get their own charming way. Just a smile and "please, Uncle Lew" did me in every time. Together, they were an enigma."

He related what he said was one typical scheme they caught him in. "They were about fourteen, I think, and wanted to go to some event—a movie or a concert—and they needed twenty dollars. I learned afterward that they had been refused the money by Edward and Ann because they'd been caught in a lie and their allowances had been cut. I don't remember exactly. Anyhow, they came to the door with a book of raffle tickets for a Sunfish, a small sailboat, that the winner was to be drawn at the Christmas Fair at school. Naturally, I bought the tickets and secretly hoped I would win so I could give the boys the boat. I forgot all about it until much later. It was sometime in the spring when the raffle book with my name on the stubs was found under the porch by the gardener. They had never turned in the raffle stubs or the money. To them any means was justified as long as their ends were served." Lew smiled, "Still, I would have done anything they asked as they had me wrapped around their little fingers." With a resigned sigh he added, "Don't ask me how they managed to do it. It must have been something mystical. You can't imagine how the planet lit up when they smiled."

"How did you tell them apart? Doesn't one have a scar or a lisp, or a cauliflower ear, or something else to let you know which one is which? I've always wished I had a twin. Think of the pranks you could play. How old would they be now?" Cat asked with obvious interest.

"Oh, they'll be thirty in August," said Edward. "About the same as you and Mark. But I don't think you'd have much else in common. And they did constantly play pranks. One never knew which one to blame for an infraction. I never did. Of course, they did it on purpose. I think, though, that more often Rennie led Teddy. But they both did their share. They were always pretending to be each other and there was no way to tell them apart unless they wanted you to—no scars or lisps or deformed ears." He smiled, "Ann said she knew, but I think she just thought she knew, and they fooled her too." He stood behind Cat and looked over her shoulder as she turned more album pages. "Their pursuits were not intellectual. They were bright enough. Their achievement test scores were always among the highest in the class."

The inevitable conclusion made his brow wrinkle and he frowned, "I don't suppose they looked at an academic life as a life. For exciting interaction, I don't paint a brilliant canvas." He tapped one of the photos as though he was pointing out something to himself. "They were drawn by the off-beat and esoteric," he looked up, "like the Bohemians of my youth. And I don't blame them one bit. I envied the Bohemians with their exotic and carefree life styles; they were as alien to me as Australian bush men. But I had only sympathy for the plight of the Bohemians because they ended up not using their talents to forward civilization." His face teased a reconciled smile, "Oh well, things have changed since then."

"And those boys could talk you into anything! I was ready to climb the mountains of Tibet with them one summer," chuckled Lew. "They had convinced me that I should take them both off to search for Karma. I think Ann put the kibosh on that. Just as well, really."

It's funny, Edward thought as he sat in the middle of a roomful of friends, how things seem to work out. He could feel resolution stirring and it made him happy. There were things he wanted the twins to know. Now that they were older perhaps they'd understand and forgive. At the least he could apologize and let them know they'd be coming into a sizeable legacy one day. He wanted them to come home.

It is right in there
Betwixt and between . . .

from PERIL OF HOPE
Robert Frost

Chapter 20

Anthony twiddled his thumbs and impatiently smoothed his napkin a few more times. When at last there was a lull in the twin stories, he jumped in, "You probably think that because the books have been recovered we've put the theft on the back burner. Well, we're still very much involved and there is something I think you'll find interesting." He didn't pause. He had the floor now and steamrolled on.

"First, the not-so-good news: the paintings have not shown up at any of the galleries where they might be put up for sale. I'm inclined to agree with," and he looked around and settled on Mark, "whoever said they thought it was like the Gardner theft and those paintings may now be in some private collector's secret lair and never be seen again.

"The good news is in the matter of the pistols." Here was his *piece de resistance* and he jumped to his feet, "One of them has been found!" he strutted around the room, hands thrust deep in his trouser pockets, "Yes! in a pawnshop on Mass. Avenue just around the corner from the Station. The ticket stub has a fake name," he was laughing, "C. Monte Cristo—but, of course, that's to be expected. Only a fool would leave his real name. At least this guy has a sense of humor." Anthony beamed, "It's the first break we've had, and there's more."

"No wonder you've been so fidgety tonight; you've shown remarkable restraint." Lew gave a chuckle and continued, "What a break! Were you able to get a description of the person who pawned it?"

"Oh, sure," said Anthony at last able to rehash the new evidence, "But it's vague, to say the least. It could be anyone. Average-to-tall height, average build, average coloring, average and grey! Of course the shopkeeper who saw him is so nearsighted that he couldn't tell me from Dicky." A little guffaw slipped out.

"Are the rubies still in the handle?" asked Mark who continued to show an interest in the pistols and the jewels.

"Oh, yes. The pistol is in excellent condition. The pawnshop owner, Mr. Schuyler, knows a little about antique pistols and said that he thought it could still be fired and forensics agree. He said it's certainly worth more than the hundred dollars his brother-in-law gave for it." Anthony indicated with a wave of his hands that that was all there was about that matter for now.

Mark spoke up, "I'd like to see the pistols and photograph them—or it. I can see an article for a magazine or the Sunday paper. I could show the beauty and craftsmanship of an antique pistol and contrast it with what must be, to many, the cold functionality of the newest thing in Colt personal defense." He looked about the room hopefully.

Anthony frowned, "Sure, sometime. More important right now is Canfield's slaying. I'm saying slaying, because, though we all know it was murder, I don't like to call it murder yet. Arguably it could be an accident. The weapon has not been found. I mention that because there is something strange which I believe is more than coincidence." When he looked up he was nodding his head as he liked to do when he had discovered something. "And the autopsy results are in."

"Well. Tell us." Edward harumphed, "

Anthony, playing with the suspense and drama, squinted through slitted eyes like a story teller about to reveal the ogre's weakness. "It's just as we thought. Death was caused by a bullet wound—35-caliber to be precise—to the heart." But Anthony was not finished. "I suspected, as I said before, that a French Dardinelle was used to kill Canfield, which is the only pistol I know that uses 35-caliber ammunition. The 38- and 22- are much more popular."

"Is that the right word?" asked Cat.

Annoyed at the interruption, Anthony put a finger to the side of his head and thought about it for a moment before he amended, "The 38- and the 22- are much more common." Cat nodded, appeased. "But this is interesting, isn't it:" he spoke slowly stressing each word again, "the antique pistols also use 35-caliber bullets and there was probably at least one silver bullet already in the firing chamber of each gun. Remember what James Wadsworth said? Anyhow, it does make an interesting connection that Canfield might have been killed with a weapon that was stolen from the Wadsworths." He pulled in his audience, "Don't you agree?" and here was his big pronouncement: "I should tell you that the 35-caliber bullet from the utopsy was . . . silver."

"Canfield said he didn't know the Wadsworths but we can be sure he knew about their collection, especially the Robert Frost books." Anthony had worked himself into a corner again and shook his head, "But, I would hardly call a theft of books a motive for murder. Would you?" Everyone in the room was shaking their heads, too, at such a vague connection.

Edward said, "If there is a connection, it must have something to do with the Frost books. What else could it be?"

Anthony paid no heed, "And, according to the autopsy, he was killed somewhere between eight and ten o'clock at night and died almost immediately. It's a little strange because the head injury happened before he died. Maybe the fall had nothing to do with the shooting. There was nothing else remarkable to report. No other marks, no struggle. Most of the prints around the room were undistinguishable, there were so many everywhere and mostly all smudged--probably because they had been there for so long and they were mostly Canfield's it turns out.

"The janitor confirmed that the door was locked in the morning and that was unusual, too. Canfield, he said, never locked his door. It's puzzling as to why anyone would lock the door when he—or she—left. The janitor left Canfield almost every night, in his office, with the door slightly ajar. They always spoke, as they did that night, and made some polite remarks about the weather or something. The janitor had not let anyone into the building before he left at eight."

Anthony went on to say that Dicky Cronin had taken statements from everyone in the building and no one had noticed or seen anything worth reporting. "Not that anyone would say anything about anyone else anyhow. These academics never see or know anything! I don't know if they won't admit to knowing or really don't know because they're floating around in some nether region and only notice what relates to themselves."

He paused to dangle a tidbit, "But they did give me some scuttlebut. Have you heard who they think will be the next Robert Frost Fellow?" Glancing around he saw there were no takers and, like the cat that swallowed the canary, he had a big smile on his face. "No? Well, if they're right, and I suppose they are, it's to be none other than your stuffy old student, Robert Ambrose!"

"Not really!" said Edward. "I'm hardly surprised though. Ambrose is an esteemed journalist and his time-honored and scholarly contributions to the world of poetry are renown. One of his first treatises was on Frost, and I included a part of it in the foreword of one of my own books. I think he's a good choice. Don't you, Cat?"

Cat pouted, then smiled sourly and said, "I guess so. I've always thought him a bit pompous. Cat looked straight at Argus, "I didn't like Canfield and I don't really like Ambrose. Maybe I did the dastardly deed and shouldn't be left to my own devices. I might do him in too!" she gave a little laugh. Then with a serious face she addressed the rest of the room, "I do think, however, that there are many women poet-scholars who would fill the bill and I would like to see a woman in that Chair. I think Frost would have liked it, too." She made her way around the room with the coffee. She never did that before. Mark's eyes followed her.

Cat poured the coffee and without addressing anyone in particular mumbled, " Now it makes sense that I've seen Ambrose around the University." She put the coffee pot down and sat on the sofa again. "I can't remember if I saw him before Canfield's death—I was away myself then—but I know I saw him sometime." She snapped her fingers, "Right! He was at the reception for new members. Remember?" She wanted Mark to confirm her memory. He nodded. "What's going to happen to the contest and the anthology, I wonder?" She didn't want to appear overly self-absorbed, she said, but as she had committed herself to a contribution, she wanted to see the anthology printed. "I'll go to see him!"

Edward smiled and nodded, "I think you should. I'm sure the contest and anthology will continue as planned." But his gaze was through the conversation. Some unspoken communication between him and Lew beamed across the room and Lew smiled at his friend and knew he was still thinking about the twins.

**"Invisible hands crowded on her shoulder
In readiness to weigh upon her."**

**from THE LOVELY SHALL BE CHOOSERS
Robert Frost**

Chapter 21

Cat was glad when everyone finally left and she was able to sort through the revelations of the evening. It was clear that she would get no sleep until she had at least clarified her position in her own mind.

It would be premature to say anything to Edward yet, but she was 99-and-44/100ths percent sure that her new bench mate and kindred spirit was one of the twins. He certainly looked like the picture Mark had taken at the School of Government and now that she had a chance to study the old photos of Teddy and Rennie she could see a stronger resemblance. But which one? As he called himself Ed now, it must be Teddy.

The Ed she knew was so understanding and sincere and intellectual. He didn't sound like the twins who had been discussed. Of course, they may well have changed.

She had met with Ed several times since that first spring day and they had had soulful exchanges on the plight of the disadvantaged, the turmoil of world politics and environmental concerns that should be everyone's. She looked forward to talking and sharing ideas with him. It was definitely something she had missed lately with the intense focus on her book. They had tackled subjects like bees flitting from flower to flower: culling the sweet nectar. All kinds of implications arose from that. Why should she feel—what was it? Embarrassment! She shuddered when she remembered the electricity that sparked between them whenever they innocently touched.

It was incestuous. She almost cried out when she surprised herself with this grubby perception. She bolted upright, as though something had pinched her. It's crazy. Even if it is Teddy, we're not related. She tried to untangle the lines that were crossing and tying up her brain. It wasn't easy. It must be because she had begun to think of Edward as more than her mentor. At least that was what was in her mind. It was easy to justify. Her own father had died long before she was old enough to have been directly influenced by him. Her mother had not remarried and there was only one uncle who had paid any attention to her and that was, now that she thought about it, only tolerance.

She remembered with a little uneasiness that when she first met Edward she had thought of him in an even different way, and maybe that's what was bothering her now. She had been flattered by his attention and had read more into it than she should have and certainly more than what was there. That's what she had been avoiding and that was the real reason for this unsettling feeling. To put it bluntly and she squirmed at the thought. She had been in love with Edward.

That, of course, changed distinctly and rapidly. She was quick to remind herself that Edward had been unaware of any romantic overtone to her very accepting posture. She had almost forgotten that one-sided facet of their relationship. It had worn off quickly and a familial relationship developed and became comfortable and balanced, but Cat remembered uneasily the fantasies she had about Edward. She wriggled and twisted trying to find a comfortable position for both her body and her mind.

Funny that he thought of himself as such a bad father. She had blossomed under his tutelage. He had helped her discover her base of self-confidence.

In an effort to solve this emotional conundrum she was just beginning to understand, she reviewed the chronology of her relationship with Edward. She had come to the university at a time in Edward's life when he needed a cause. Ann had been dead for a while. There were no pressing duties outside the department to capture his attention. He had been ready for a cause and Cat had been it. He needed a vital, unfettered presence to carry him to a place where perspective balanced reality. Like a person finding a new religion, he embraced her work with passion and devoted time and energy selflessly. She had accepted his involvement without question. No wonder she had read more into it.

Cat remembered that it wasn't until after his retirement, when she was pretty much on the road to success that the attention he had showered on her waned. Now she wondered if she had been so self-absorbed she hadn't noticed the general malaise that had overtaken Edward because she thought it was just that she no longer needed his constant support. By the time she had alerted Lew and Anthony to a detached Edward, he had sunken into an abyss of despair; he had been disjoined and unfocused.

She sighed. All that was behind them now and she hoped never to see it return. His attitude had done an about face. It wasn't just the collaboration on the theft, but that had clearly started the upward swing. He'd begun to tap into his inner resources and found a spring of enthusiasm that had been dry for a long time. Cat thought that if anything were to pull him out of the chasm it would be reemergence into his own work. Was the reappearance of the twins going to be a help or a hindrance?

She knew what the next step had to be—a meeting or gathering or maybe a dinner with everyone. It was going to take planning and she would talk with Lew who always knew the right thing to do. He knew the twins and the problems.

It was at least an hour before she eased back into the pillows on her bed and picked up a book. She read a few pages and put the book down. Although she wouldn't have been able to tell anyone what she had read, it had served the purpose of distancing her from her desultory thoughts. The tumblers were lining up to unlock this paradox. She started to relax and felt the comfortable fuzziness of sleep descending. Even though she hadn't completely straightened out the twists, she felt more secure in her own understanding of the situation and she drifted off with a vision of reconciliation in her head.

**"The bud must bloom till blowsy blown
Its petals loosen and are strown;"**

**from OUR DOOM TO BLOOM
Robert Frost**

Chapter 22

Berkeley Street residents were early risers, often they could be seen waiting at the door for the newspapers to be delivered. This morning Lew caught the papers as the carrier tossed first the *Globe* and then the *Times* to him. Lew winced as he stepped up to the threshold to go back inside. Through the open door he could smell the toast burning and raced to eject the toast from the old toaster.

Next door, Cat threw back the curtains letting the early sun flood her room on the third floor. She showered, put on jeans and a sweatshirt and reviewed her thoughts of the night before. Her mind was made up. She'd see Lew and see what he thought about this tangle of relationships. Together they'd figure out the best approach for a how and where for a reconciliation. She was sure now that the Ed she had been seeing almost every day was Teddy. She hurried down the stairs, coaxed by the Juan Valdez brew wafting up the stairs.

Edward was not in the kitchen but the coffee was made and waiting. He must be in his study writing. She liked to think he was writing again. She poured some coffee and searched the cupboard and breadbox until she found her breakfast of the remaining piece of torte from the night before. Then she walked between the two houses, rapped at Lew's door before opening it and walked into his kitchen. Lew was already halfway through a cup of coffee and had the *Globe* spread out across the table. He looked up, smiled, and motioned to the toast on the table.

"Thanks. I've already had my breakfast. I've brought my own cup." Before her on the table was a pile of burnt toast. "Do you do this on purpose--or is it a syndrome of Berkeley Street?"

Lew looked up, "No, I hate burnt toast, but that's the way the toaster makes it. I really should get a new one. But now most of the toasters have some other features—like grilling or baking or something. And all I want is toast—nice and lightly browned!"

Cat sat with a thud. She didn't say she had finished off the torte but it must have been in her mind when she said, "You're always so thoughtful. You know just what will please. You're a good friend." She looked around the kitchen. There was dust on the stove hood and the countertop needed a thorough scrubbing instead of the quick wipe she suspected it got between visits by the cleaning lady. But that wasn't what she was here for. "Nothing's ever easy, is it, Lew?"

Lew steadied his hand and sipped from his cup, "No. But what is it that's got my favorite optimist troubled?" He put the cup down and reached for the coffee pot to refill her cup.

"Thanks." She looked at the coffee as though it was going to speak and sloshed it around in her cup. "I have something I need to talk about and I don't know how to begin. I've been trying to sort it out and I guess the best thing to do is to throw out the pieces and then try to assemble them into some logical or reasonable order."

"Sounds right to me, Cat. Perhaps I can help," he looked up from his paper. "You have my undivided attention," an encouraging smile turned up the corners of his mouth as he pushed aside the paper.

"Oh, I know you can help," Cat said and as though she were embarking on a different subject said, "Do you know that feeling of actually being in tune, of knowing something is special and not saying anything because it's obvious to you and to define it or defend it would look like there was some doubt?" She looked as though she hadn't quite said what she wanted to, as though she was going to clarify it, when Lew spoke.

"That sounds pretty serious, Cat," Lew smiled but looked puzzled, "Is this a person or a situation that's confounding you?"

"It's a person. And, I guess it's a situation, too."

"You'll have to tell me more." He was mystified and wondered where this was going. Cat had never come to him with a romantic issue and if that's what it is, he thought, he wasn't going to be much help. He wondered if the uneasiness or awkwardness he had seen with Mark was a manifestation of the trouble she was having.

He watched her for signs and stirred his coffee. By staring blankly at the aging kitchen wall she was not giving a clue. "Of course," he said, tightening up and taking a tack he could switch if he needed to, "I felt complete harmony with Sarah, and there is no one I'm more comfortable with than Edward. But I suspect what you mean is something a bit different." To take up a little time, he refolded the paper and sat back in his chair. "Let me tell you about the most heady feeling of harmony I can ever remember. It was so strong that even though it happened years ago, I can still sense the euphoria."

Lew had stepped back into another lifetime. "It was the intensity of oneness that, as a crew, we never mentioned. To try to define it might upset the harmony and balance of both the boat and our psyches. It was the elation of feeling eight pairs of arms and legs moving as one in a god-like harmony." His eyes were closed and he was reliving the rhythms. He opened his eyes, "Have you ever rowed? I've never felt in more complete harmony, and if what you're talking about is anything like that, then, yes, I understand. It's not just physical, it's a mental and psychological state." He looked at Cat as though he had just had a revelation, "I'm sure musicians understand it. It's as close to ecstasy as we mortals will ever get," he said in a lighthearted voice. "It doesn't always happen, of course, but when it does, it's worth the agony that follows." He smiled at some distant thought. "The agony comes, too, from that same ecstasy. You know, after a race we would be nauseous and absolutely drained of everything: strength, emotion, physical feeling. But we kept doing it and looked forward to it!" He picked up his cup, saw that it was empty and set it back down again as he smiled across the table. "So what's disturbing you? The agony or the ecstasy?"

Cat's eyes took in Lew like a wide-angle lens. She had always thought of Lew as emotionally shallow. He was always sweet and kind, consoling and considerate, but he never seemed deeply affected by what was going on around him. Maybe she had been wrong and he had sloughed off those emotions to protect himself and keep himself private. It was another thing she didn't want to think about right now.

"It's the twins," she blurted, "I'm sure I've met one of them. I call him Ed."

"This is wonderful news. Where? Can we get in touch with them?" Lew was excited. He stood up and then sat right back down again, as though he wanted to do something but didn't know what. "Tell me about it. How long have you known him? Is it Teddy? Or have you met them both?"

Cat sighed. "Let me start at the beginning." She recounted how they met in the Quad. How she had found herself going at the same time every day with more lunch than she could eat. How hours sped by. How they talked about all kinds of things. She confided, "I feel, and I think he does too, a poetic harmony, a meeting of minds." She hesitated before she went on, "One part that scares me, now that I'm pretty sure who he is, is that I know so much about him and his brother that I wonder if I'm being taken in and why or, and I pray this is the case, that they, or at least Ed-Teddy has changed. I've only met the one."

Lew said he could see Cat's dilemma. He was delighted to think that the twins—he hoped both—were here in Cambridge. In the same breath he said he hoped they had matured and become more responsible. It sounded from what Cat said, that at least one of them had. "They were always pretending to be which ever twin they weren't. In any case," he said, "I'm eager to see them and I hope that any relationship you've started will carry over." He thought Cat's problem of identifying the bond that was forming between her and Ed-Teddy could only help with a reconciliation of the twins and their father. He pondered it a moment and said, "I think we should make a plan to get everyone together." He sat back in his chair and crossed his leg over his knee, "'Aye, there's the rub.' But first, I'd like to meet Ed and make sure it's Teddy. Are you going to see him today?"

"I think so. We never make definite plans, but he comes every nice day. And today looks like it's going to be a winner." Cat got up and peered out the window, her arms leaning on the sill. The daffodils were beautiful in the front yard and the lilacs would be bursting out with a few more warm spring days. Just seeing the burgeoning season all around her made her feel good. She flung her arms out in a stage-like gesture and sounded like her old self. "I could invite everyone to dinner." Almost as soon as she got the words out, she started to see problems. "They might feel uncomfortable about going to the house. And what if they don't want to come? I've only met Ed and if his twin--"

Lew interrupted, "Rennie, his name is Lawrence--named for me."

". . . Rennie," she continued, "is around, I'd have to explain the whole thing to both of them, wouldn't I? I wish I had a video of the other night when you all were reminiscing. Edward so wants to set things right." With a slight pause, Cat added, "He's taking the lion's share of the blame for their leaving and just wants to have and maybe enjoy some time with them."

"I think you're right, Cat. Nothing would please Edward more than having his boys back, getting to know them again, getting them to know and understand him, and having them forgive him."

"Then let's get started." She looked up and said, "Today. Can you come for lunch today?"

"Yes . . . " then he looked at the calendar and at a notation on the day's date. Oh, I'm sorry—not today . . . or tomorrow. How about next week? That won't put it off for too long. I'm really sorry, but I have appointments I can't break."

A dinner for everyone would be an easy way to begin. She shook her head, "We need a neutral turf. Think about it." She looked at her watch and picked up her coffee cup as she prepared to leave, much happier than when she came in. "Twelve-fifteen in the Quad on Monday."

"Right, I'll be there." Lew started unfolding the newspaper. "I know! Tonio's! Perfect! As soon as we decide when it should be, I'll call and make a reservation. It'll be my treat and my pleasure. And who else should be there? Definitely, Anthony."

Cat nodded agreement. She liked it. It was a good idea. "See you at lunchtime on Monday, if not before," she said as she closed the door behind her.

She hurried down the path from Lew's and into the Whitman kitchen, set her cup down on the sink counter and raced upstairs to change. It was late and she wanted to drop in on Robert Ambrose. Now that she knew he was to be taking over the Chair and the anthology, it would be politic to secure her position within the Department. It wasn't going to be hard. He had responded favorably to her in the past. She put on a black sweater dress and tied her one extravagant possession--a pink and white Hermes scarf--around her shoulders. She turned around and studied herself in the mirror. Professional but not intimidating. Good!

The black letters on the door to his office had been scraped off. Canfield's name was no longer there, but neither was Ambrose's. Of course, his appointment as the new Chair had not been announced publicly yet. "Next week," he said when she asked.

He greeted Cat with a warm smile and offered time right then for a chat. He confided to Cat that he was happy to be back in comfortable academia. He had thought about moving back, he said, even before he was offered the Chair. "New York is exciting but too fast for a ponderous, native Bostonian like me." They spent a while on Cat's verses before either of them spoke about anything else.

With little prompting, Cat brought him up to date on what she knew about the investigation into Canfield's death.

They agreed it had been a terrible shock for everyone in the department but that things were pretty much back to normal. Even the anthology was moving along.

"No one here," Ambrose said, "can imagine a reason for it. Canfield was a quiet, unassuming fellow with a great deal of professional expertise. He went about his mission of elevating the department in the eyes of the University with style and grace." The spring gardens beyond the window had captured his eyes so he didn't see Cat shudder.

"Canfield," Ambrose said turning back to Cat, "would have been pleased with the anthology. It was his baby and it's going to be a great success. I'm going to see to it that he gets the credit." He asked about Edward and how to get to his house. He said he hoped things were better than the last time he saw him. "And how is Lew? He has always been such an approving and staunch friend."

Cat filled him in and as she was about to leave, she asked what he thought about Mark's cover designs. His confidential information was that the cover had been narrowed down to three designs and two of them were Mark's. That was good news. "We intend to make an announcement soon. The Department meeting next week would be a good time." he said.

She couldn't wait to tell Mark. He had worked so hard on those designs and he deserved to be chosen; they were good. Still, she took a little fiendish pleasure in knowing something Mark didn't and keeping it from him for just a little while—like a big sister teasing a younger sibling.

**"Then for a moment all there was, was size,
Confusion and a roar that drowned the   cries."**

**from THE EGG AND THE MACHINE
Robert Frost**

Chapter 23

Cat waltzed into the Quad at lunchtime—one, two, three; one, two, three. She felt good about everything. The meeting with Ambrose had given her an extra lift and she felt pretty good now about her place in the Department. With Ambrose and Edward behind her, she had a leg-up on the shaky ladder and felt her book was going to give her the fortitude to reach the next rung.

Even so, she was glad she had completed that application for a two-year fellowship at Oxford. At first, it was a lark she pursued because it was easy. She filled out the application during last summer when she was bumping along what seemed a dead-end road. Since then, things had changed, but it's always good to have options, she thought, choosing from among favorable alternatives is good for the psyche.

Unlike most of the time when she didn't feel glamorous at all, she felt a little worldly glamour and with that came an aura of sophistication usually hidden under jeans and sweatshirt. Would Ed notice, she wondered? And what if he did?

Pink and white petals from the apple blossoms fell on the bench like confetti. She brushed them off and settled herself at one end. All in all, she was pleased with herself. She closed her eyes and let the sun wash her freckled nose; she was adrift in a warm, soft, fresh spring day. After a few minutes, she opened her eyes and looked up to see Ed turn onto the path with someone walking beside him. He was tall and blond with Ed's smile and walk. Another plus for today, thought Cat as she watched Ed-Teddy, and his brother Rennie walk toward her.

She rose to meet them and put out her hand as Ed said, "This is my other half," presenting his brother with a hand flourish like a magician brandishing a trick. "His name is Lawrence but we call him Rennie, and you can call him anything you like." With a little qualifying grin he added, "But he doesn't answer to Larry! You look great--something important going on?"

She wasn't ignoring the compliment or the question; all she could think of was that now she knew for sure. "You look awfully alike." Though she knew why, she wanted to hear it.

And Ed obliged, "We're twins. I guess I neglected to tell you that when I mentioned I had an older brother that he's about two minutes older and likes to remind me of it. He says it makes him the wiser; but he's not." He was joking but something in his voice told Cat he was a bit more serious. "Without Rennie's beard, you couldn't tell us apart. No one has ever been able to," he shrugged his shoulders as if to say he couldn't understand the problem. Cat scrutinized the two faces, first one then the other. Ed had sometimes had a scruffy stubble of a beard, too. Today, though, he was clean-shaven. So, today, at least, she knew which was which. She thought maybe she could tell anyway. There seemed to be a softness about Ed that was lacking in Rennie; or maybe it was a hardness she perceived in Rennie that was lacking in Ed. Or maybe she was projecting some of the previous evening's tales and giving Rennie an unfair disadvantage? There was, though, an attitude or posture . . . something she couldn't quite put her finger on that made her think she could tell who was who.

"Which twin has the Toni?" Rennie joked as he offered Cat all around views of himself. "Do you remember that old ad?" He raised his eyebrows, "I think they both had Tonis!" They all laughed.

Rennie was as charming as Ed—whom he called Teddy—and they easily fell into comfortable bantering. At one point, Rennie asked, "Do you have a University ID card that can get us into the Observatory?" bringing Cat back into the conversation she heard hovering on the periphery of her perplexing thoughts about what to do next. He noticed her confusion, must have thought it was his question, and offered an explanation, "The lunar eclipse. Wouldn't you like to see it through a good, powerful telescope? I sure would." He turned to Teddy. "You would, too, wouldn't you?" He turned back to Cat, "What department are you with?"

"The English Department—modern poetry is my field," she answered automatically, "and sure. I have a card, but you don't need it. The Observatory has programs for the public, and any time there is a unique event like an eclipse, they always have an open-for-viewing time and a lecture." She looked back and forth before she said, "When is it?"

"Tomorrow."

It seemed to Cat that Rennie was boldly claiming that trait of his she had heard discussed of being opportunistic. Was his reason for coming today to charm her into letting him borrow her ID card? Did he really want it to get into the Observatory?

The quandary she was in was for reasons other than trying to figure out Rennie. Should she say something to them herself or wait for Lew? If only he could have come today. But as she often complained, nothing ever happens the easy way. If she said nothing, Rennie and Ed-Teddy might think there had been a conspiracy of sorts when they finally met with Lew. She didn't want to risk the friendship because of a . . . the word cover-up came to mind but that was too sinister . . . misunderstanding was the better word.

"I'll find out more and let you know. Will I see you tomorrow at lunchtime?" Her question was directed to Ed and he answered quickly with a nod and a smile. She glanced at her watch and explained, "I have a seminar at one o'clock and I'm going to be late already so I'll see you tomorrow. Wish I had more time now." She turned to Rennie and said, "Happy to meet you. I'm sure it'll be fine to go to the observatory, so you should plan on it. If you get anxious, you could call the observatory yourself."

"I'd rather have you do it," Rennie smiled boyishly.

"O.k." Cat cheerily agreed. Under her good-natured smile she had a lot of questions. There seemed to be so many things to explain or that needed answers and she wasn't sure she was going to be able to cope by herself. She was bursting to say something. In the end, she had decided to wait until the next day, Friday, and broach the whole thing with Ed-Teddy--alone. It turned out to have been the right thing to do. There were no lights on at Lew's by the time she got home after the seminar which continued after dinner and well into the evening, so she couldn't consult with him. Friday morning she had an early breakfast meeting with the Equality in Women's Tenure Committee. Fortunately, she missed Edward last night and this morning too so she didn't have to feel guilty about keeping something from him.

Friday at lunchtime she met Ed with a couple of sandwiches and cold drinks. First she handed him a note where she had scribbled down the hours the observatory was open and the lecture and time she had signed them up for. Then she plunged head first into her rehearsed confession-explanation. She began with the photos and the album and their father's sincere wishes for a reunion.

Teddy was dumbfounded. To say it was a shock to him was an understatement. Cat's presentation had been abrupt at best; completely unnerving at worst. While Teddy sat dazed and overwhelmed, Cat related most of the conversation and some of the stories told the evening the pictures were found. She emphasized how excited Edward and Lew were about the prospects of a reunion.

All the while she was talking, Teddy seemed to be sorting things out in his mind. When she paused he said,

"Rennie was right about a connection between you and our father. It was stupid of me not to have guessed it before. But, we never really talked about personal arrangements like where you live and what exactly your position is in the Department. In fact, I didn't know you're a poet. I thought you liked poetry like I do and just knew a lot about it." The friendly robin strutted before them teasing them to watch him and abandon all other subjects. Cat tossed a bread crust to him and he flew off with it up to the nest they had seen him building earlier. They both watched.

"How long have you known? Really." asked Teddy.

"Like I told you, the whole thing just unfolded and became obvious a couple of nights ago. It was an accidental connection; a joke of fate that those photos were of you and Rennie. Joke is the wrong word--jolt is more like it. I was just as astounded as you." She brushed some more crumbs onto the grass. "What would be the point in keeping it to myself? I probably should have been smart enough to have guessed it before, but it never occurred to me. If you had told me about your family or past, I might have clued in. But, as you said, we never pressed each other for personal facts. Did we?"

"No, we didn't," Teddy barely whispered. "Just for the record we really have tried to see him," he sighed, "and every time we steeled ourselves and almost got to the door, something happened to put us off. Once, or maybe even twice, we got to the front door and no one was home." He smiled at Cat, "If we had succeeded on one of those tries, we would have met sooner."

Cat saw that Teddy needed time alone to place these revelations into his own perspective. "I'll work out arrangements for the meeting. Lew was planning to come on Monday at lunchtime to meet you." We were going to set a time and date then." she said, preparing to leave.

He snapped out of his silent ruminating, "Meeting?"

"Well, sure. You want it to happen, don't you? Your father and Lew and I certainly do. And, soon." Cat was so caught up that she blurted out: "How about a lunch on Sunday? At a restaurant? Do you think Rennie will agree? If only Lew could have come today, we could have already started planning. But I'm sure he and your father will agree. Can you give me a 'phone number or if you want, I could meet you here tomorrow to confirm everything. I'm sure you can plan on Sunday, though, for lunch."

Teddy nodded absently. "I guess so. I don't know. Will my father agree?"

"It's what he wants most in the world!"

Later, when Teddy told Rennie about this meeting, he quoted Cat, "It's what he wants most in the world. I can't believe that this is going to work out so easily and I sure hope he will be as forgiving and accepting as Cat said." There was more now to consider than the return of prodigal sons—their wastefulness had been with time, energy and thoughtfulness. "And let's get our stories straight. I, for one, am not going to mess it up with a bunch of lies and you'd better think carefully about it too," Teddy said, opening the door for a dialog, but Rennie had nothing to say.

So back and forth. It almost scares
A man the way things come in pairs."

from TO A THINKER
Robert Frost

Chapter 24

Cat stopped at Lew's with the news confirming that the
twins were, indeed, in Cambridge. She told him about meeting
Rennie and in detail about the long and enlightening
conversation with Teddy. That there would be a reunion, clearly
delighted Lew and he gave Cat a hug and a kiss on the cheek.
"Is your muddle any clearer?" he asked.

"All that will just have to wait, and I guess I should call
him Teddy now. He called himself Ed when we met," she said
with a little grin. "Anyhow, I feel comfortable with things. We
spent practically the whole afternoon asking and answering each
other's questions. I told him about how Mark's photos played a
role and how Edward regrets the years they've been gone and
been incommunicado; that he doesn't blame them for anything
and wants to start on a new page."

Lew nodded agreement, "Let's go tell Edward."

Together they walked next door. Edward, sitting in the
living room reading, looked at them over his glasses as they
entered. "You two look pleased with yourselves. What's up?"
He closed his book and put it down on the table beside him.

Cat and Lew made their way to the edge of the sofa and gingerly sat down. They both started talking at once, stopped, laughed and Cat gave Lew the floor, "You tell!" she said.

Edward was puzzled but watched, eyes moving from Cat to Lew, trying to see through the fog of uneasiness. Lew harumphed, straightened up and started by telling Edward that not only were the twins living in Cambridge as they had all suspected, but that arrangements for a luncheon at Tonio's on Sunday, were complete.

Edward's face lit up like fourth of July fireworks and he exploded in his low-keyed, understated way. "Good! Good! How do they look?" He had a million questions, "Both of them? You found both? I'll call them. How do I do that? Where are they?" He was out of his chair and walking back and forth and around the room. "Where do they live? How long have they been here? What are their plans?" He stopped, "Edward," Cat said, "I told them briefly what has happened since they've been gone so they know that Ann died and that you retired. They already knew about Ann because they had seen her death referred to in a newspaper. That's one reason they came back. You'll have to give them details because I know they want to know more: how she died, where she's buried, all those things that have been making you feel it's an unclosed grave. And, Edward, they've tried to see you but Murphy's Law always interfered. They seem really glad to be here and are just as eager to see you." She watched to see what his reaction was to that. He was nodding his head. Cat continued, "I would never have recognized them from the descriptions of the other night. They both are charming. They are both as anxious as you for a meeting." She knew that was an assumption, but she honestly thought she was right.

Lew had been watching, too, and broke in with, "And you'll have to ask them what their plans are. You'll have plenty of time to get caught up. As Cat said, they've been hanging around mustering up courage for a while and honestly tried to come here a few times but were thwarted." Cat was smiling and nodding her head as Lew spoke. "We've asked Tonio to prepare the fatted calf! Sunday at two o'clock!"

Edward was so pleased and happy that they only barely managed to dissuade him from tearing out of the house and racing down to Central Square to look for them. They left Edward thumbing through his photo albums. Questions would pop up and answers would be found. The all-important start had been made.

"From now on, that's what I'm always going to do," Cat said to Lew at the back door before they walked down the path to his house.

"What's that?"

"Anticipate the worst possible scenario and then find I'm completely wrong when everything turns out rosy!" She was laughing and stooped to pick a dead daffodil from the midst of bright yellow heads. "We're almost home free. The twins will be back. Edward has forgotten all that morbid stuff. The Wadsworths have most of their treasures back." She frowned. "We'd be on our way to a wrapped-up movie ending if it weren't for what happened to Canfield. We'll probably never have answers to that."

Lew said, "Probably not. Maybe we wouldn't want to know. Sometimes things are better left unanswered. Right now we have more pleasant and happy times to look forward to, so let's begin by being optimistic. I can feel it. Everything will be worked out to the benefit of all." He turned the door handle, "Like to come in for a drink? Tea? Coffee? Soda?"

"Oh, thanks, but not now--I have some things to think out before Sunday. I'll come by early and we can go to Tonio's together. See you then." She stooped down to pick a few more dead heads.

Too good to be true, she thought. Everything so far had gone well and without a hitch. Still, Mr. Murphy and his law are bound to drop in and Cat hoped she would be prepared to deal with unforeseen circumstances though she couldn't think what they might be. Tonio had been agreeable and, in fact, said he would enjoy preparing a special menu. "Maybe," he said, clasping his hands together, "family reunions will be one of my specialities."

Anthony had agreed wholeheartedly that Tonio's was the best possible setting. He was delighted to be asked to be there.

Lew had ventured, "We can orchestrate the whole affair and keep it in tune and underplayed. I don't think it will be in Edward's best interests to get too enthusiastic about all this until we know exactly what the twins are up to; if they're up to anything. I am just a bit leery about turning over heart and soul and estate to the former champions of mistrust."

*   *   *   *

Cat and Lew arrived at Tonio's before anyone else on Sunday. Edward had insisted on walking to the restaurant alone and hadn't arrived. Mark came in with his camera loaded to record the event. They seemed nervous but Tonio assured them that all was under control on his front and that he had planned a fantastic menu starting with antipasto and ending with his own panna cotta. He smacked his fingers in a classic Italian gesture.

They were standing by the small bar applauding Tonio's menu and no one heard the door open or saw the two who entered. Lew felt a light tap on his shoulder, "Excuse me, we're looking for the Whitman party. I think we're early," said a voice from behind. Lew turned.

"This . . ." Lew could say no more; he opened his arms and clutched both boys close. Unnoticed, Mark was clicking the shutter from his place to one side.

"Uncle Lew . . ." said one of them and there were no more words until Lew spoke through muffled, choked greetings.

"There's so much to say," said Lew, "that beginning anywhere will do." He had taken his handkerchief out and wiped his eyes. "I'm so happy to see you both, to have you here among us again. I hope this will be the beginning of a new time for all of us. We have missed you so. . . I have missed you. Later, we'll trace all of what has happened in the years you've been gone," Lew looked back and forth between them, "And who is who?"

They laughed and Cat said, "This is Rennie," taking Rennie, with beard intact, by the arm, "and this is my lunch and bench partner, Ed-Teddy." She giggled a little, "I think I should call you Teddy, like everyone else does." They do look alike, she thought, but she knew which was which, at least, until Teddy grew another beard. The beard Rennie was sporting was only a scruffy, Al-Pacino-stubble growth and looked even less full because it was fair.

"Fine," said Teddy and moved closer to Cat with an extended arm, pulled her closer, and gave her a squeeze. "If it hadn't been for Cat, I guess we wouldn't be here now."

"Well, that may be but I prefer to think that this meeting was destined by strong wills and maybe the stars." Lew was smiling his crinkled-eye smile. "In fact, there are so many variables that pointed the way that it will be interesting to chronicle them and see if it would have been possible to avoid each other." They all laughed.

"Speaking of stars, as in star-kissed." Rennie said, "the lunar eclipse last night was spectacular. Thanks, again to Cat, we saw it all." He inclined his head to one side and bowed, and Cat saw the charm radiating and capturing his audience.

They talked about other eclipses with chatty conversation, postponing the more substantial talk about the past until Edward was there to hear first hand. Anthony arrived with a jovial and friendly handshake and welcomed everyone as though it was his party and his home. "Maybe you remember me from years ago when I used to call on your father, sometimes with police problems that needed a methodical mind to unravel.

Please call me Anthony," he said with a smile in his voice, "I was quite sure I recognized the picture." He paused, pressed his lips together and said, "I think I've seen you around that geode shop,"

"Celestial Lights?" asked Rennie.

"Yes, that's it. And . . . did you play basketball at the youth center a few times?" Anthony looked first at one and then the other, "One of you, I'm sure--but which? Must be," he pointed first at Rennie, "you. Or I suppose you," and he pointed at Teddy, "could have shaved a beard off, or conversely you" he pointed at Rennie again "could have grown one. You'll have to tell me." They were all laughing by this time.

Teddy looked and tried to place Anthony. "I'm the one. I may have had a few days' growth on my face then. You look very different in sweats. I wouldn't have recognized you from the basketball court or from years ago either. And, though I didn't go to the Center last week, I intend to go back. I've been job hunting. Those kids are really good and keep us hopping, don't they?" He said this to the others who were wondering what was going on.

Anthony explained further by saying that he played basketball with a teen group at the Community Centre every Thursday and welcomed any help he could get. Mark, on the sidelines, was drawn in and said it was something he would like to get involved with, too. Basketball talk eased the initial awkwardness and they were well into an animated discussion of the NBA playoffs when Edward arrived.

All heads turned as he opened the door, spread his arms and beamed. "Teddy! Rennie!"

"Dad!" one of them cried. There were mumblings that no one else could hear. Words were preempted by emotions. The small gathering turned, like a flock of birds changing direction in mid-flight, and left the three of them alone.

If Edward were nervous, he didn't show it. He seemed overjoyed. Tears ran down his ruddy cheeks as he held the boys close then at arm's length to look at them, then close again. He freed them from his grasp and made no attempt to hide his pleasure. He laughed, "My, how you've grown!" They joined in the joking by hamming it up and strutting their size.

Edward drew everyone into the drama by reintroducing his sons to his friends with a flourish even though they had already met Teddy and Rennie. It made no difference to him that there had been years of no news. The only thing that mattered, and he said it many times that day, was that they were all together again.

The twins sat on either side of their father at the large round table. Edward asked questions that were easily answered about how they liked Central America and Mexico and how long they had been there. He tried not to ask awkward questions. There would be time for that later. Lew was interested in the economics, the general state of the country, and the people. How did they cope with such poverty? Did they notice any changes while they were there? How did the population exist?

They answered thoughtfully and intelligently and Rennie told funny stories about riding on an ancient, dilapidated bus with chickens and goats. "They get on first, you know, and then if there is room for interlopers like us, we get to stand in the aisle, bumping and tripping over our feet and a million baskets of tomatoes and beans, while the goats take up the seat space! VIP's first!" he joked. Everyone was enchanted and attentive and he continued with tales of digging with a teaspoon and paintbrush on a dig at a newly excavated Mayan site.

"Like the old days," Lew mumbled, mainly to himself.

The afternoon flew by and they had to leave to allow Tonio time for
dinner preparations.

"To be continued tomorrow at lunchtime on Berkeley Street. O.K. Edward?" Cat invited everyone.

"Of course. Good idea." Edward beamed, "There's so much to catch up on. I know it'll take time, but I want to get started right away!"

They all parted and Edward and Lew walked home. It was a necessary diversion. Edward was so keyed up he could hardly contain himself and he kept bursting forth with a swing of his hands or an out-loud laugh. Lew said nothing but felt a wave of contentment and happiness. Edward was back in good spirits. Peace was within reach.   When Lew remarked about the wonderful meal Tonio had served, Edward said, "It was the best meal of my life." He clapped his hands together like a prize fighter and grinned, "I'm happier than I have ever been." He chortled, "It was like a plum pudding--full of surprise delights. This is what I have been praying for," he said and put his hand on Lew's shoulder, "I can never repay you, Lew, for all the years of undying support of me and my family, but if I could, it would take forever, and I would still be indebted." When they came to the path between their houses, they stood in the middle, quietly reflecting on the afternoon before they each went their separate ways. Lew accepted Edward's words with a manly hug and a thump on the back and turned up his walk with fogged-up glasses and a less heavy heart.

Edward sat at his desk in the study, pulled out a copy of his old will and began to outline a new will. This was not something he felt had to be done right away, but starting it helped him set him mind straight. He was happy to be able to think positively about the disposition of his estate and he wanted to be sure as to how Teddy and Rennie would be best served. For years now he had not wanted to think about it because although he had named his sons as heirs, he was not happy. It seemed like signing *carte blanche* to strangers. Now, at least, he would know that Whitmans were going to be carrying on for at least another generation—more he dared hope. He allowed for the contingencies he hoped the twins had outgrown by putting restrictions on the sale of property. He planned to place a major part of his estate into a trust that would eventually, if no heirs appeared after the twins, revert to the University. He didn't, of course, intend to wait until his death to have Ann's estate distributed.

"The lowly pen is yet a hold
Against the dark and wind and cold
To give a prospect to a plan
And warrant prudence in a man."

from **A BLUE RIBBON AT AMESBURY**
Frost

Chapter 25

Edward scrutinized the mostly quiet and subdued ties on his rack. Dull. He was in a happy place and was eager to reflect his joy in every little way he could. Towards the back some color leapt out at him and he pulled it from the somber mass. It must have been a gift from Cat he thought, as he knotted the pink and red silk and gave a pleased smile to the mirror.

On his way downstairs, he stopped in the middle of the staircase and studied the studio photographs and blown-up candids of himself, Ann, and the twins, sometimes together and sometimes alone, that wound their way, step-like, from the bottom to the top of the staircase. They had been part of the wall for so long he usually saw them without noticing. Ann had labored for ages over the placement for each photo and finally came up with this configuration and, of course, he had never even given thought to changing it. He stopped halfway down the staircase in front of a formal photograph of Ann taken when she was named to the board of the Art Society. She was beautiful in a quiet, arty way. He always liked the way her short ash-blond hair turned under at the ends; there was a name for it, but he couldn't remember what it was. "I do miss you," he said aloud and continued down the stairs.

At the bottom of the stairs a brilliant ray of spring sunlight through the French doors lit up a pathway through the living room to the bottom of the stairs. He stepped into the sunlight and vowed to dismiss the somber shadows and step into the light of day; and as Ann would have said: turn to a new page. Realization dawned like a flash brainstorm that he had been a fool to think that being miserable was a way to punish Ann for leaving him. He was only punishing himself. She was still here in so many ways. In fact, he thought, too many ways, as he looked around at the paint and wallpaper that was old now and outdated. Ann had updated the painting and papering of the house years before she died. It must be at least twenty years, and it was time to make a fresh start from the inside out. She would have been disappointed in the detached role he had assumed since his retirement. He really had been a dismal bore. Well, she'd be proud of him now, flashy tie and cheerful countenance. He quickened his step.

The kitchen was quiet. He liked it. Instead of thinking of it as lonely as he would have a short time ago, he thought of it as peaceful. Even though it was nice to have Cat taking care of things, it was nice, too, to have a little silence. Cat's presence burst the sides of time and space; there was always too much of her to contain or fence her in comfortably. He chuckled as he thought of her spilling over the edges of herself. Still, what would he do without her? I'd manage, he said to no one. He filled the coffeemaker with water and measured out the coffee. As soon as the coffee started dripping into the pot he artfully pulled out the pot and placed his cup under the steady, steamy, stream. Some of the coffee spilled onto the warmer when he pulled his cup away before replacing the pot. He liked the fresh burning smell.

He took his cup into his study displacing his usual custom of sitting at the kitchen table with the newspaper, took a few big gulps as he looked out the window, and placed the cup on the edge of his desk. The chair squeaked as he sat down and he moved it around on its casters to find a comfortable spot. He picked up his pen and within seconds was furiously scratching away on a pad of composition paper. It was as though the pen had taken on a vitality of its own. and like the Red Shoes, he couldn't have stopped if he had wanted to. Words spun around like an eddy in his brain funneling his images into a simple urgent flow. He struggled to keep up and scribbled faster.

And he had thought he was out of words—written himself off—out of the scene and off the stage. He had been a zombie. Yesterday marked a new mortality for Edward. It was the end of neverness, and inspiration welled up to fill and overflow in the curlicues of his mind. It was as easy as it used to be. He wrote and wrote, and finally sat back in his chair pondering each word and savoring these moments. His life had renewed meaning and he was expressing himself in the way he knew best—with his poetry. This, he thought, is why I am.

Some banging around from the kitchen jarred his thoughts. He glanced at his watch. It was almost noon. He shook his wrist thinking his watch must be wrong; but it wasn't. Three hours had passed like three minutes. His cold coffee sat on the edge of his desk and he heard and felt his stomach grumbling at him. Cat was out there putting together the promised lunch. Teddy and Rennie would be here soon, along with everyone else who could get away.

He turned back to his desk for a last few words before the elusive meter got lost in wordiness. Like an artist with a brush, his finishing touches were subtle and barely caressed the thought. Satisfied, he put his gold pen back where it belonged in his breast pocket and pushed his work under the blotter before he got up from the desk to gaze out the open window and breathe in the fresh air. He couldn't remember when it had smelled so good.

The twins were what he had written about—his joy.

He wanted to do what would be right for them and not project his own wishes upon them. After the reunion yesterday at Tonio's, he had wanted Teddy and Rennie to move right back into the house. But it was time for those rooms to be repainted and redecorated. In fact, it was time for the whole interior to be painted, and maybe the outside too. He wanted everything to be perfect—at least in the superficial that he could do something about.

Now, after the emotions had settled for twenty-four hours, he chided himself. It's unrealistic for me to try to fix their lives up with paint and polish. They might have other plans and they will need time and space. Would their plans include him and staying around Cambridge for a while? He hoped so. What were they good at? He realized he had no idea of their individual adult capabilities. There were so many questions. Were the answers ones he could cope with? A little voice inside him told him to take it easy, to be happy, but not to smother. His biggest worry was that he would drive them away again.

Edward made his way into the living room and the banging around in the kitchen got noisier. He was about to investigate the latest clatter when Anthony breezed in. He was brushing himself off. Edward noticed, he wasn't wiping and pushing at his nose; it was no longer red and swollen, at least not much.

"I tried to help Cat, but only succeeded in messing things up." He looked down at his feet and stumbled around, and almost as an afterthought added, "That little step-stool is dangerous—it tried to throw me off and tip over—it's not balanced." Edward smiled at his funny friend while Anthony brushed himself off some more and rubbed the toes of his shoes on the backs of his pants legs. "I told Cat she ought to keep things within easier reach. If I can't reach them easily, she certainly can't.

"I've noticed that you hardly sneeze anymore." Edward said. Anthony pulled a prescription vial out of his pocket. He shook it and pills rattled, "Doc Appleby may be an awful grouch but he knows his job. He diagnosed my problem," he snapped his fingers, "Gave me this prescription, and my nose has stopped sneezing and itching." He always spoke about his nose as though it belonged to someone else. He gave it a quick rub.

"Speaking of Appleby, how's the case? Anything new?" Edward asked. Anthony shook his head and nodded at the same time, and had his mouth open to elaborate, but just then Teddy and Rennie walked in and stole his attention. It was a tentative entrance.

Edward greeted them with a hug. He couldn't hide his delight--and didn't want to. He led the way and the twins walked around testing their memories and making confirming gestures. Rennie picked up the photo album from a shelf of books. He thumbed the pages and laughed, "Look, Teddy, here's us with the Wadsworth kids. Remember their dog—what was his name?" No one could remember. "I wonder where Dana and Jeanne are. Jeanne wanted to be a vet. Anyone seen them?" He looked up from the album with raised eyebrows and a questioning eye. Teddy was very quiet.

"I haven't seen the children for a long time. I think they're both in another country or at least another part of this one." Edward closed his eyes and strained to remember. "But I have seen Barbara and James. There was an unusual theft at their house and Anthony and Lew and I have been trying to make sense of it. We've spent quite a lot of time with the Wadsworths recently."

Anthony went on as Edward paused, "A bunch of first edition books went missing but were found nearby a few days later. Some thieves broke into the house, caused a minor havoc by taking the books that were destined for the Heiniken Museum and also some priceless Fragonard miniatures which haven't been found. And they took two antique, ruby-handled pistols. You," and he looked from one twin to the other with meaning but not knowing who was who, he addressed both of them, "probably remember them. You tried to walk off with one of them when you were a youngster."

The twins looked at each other, Rennie smiling and Teddy looking like he had seen a ghost.

Edward, seeing they were uncomfortable, said, "It was just a childish whim--you probably don't even remember, do you?"

Rennie said nothing, just smiled some more, shook his head and turned back to the photo album.

Anthony continued, "One of the pistols has been found in a pawn shop, but the other is still missing." He spoke slowly, narrowing his eyes and sounding mysterious. "And there's a strange coincidence about that pistol. I think it's quite possible that it was used to commit a murder."

Both Teddy and Rennie stopped mid-step and looked genuinely shocked. One of them said, "A murder?"

"Yes," said Anthony, "the victim, Joshua Canfield, was the poet who took the Frost Chair at the university when your father retired. You wouldn't know anything about that, though, would you." It was a statement, not a question. "He was found shot dead in his office. The pistol, we think, fired a silver bullet. That's not something you hear every day." He watched the reactions of the twins and thought they looked guilty of something. He hoped it wasn't murder. Little slots in Anthony's brain were filling in and he was adding up coincidences without conclusions.

Teddy looked dumbfounded and kept quiet.

"So you see," said Edward, "we've had quite a bit of contact with the Wadsworths. I know they would love to see you both; they asked about you. Why don't you go over and get caught up with the lives of Dana and Jeanne." Then he thought to himself, they'll go when they want to; leave them alone.

Lew and Mark arrived. Cat called out, "lunch!" They all adjourned to the dining room and the lunch got underway. Lew had made his stop at the Blacksmith Shop and had a delicate Dacquoise for dessert. Cat had homemade vegetable soup, green leafy salad, and French baguette ready. The conversation was easy and comfortable. Teddy asked Mark about his studio and how he got interested in photography in the first place.

Mark was more animated than usual and told them, "When I was in sixth grade we had a teacher who was always taking great pictures of whatever was happening around the school. He always had this extra, all-seeing eye working for him. He caught the kindergarteners' awe at the Parade of Horribles, which was much more telling than the Horribles themselves. And there was the time a bewildered sixth-grade violinist didn't know what to do when a string broke. A photo captured the essence and pathos of the moment."

There was a lull and Cat spoke up, "I didn't tell you, Mark, but I stopped in to see Ambrose last week and the committee has narrowed it down to three covers for the anthology—and two of the designs are yours! I don't think it's been announced yet. but I think it's almost a shoo-in." She went on to explain—though no one asked. "I was afraid the anthology would get lost in the murderous mire, but now that Robert Ambrose has claimed his new Chair, things have started happening. Maybe he won't be so bad. I had better not make a judgment on him like I did on Canfield," she said before she very softly, hardly audibly, said, "I still think a woman should be considered sometime."

As everyone at the table was still considering Cat's quiet proclamation, Rennie said, "Where's the TV?"

Everyone looked at him as though he had asked where their secrets were hidden. Edward broke the hush by putting his hand to his chin, obviously straining his brain in thought and saying, "I don't know. Cat, don't we have a television somewhere? I mean besides the little one in the kitchen?" He looked around the room and saw it was not in the dining room.

"Of course! It's in the closet by the front door. Is there something you wanted to watch?"

"I just like to have it on.

"Oh."

Rennie said, "When you only have a rented, not too nicely furnished, room to spend rainy days and dull evenings in, there's not much to occupy your mind and it's easy to resort to old movies and talk shows. Some of them are pretty good. They discuss topics like the environment and education and family values."

"There are always books," Mark said.

Rennie ignored Mark altogether and cut him off before he could say more, "I like the talk shows where they have these poor people with AIDS or battered wives or impotent lovers or, better yet," he was laughing, "a mother and a daughter dating the same boyfriend, on stage together like they're on a precarious perch where a well aimed delivery could plunge them into a tub of cold water, like at the fair." Rennie was enjoying himself. "Remember how we hit the bulls eye and took Mr. Cummings off his perch and into the tub of water—which I think was cold water? Except, on TV, the host pretends to be sensitive to the plight of these losers and then batters and beats them down again and again. It's so funny! And the audience! They're even better. . . or worse!"

"Rennie," Teddy looked apprehensive, "that's not funny. Stop trying to shock everyone."

"It is shocking. That's what everyone wants--to be shocked. Or to vicariously commit some crime--that's why they have all those shows. You don't suppose for one minute they'd spend all that money if they didn't get the ratings, do you? Murders and incestuous tangles and car chases and bloody fights make money!"

He had everyone's attention and embarked on a new topic that he seemed to be trying to present just as shocking. "Well, what are we going to do now that our dear Dad has opened his heart and his door to his wayward progeny?" He was still grinning. "Watch TV all day? I could get used to that. And this food is pretty good." He was eating as he spoke. "I wonder if you're prepared to take us on again." Rennie put his spoon down and in the deafening silence he pointed at Edward.

Lew started squirming. He should have foreseen this. How would Edward cope?

But Edward was ready and he surprised not only Lew, but everyone else too. He took a deep breath before he started on something he had obviously thought about, "I want you both back. By that I mean I want you here only as much as you want to be here. If you prefer to be elsewhere, that's fine. I do want you to know that I love you both no matter what the past years reveal. You've shocked me before and I'm sure you'll do it again. But I don't care and I think I can keep my perspective. I'm ready to share any and all my worldly goods and wealth. Your mother's estate is yours now, or will be next week, and you can take it and squander it or put it to work for you or anything you'd like. I am not going to try to control either of you with rewards for promises you can't or don't want to keep." He looked around the table. Everyone seemed caught in mid-move, barely breathing. "I do hope you'll let me be a small part of your lives. All I ask is for forgiveness and that you see it in your hearts to accept me."

It was a lengthy speech for the lunch table but Edward still had his composure and smiled as he gestured for everyone to continue with lunch.

"Even the bravest that are slain
Shall not dissemble their surprise. . ."

from THE TRIAL BY EXISTENCE
Robert Frost

Chapter 26

There was only a moment of that kind of awkwardness that surrounds a hidden truth when it has at last been voiced. Edward's words cleared the air, Cat thought, as she watched the reaction of the twins.

For all she cared, Rennie could take his share and leave and she hoped he would. He wasn't even trying to make himself agreeable. Thinking she might be unfair she moderated her view. Maybe Rennie could find something to do instead of sitting around watching television thinking up ways to be itchy. He is so different from Teddy.

There is any number of things Teddy could pursue to fill his life in a meaningful way. He could, for instance, become a teacher, maybe a sports teacher at one of the independent schools in Cambridge. They're always looking to fill part-time posts for part-time wages. Could Cat vouch for him? She thought she could; but really, what did she know about either of them? There was a huge time gap to be filled in.

She had asked if they would like to go back to school. It would be so easy here in Cambridge where there are so many choices in education. She turned toward Teddy and said, "You know, there's a lot of experience and expertise right here in this room, and I think I speak for everyone," she looked around the table, "when I say we would welcome the opportunity to use it to help you—both of you—find a niche."

Of everyone who jumped in with ideas, Anthony had the most immediate, practical solution. They, one or both, would be welcomed at the Community Center—he could call the director. "There are youngsters there," Anthony said, "who need all the help and guidance they can get." It occurred to him that these two really hadn't proven themselves to be pillars of the community. Then again, Teddy had already shown he was willing to take on a mentor role with the basketball team. "These kids are much more impressed by someone who has strayed from the usual orthodox paths and found a way back into community life with renewed vigor than they are with those of us who have always had empathy for the plight of others but no first-hand experience with it. Some of these kids," he said, "have no positive influence in their lives other than a few teachers and people like Dicky.

"And you," Lew put in.

"Yes, and me. But it's better to have younger images they can identify with more easily. Face it, it's pretty hard to call a police commissioner your friend when you're sixteen and scared of him or that he'll find out something you've been trying to hide. I don't do that, of course. I try to be an authority figure with a heart, but they really need young people like you. They need examples of good sportsmanship and gamesmanship to foster team unity and self reliance and discipline."

Cat made the case that it would be a good move. It would get them back into the mainstream where they could paddle along until a fortuitous current pushed them into a new direction. It would give them some stability and meaning.

Mark surprised everyone with interesting news about the new spring theatre productions. "I've been commissioned to design a photographic backdrop," he added, "and they're always looking for set people. It's interesting work with creative people." Rennie seemed interested and asked questions about who hired and how long a project it would be.

"We just need a little time to figure things out," said Teddy..

Anthony swabbed the end of his soup with a crust of bread and popped it into his mouth.

"Who would like more soup? There's plenty," Cat offered. Everyone was ready for dessert it seemed. There was more talk about the Community Center while Cat served the dessert. She cut the Daquoise into eight pieces, leaving one piece temptingly on the plate—for later and whoever got to it first.

Anthony made short work of the torte and coffee and apologized but had to get back to the station. Everyone else stayed at the table, drinking coffee and enjoying the conversation rising back to an easy, manageable plane. Prodded by their audience, Teddy and Rennie started to talk about some of their amusing junkets. Teddy's agreeable humor neutralized Rennie's anecdotes that seemed over-the-top or not quite true.

With some further prompting, they told about life in Mexico and Guatemala. It was obvious that there was something that Teddy didn't want Rennie to talk about and Rennie seemed to be playing on it with some success. Teddy looked uncomfortable and changed the subject several times telling about some of their later adventures in Texas when they were cowboys. But Rennie wouldn't let it rest. "What do you think Maria-Elena will say about all this? You going to tell her? Think you can get her to come?"

There it is, thought Cat. She knew there was something she wasn't going to like when Rennie kept looking at her with a devilish I-know-something grin. Then he came out with it all at once: Teddy had a wife and daughter in Mexico.

The room was still. Teddy was annoyed and it showed as he turned to Rennie and said, "You had to do it, didn't you?" He spoke to a point in the corner of the room before straightening up and looking at first his father and then at Cat. "I was going to tell you. I just wanted to do it my way. I'm in touch with them and I hear from Maria-Elena often. Edwina—yes," he smiled at his father, "named for you—is almost six years old now. I haven't seen her since she was a toddler, but I would like to bring her and Maria here." He cast a deathly, shattering look at his brother. "They are not peasants as Rennie likes to say, just not rich. They live with Maria-Elena's family on a small ranchero in

Guanajuato. We worked for them for a while. When there wasn't enough work to keep us both busy, we went north. I've always wanted to either join them or have them join me. Which brings us to another touchy point—about joining them. I'm not sure we would be welcome there."

He was glad Anthony had left and he wiped his face with his napkin before he started, "We had a spot of trouble just before we went to Texas. We were eating tacos in a bar when some drunken Mexican cowboys started to razz us. They stole our wallets and started a fight. In the end, the bar was badly broken up and when the local police showed up, I was outside getting the truck revved up. They had Rennie by the arms and were about to lead him away."

Rennie slapped his thigh and continued the story, "They looked at me and then saw Teddy outside and I started yelling they got the wrong one. Everyone in the bar was laughing and pointing. While they were figuring things out, I hopped into the truck and we roared away." He was laughing and said, "I don't think they had a police car or if they did it was in the shop!" A little self-consciously, everyone else laughed too.

Cat was quiet; a jumble of images simmering in her head. This was just too much. She knew she and Teddy were communicating on an intellectual level; they were *sympaticos* but there was an invisible barrier between them, something made him cautious about saying or showing too much. She had attributed it to his trying not to come on too strong. Now she knew what it was and that was that he was trying to not come on to her at all! When she thought back she could see she was right.

And she had been right in the first place; it was a familial affinity they had. The past few days she was convinced it was because of her bond with Edward, but now. . . . This was confusing! She was glad she had started to identify these sentiments, but she was not happy.

It was her naïve, poetic soul, she thought, that drove her to unsuitable partners in the past. It seemed to her that she was destined to be in a romantic muddle. Things always started off explosively and blissfully, then like most big bangs, fizzled and she was left with remembering the sound and the fury and not much else. Well, maybe not quite that bad, she thought.

With every relationship she could remember, it seemed that no matter how she tried to control and subdue the amphetamine-like chemical drenching her brain and making her feel a frenzy of excitement and euphoria, before long she felt the crumbling, lovesick despair of rejection. She never drifted into a relationship except with Mark and that didn't count because she didn't feel that tingling and spark. Theirs was a comfortable comradeship and he was always there accepting her capricious behavior.

Her overwhelming thought was to just get through this lunch without anything else happening that might upset the comfortable balance Edward was teetering on.

It was late afternoon when everyone finally left and Edward could adjourn to his study. But before he did he wanted to tell Cat how much he appreciated all she did to make this a successful occasion. As an afterthought, he said to Cat, "Let's not bother with supper tonight. Some of this leftover soup will be fine for me."

Cat nodded agreement. After straightening out the mess in the kitchen, she walked out the door and down to the river. There was an empty bench at the water's edge. Her notebook and pencil were in her hand as she sat down, but she didn't write. She sat for a long time trying to thread her way through the labyrinth of paradoxical truths.

When she went to bed that night she shut off all the relationship puzzles that were not fitting together and soothed her addled brain with poetry. Hers. She was comforted, too, by the fact that her new book was almost at the printer. It was good. Robert Ambrose said so.

"We allow some time for guile
And don't come out for a while,
Either to eat or drink.
We take occasion to think."

from A DRUMLIN WOODCHUCK
Robert Frost

Chapter 27

The next morning was a poet's spring day. Cat opened the back door to let some of it in. Because she couldn't tease Edward about New England weather today, didn't stop her from baiting him a bit: "New England is finally giving in to California Technicolor," she joshed.

Edward, ever ready to ignore her proffered comments, looked up from the paper for a second, "Good morning," he said. "It says here that the Cambridge police have made progress into the recent slaying of a University professor and that finding the pistol is key. It doesn't say anything about the fact that there were two stolen pistols and that only one has been recovered." He watched Cat straighten things and pour coffee. He picked up a piece of toast—burnt—and put it back on the plate. "I have no doubt they'll trace whoever pawned it. They always do."

He turned a page and sighed before putting it down, "I wouldn't want to be a criminal these days there are too many ways to get caught and the minuses definitely outweigh the pluses of becoming an outlaw." He was smiling at Cat and continued with a twinkle, "With all the new electronic expertise, and it isn't just fingerprints and blood typing but DNA positive identification and infrared imaging, and who knows what else. Covering up and evading would take more time and thought than the crime itself." He went back to the paper. "It'd be easier to turn legitimate and earn a living."

Cat hmmmed and drank her coffee. "I hadn't looked at it from the criminal's point of view. I guess it does rather throw a spanner into the works." She picked up the same piece of toast Edward had discarded and took a bite after heaping on some raspberry jam. It was crunchy and a big piece of it dropped into her coffee. Edward peered over his glasses just in time to hear a plop and see a splash. She giggled. "I can't even eat a piece of toast without leaving clues."

Edward glanced at Cat, relaxed the newspaper barrier between them and said, "Sometime when you have a few minutes, we should sit down and talk about getting this place painted and redecorated. I decided yesterday that should be done--look at these dingy walls."

Not long ago Cat's reaction would have been amazement. For more than two years he never noticed dingy walls, chipped paint, or anything else to do with the house. He didn't give her enough time to respond before saying, "Actually, if you wouldn't mind, I'd rather just have you see to it. I'd like whatever you do. And, I want you to do the third floor however you would like, anyway. It's for you and always will be." His eyes were aimed at the ceiling for a few seconds and then he looked beyond Cat to the rear of the house. "Do you think I could convert the back part of the house to a little suite for me? I could change the big pantry into a closet and there's already a bathroom. Maybe I could keep my study where it is and connect it to my own quiet space. That would leave the whole house for Teddy and his family. And Rennie could have his own area on the second floor in the back." All this, he assured, was only in the embryo stage and he would gladly listen to suggestions.

Cat agreed to get things started. That part was easy. Whether or not she wanted to stay on the third floor was another matter. She didn't want to be housekeeper to the twins and some extended family. She couldn't. But she would see the refurbishing through. Now, in the light of day, sitting here with Edward, she was thinking a bit more clearly about her relationship with Teddy. Perspective, she thought, is everything.

Edward didn't know yet about the fellowship at Oxford. She hadn't told him because, she argued with herself, she only did it to see if she would be accepted and was almost sure she wouldn't go even if the fellowship were offered. At the time, she had been worried about leaving Edward in his precarious mood. Now with Edward's life changes and some of her own thought out, she'd changed her mind and was pretty sure she would take it if it were offered. She surprised herself by assuming she would be accepted and would go.

Edward put the paper back together, finished his coffee and headed for his desk in the study, announcing, "I'll be writing for a few hours," and left Cat in the kitchen.

It seemed abrupt, but she was getting used to Edward as she used to know him. A little self-centered, not nasty or selfish, but, to put it nicely, goal oriented, and she accepted that.

Cat stacked the few dishes, made a couple of sandwiches and hurried to the university. She wanted to be on time for her appointment with Ambrose at nine-thirty. There were a few changes in her submission she wanted to discuss with him. But she also wanted to see what he thought about the fellowship at Oxford and what it might mean for her. Ambrose, she remembered, had spent some time at Oxford.

The glass door in James Hall now proclaimed Robert Ambrose as the Robert Frost Chair in bold black letters. Cat pushed at the slightly open door, squared her shoulders and smiled warmly, "Good morning. Thanks so much for seeing me last week and offering words of encouragement. I needed them. And, now, I have some unrelated questions I'd like to ask you."

"Good morning to you," Ambrose looked up from the manuscript he had before him on his desk. He was smiling and in casual Cambridge dress of no tie, an open shirt under his tweed jacket, and jeans. "It was easy, your work is good and deserving of a place. I wish others would come to see me with such good work and in such good order. Maybe more will come as we get more publicity." He went on to offer a few suggestions for subtle changes ending with, " . . . and what were the other questions."

Cat told him about the application, and after some prodding, he talked a little, with that far-away-look people often get when they reminisce, about his two years at Oxford, and he said, ". . . it was the most intense and broadening intellectual experience of my life. Milton, Shakespeare, Coleridge, Wordsworth, Shelley, Keats, Burns—the essence of these mighty versifiers inspired all of us who walked the hidden footpaths and found the lodestones scattered along the way." It was a slightly embarrassed Ambrose who bridged the years back to his office to Cat who sat with an open mouth. It was as though he hadn't meant to show himself but couldn't help it. In spite of his reluctance to over state, he gave Cat reassurance and she felt a spark of enthusiasm from across the desk and knew she was right in wishing to go. Now she just had to wait for the acceptance letter.

Once again, she left the office of the Robert Frost Chair floating a few inches off the ground. A spring breeze spiraled around her ankles and chased a wayward paper across the path as she turned the corner into the Quad.

Cat eased onto the bench and hoped her telepathic messages to Teddy were working. Even though she had given much thought about how she would open the conversation, she was still not sure. Learning about his wife and daughter hadn't devastated her because she hadn't projected their relationship that far. Had she? How had she thought of it? Was this merely something she recognized and identified as her "infatuation syndrome?" She sighed. This kind of ruminating was not productive.

Instead she rerouted her energies and focused her thoughts on a completely different level. And that was the impact of all this on Edward: the twins' return, the theft, the murder. and how the scenario would be played out. Each day she saw improvement in Edward's outlook and he had taken all this shaking up with equanimity. His despondency and ennui were a closed chapter and she saw no more of the disturbing characteristics that had worried her so much. In fact, she thought, he's getting quite demanding, to say nothing of being a little insensitive. Of course, she argued, how could he be sensitive to something he doesn't know about? Maybe she was so close that she saw things out of context and proportion, had put too dramatic a spin on his detachment and now she was standing back and could see more clearly.

She looked up again, saw Teddy across the Quad and waved. It seemed to take him ages to walk the little distance down the path to the bench and sit down. She was ready for him when he finally reached her.

No superficial pleasantries for Cat. "I'm glad to see you alone, and I've been trying to understand why you didn't tell me about Maria-Elena an Edwina. Didn't you trust me?"

"I do and I did," he hesitated and clamped his lips together as if to say it was a puzzle to him too. Then he said, "It all happened so fast. You have to understand that I didn't know who you were or anything about your situation with my father. As far as I knew, you might have had a husband or boyfriend. "We never talked about our own relationships, remember? You never said." He was tapping his fingers together. "Neither did I--not for any hidden reason though. We were two kindred spirits who met on a bench. I never intended to hide my family from anyone; not you and certainly not my father. I just hadn't had time to figure it all out. I'm still not sure what to do or how." He stood up and walked around the bench before sitting down again.

He continued, "I wasn't being deceitful. I do like you a lot and I love Maria. I tossed and turned all night thinking about this and how to say it right. I want us to remain friends; it never got further than that anyway and I think that if it did, it would have been a mistake. We're more like siblings." He looked her in the eye, "Be truthful. You don't feel that infatuation thing." It was not a question. "I feel like I've known you for a long time; like a good friend or a sister or a cousin."

Even though Cat knew what he meant, she wasn't ready to admit it. She felt hurt but wanted to hide it. So she said, "I have to admit that I have been ambivalent about it but I thought it was because you never said much about your personal life and I worried," she looked up at him and realized the truth of what he had said as she finished her sentence, "that there was someone else to consider."

The jumble that had been tying her in knots she couldn't undo was loosening, and she was beginning to feel some slack enabling her to slip the knots. He's right, she thought, we are more like brother and sister and we can be friends on those terms without any hurt.

People walked back and forth engrossed in their own worlds while Cat pulled some pita bread sandwiches and grapes out of her bag and they picked at the food, barely touching it. After a while Teddy said, "Please don't give up on me. I'm confused about the whole situation and need time to set things straight in my own head. Then I'll tackle Rennie and his attitudes. He's really just scared he won't live up to expectations so he acts up." He took hold of her hand, "In many ways, you are very like Maria-Elena. I would like you two to be friends, too." He patted her hand and placed it gently back in her lap. "I can start the mending and I mean to be open and nonjudgmental. To myself as well as to my father and Rennie." They sat in silence.

Cat put things away crumpling the wrappers, stuffing them back into her bag and brushing off crumbs. "I have to go. I've a meeting with Ambrose," she explained, though she couldn't have said why she felt she had to, particularly as it wasn't true. She had already seen Ambrose. In her buried consciousness she wanted to tell Teddy about Oxford, but she didn't say a word.

"Yes." he said, "I'll see you soon. I need some time." He didn't sound happy.

Cat went in one direction and Teddy went in another out of the Quad that had been their secret garden.

**"I shall set forth for somewhere,
I shall make the reckless choice. . ."**

    **from THE SOUND OF TREES
Robert Frost**

Chapter 28

Teddy's head was spinning with more than Cat's misunderstanding about their relationship. That only added to the tangle, and he cursed Rennie for jumping the gun by telling everyone about Maria-Elena and Edwina. It was something he had wanted to do, in his own time and in his own way. But that seemed trivial at the moment. What he never got the chance to explain to Cat was the Wadsworth fiasco.

He had made up his mind to tell her the whole story and to ask her advice. It had been weighing on his mind because he knew that if he and Rennie continued to hide it, they could never return to life in Cambridge. He wanted to come clean, be forgiven, and take his punishment. Everything could be accounted for except that other pistol and it was sure to turn up. The whole thing was messy and he cursed the stupidity, his and Rennie's, that led them, uninvited, into the Wadsworths' house

that night. Then, when he found Cat so deep on another page in
the saga, he couldn't bring it up. It had taken all the courage he
could muster to just get himself to the Quad to meet her.

Back at their room, he lashed out at Rennie. "Well, this
is just great. How are we going to get around this one?" Teddy
stood over Rennie in an uncharacteristic stance. Usually he was
the one defending his actions with Rennie asserting himself by
ramroding dominance over a situation. As though his mind was
made up, he said, "I think we are going to have to tell the
commissioner . . ."

"Call him Anthony. He said to." Rennie looked down at
his stretched out hand and flicked his wrist in dismissal. He got
up and started to walk away.

"No!" Teddy tugged at Rennie's arm, "You're going to
sit here and pay attention until we reach an agreement." Teddy
was angry. "If you can't be bothered, I'm just going to go to . .
. Anthony. . . and tell him what we did."

Rennie, of course, refused to listen. He got up and left
the room.

So, later that afternoon Teddy walked to the station. He
felt a little unsure of himself as his sneakered feet quietly stole
up the stairs to the Commissioner's office. When Anthony saw
him on the other side of his desk, he knew he was not going to be
happy with whatever came next, and he had a suspicion about
what it would be. He called Dicky in, closed the door all the
way, and they listened to Teddy for the next half hour.

Teddy told them about how Rennie had remembered the
code to the Wadsworths; lock and security system. It was easy.

"You'd think they'd have changed the code at least once in all these years," he said. "Initially," he said, "we just went in to raid the icebox, the Wadsworths wouldn't mind that. We made sandwiches and took them into the library to be comfortable like we used to do with Jeanne and Dana. It didn't feel like we were committing a crime."

Then they saw the books all stacked as though, by some prior arrangement, they were waiting to be taken away. "At first we thought we could pawn them but," he said, "after we carried them out, they got more awkward and heavier and it seemed like less of a good idea. It was really stealing and we've never done anything like that."

Anthony quietly watched saying nothing about the time they conned Lew by keeping the twenty dollars he had given them for raffle tickets. They were young but that was certainly stealing.

"We probably would have taken them back into the house," Anthony looked skeptical when he heard that but paid attention while Teddy continued with his story, "but while we were outside, a station wagon drove into the driveway and we just left the books under the bushes and got out of there. They were in boxes . . . but the paintings didn't fit and neither did the pistols so we took those along with us," he reasoned, "they seemed easier to deal with."

"We went back the next night," he said, "and the books were still there, under the bushes, undiscovered. We knew we could get Mrs. Oliver to call the police who would find the books. She always did if she heard anything out of the ordinary, so we made wild noises and scattered newspapers all over her lawn. We wanted to be sure the books were rescued before it rained or they blew apart. It was just lucky that the weather had been dry."

"We were wishing we hadn't taken the stuff in the first place." He looked like he was trying to convince Anthony that it was no big deal by giving a little shrug. "That night, we were hungry and had no money. We had tried again to see my father, but the house was dark and no one was home. After we stopped there, we ended up on Brattle Street in front of the Wadsworth house. It was really a spur-of-the-moment thing. A prank. If we hadn't been so hungry, we wouldn't have gone in at all."

Anthony thought for a moment and said, "That was a Sunday night. You should have gone to Lew's. We were there for a brandy after dinner in the Square. I suppose we didn't leave until shortly after ten. So go on. What about the Fragonards and the pistols?"

Teddy continued, "If you look in the Heineken Museum coatroom behind the table at the end of the room, you'll find the Fragonards, wrapped in newspaper. I couldn't very well put a sign on them or say anything, but I was nervous that they were being overlooked when I saw they were still there yesterday. It was Rennie who took the pistol to the pawnshop. . ."

Anthony interrupted, "What about the other pistol?"

Teddy sighed shaking his head, "I lost that one. I know that sounds feeble, but I don't know what happened to it. So I must have lost it. One day I had it and then when I went to look for it later, it wasn't there."

"Could Rennie have taken it?"

"I suppose so."

Dicky's head snapped around to Anthony. He knew what Anthony was thinking: if that lost pistol was the one that killed Canfield, and it seems now it probably was, was Rennie the one who pulled the trigger?

"Though he could have taken it I am pretty sure he didn't. He can't hide much from me."

"When do you last remember having both of them?"

"It was a few days after we broke into the Wadsworths'. I remember shifting them around in my pack because they were uncomfortable—one was sticking into my back. I set the pack down for only a few minutes to rearrange while I sat down in the Quad. But I was sure I put them back in my pack. It's possible, of course, that one slipped out. It's possible but not probable.

"It was after the theft that Canfield was murdered," Anthony was mumbling and assessing the situation out loud. "But where does that lead? If you lost it as you said, then anyone could have picked it up and anyone could have used it to kill Canfield."

Dicky's scribbled notes took over where Anthony left off: "Unless it was Rennie and he had taken it without Teddy's knowledge." Dicky wrote, "Or, that Teddy was covering his own tracks."

Anthony hadn't stopped, "There is a string of coincidences to be explained."

Dicky had already started a list that included not only the pistols that came from the Wadsworths' and the Frost books,

Canfield's Frost Chair, and Edward, a Wadsworth neighbor and former Frost Fellow and . . .

"I can't tell you why we did it. As I said, we really broke into the Wadsworths for something to eat. I don't mean to make excuses for either of us. We did it. We are sorry if we caused any trouble and we are ready to take the consequences. At least, I am," he considered for a moment and said, "Rennie, too."

"It will be up to the Wadsworths to press charges but I'll take your statement, have it printed up and ask you and Rennie to sign it. Then we'll take it from there." Anthony motioned to Dicky that that was all for now and Dicky left, closing the door behind him.

When they were alone, Anthony got up from his desk and went over to the window. A spring shower was splatting on the windowpane washing off some of the city dust. "I'm glad you came to me on your own. That's one thing in your favor. This case has been a stickler. We just couldn't figure a motive. That there is none makes sense. My only problem with that is that the missing pistol is probably the one that was used to kill Professor Canfield and that puts a much more serious spin on the situation."

Teddy jumped up, "You can't be serious. We broke into the Wadsworths' but we sure didn't kill anyone!" He stood up and started pacing nervously.

"Maybe you didn't. Why didn't Rennie come with you today?"

This was not going as Teddy had planned and he wished, again, that Rennie had come with him. Stealing was one thing, murder was something he didn't want to even think about.

"He wouldn't come with me, I think, because he never wants to admit he has been wrong about anything or has made a mistake. He has always been a show-off and a bully, but he has never physically harmed anyone. Not even me. His game is mental one-ups-man-ship and stuff like that. When did this murder take place anyhow?"

Anthony had his calendar out to check the date. "It was a Wednesday night. I remember I was late getting to the station the next day—the day it was discovered—because I had to stop at the court house to check on a summons that I couldn't do on Wednesday afternoon because I had to get to the Community Center early," he stopped talking, started nodding his head in confirmation, "and you were there with us at the Center and afterwards at the pizza joint." He looked relieved and so did Teddy. Then he said, "But Rennie was not with us. Where was he?"

What a snarl thought Teddy. Ten minutes later he left, assuring Anthony that he would get back to him and have Rennie give him a run-down of his alibi, and they would both sign the statement. Teddy didn't know where Rennie could have been and, of course, had no reason to even ask. Rennie was always taking off somewhere and was not in the habit of saying where. Teddy hoped he could remember where he had been that Wednesday and could find someone to verify it.

When Teddy told Rennie about his confession to Anthony, Rennie was tearing mad. "We could have gotten away with it and never had to answer for it. Now, you've practically got us charged with murder!"

Teddy wanted to say, "Not us. You." But, more, he wanted to be sure where Rennie had been, so he said, "I was at the Community Center the night of the murder and Anthony was with me. I think you were at Celeste's. Weren't you?"

Celeste was the owner of Celestial Lights. She had taken a fancy to Rennie and he had taken advantage of her receptivity to explore one of his business fantasies. He could be her buyer rep in Central America where he knew the people and the goods, he had told her. There was a world of jewelry and stones that was ripe to be tapped into. Silver, he told her, and obsidian, turquoise and other semi-precious stones like topaz were in abundance there; and cheap. He was convincing and she was ready to be convinced.

"Yeah. That's where I've been most nights. I've just about got her persuaded to send me to Central America." He added, "I could make a killing for her in jewelry and stones. Maybe we could even become partners. With a little capital I could become a thriving entrepreneur." He was putting on his I-know-what-I'm-talking about act. "I could sure use some of mother's estate."

Teddy was unconvinced. He had seen schemes for making a killing come and go and mostly fail abysmally. But he was really interested only in where Rennie had been that night not in another collapsible enterprise. "But were you there that night?"

"How should I know? Do I have a secretary? When was it again?" He looked like he was straining to remember."

"It was Wednesday, the Wednesday after we broke into the Wadsworths' house. On Tuesday, remember, we put the papers all over Mrs. Oliver's lawn. The next day, Wednesday, or rather Wednesday night, is the critical time. I was at the Community Center playing basketball with a bunch of teenagers and Anthony himself though we didn't know each other then. Where were you?"

"I remember now! Of course. You're right. I was at Celeste's. She had made a great meal and we had stew and bread and wine well into the night. I stayed there all night. She'll remember, too. It was somebody-or-other's birthday. She made a big deal of candles in the yogurt." He sounded relieved. "I'll just be sure to get to Celeste and prompt her memory tomorrow."

Teddy felt better and hoped Celeste would remember without coaching. Then the two of them started arguing about something else. Everything was back to normal.

In the meantime, Anthony called Edward and asked that he and Lew give him a little time in the morning to go over something serious. Something that they must find answers to. He said time was of the essence.

"Were not, as 'twere, the merest mark
of gloom
But stretched away unto the edge of
doom."

from INTO MY OWN
Robert Frost

Chapter 29

Another beautiful morning. Spring was in full bloom.
Cat had picked a few daffodils for the table and Anthony and
Edward ate burnt toast and jam with coffee while they perused
sections of the *Globe*. Anthony had the sports section, as usual,
and Edward was thumbing through the arts section. Edward read
aloud, "the Boston Opera is doing 'La Boheme' this year. Want
to go?"

No response came from Anthony.

Edward repeated a little louder, "Want to go?" and
moved the paper from in front of him so he could see his
breakfast partner.

"Huh." Anthony looked at the section Edward was
holding, saw the opera feature and said, "Yes, sure. 'La Boheme.'
I'd like it better if it were in Italian—but, yes, I would like to go.
What else is on the run?" He focused, "At least there'll be one
everyone will like. Usually they revive some old war horses.
There's a reason no one does them? They're not interesting and
the music is o.k. but not great." At least, he had spoken for

himself. He went back to the paper. "But, yes, let's go to La Boheme."

Anthony was preoccupied with the coming-down-to-the-wire NBA results. "Say, wouldn't you like to take in some of these last games—maybe the boys would like to. I'll ask. Would you like to go?" He was thinking he'd get a bunch of tickets. If no one here wanted to go he could always take his basketball players.

Underneath his joking was the real reason for his preoccupation. Very soon he would have to make some decisions in his capacity as commissioner. Today. He was ambivalent about what to do and how, and it showed in his unusual. unjovial manner. Maybe there was nothing to his worries, but it looked bad. He had made up his mind to tell Edward and Lew about meeting yesterday with Teddy and his ensuing confession. He wanted to do it face-to-face—that was why he arranged for this morning meeting. The good thing was that in all probability, the Wadsworths would not even press charges once they listened to the circumstances of the twins' break-in. They had meant no harm, intent again. was key.

His worry, and here was the problem: the murder. The pistol connection was clear. He felt as sure as anyone could without proof positive that one of those antique pistols had done the job. His gut feeling, though, was, that it was not Rennie who killed Canfield. And an alibi would go a long way to proving it in the eyes of the law. They had to find something concrete to put Rennie in the clear. He was sure that if they sat down and went through the chronology of events they would find the key they were looking for, even if Rennie were so egotistical that he deemed it unnecessary to defend himself against something he said he didn't do. He truly thought everyone should believe him and he was insulted to think they mightn't. Did it never occur to him that he presented an amoral, completely untrustworthy posture? Anthony hurriedly refolded the paper and started to clear the table. At nine o'clock they walked out the back door. Lew, he thought, will have some ideas. He always does.

He and Edward walked down the path by the lilacs to Lew's back door. The hedge between the properties of the two friends was heavy with blossoms and lilac scent wafted on the morning breeze. The daffodils had been naturalizing in the front yards for years: ". . . a crowd, A host, of golden daffodils; . . ." were nodding in the ivy-covered ground where the sun never broke through in the summertime after the ancient copper beech had leafed. Right now it was a glorious array. Passers-by stopped to admire it.

The door was unlocked so Anthony gave his rat-ta-rat-tat-tat-tat knock, rattled the knob and entered.

"Lew! Lew! Are you here?" called Edward. "He must be here, he knew we were coming. We're only a little late; he looked at his watch. Maybe he's so engrossed in some dusty volume, he can't hear us." Edward was talking to Anthony as he led the way through the house to the study where Lew kept his desk and files.

The door to the study was ajar, light shining through the crack cast a dim beam on the oriental hall runner. Anthony knocked. And again, louder this time. The door opened a little

more as he knocked. He called, "Lew, are you in there?" He
sniffed. There was a funny smell in the air. He recognized it
immediately. He tried but he couldn't seem to go any faster. It
was as though they were frozen in a time bubble. In slow motion
Anthony raised his arm and pushed open the door to the study.
The cordite odor slapped their faces and stung their nostrils. It
was sharp and fresh. A nightmare-like scene telescoped before
them as they passed into real time. Anthony gasped. Edward
bellowed and stumbled to hold on to something, practically
knocking both of them over.

There, slumped over the desk was Lew. Most of his
handsome head was gone, scattered across the desk and splatters
of something: blood? on the bookcases behind.

Edward, moaning, started across the room. "Don't,"
Anthony stopped him with a raised hand and wondered if he had
the strength to subdue his friend; if he had the strength to make it
through this scene himself. He was back in the time bubble and
felt his energy draining and melting leaving his knees wobbling
like grape jelly. He couldn't comprehend what he saw! It
couldn't be! How did this happen? Who could have done this?
Why?

"Lew! Lew!" Edward shouted, as though if he shouted
loud enough Lew would raise his head and say hello, I've been
waiting for you. Reality told him there could be no response but
he didn't seem to believe it. He couldn't believe it. "Anthony,
what has happened? What has happened?" Edward looked to
Anthony to give him an answer he could grasp. He was

trembling and wailing an unearthly moan, his face screwed up in a grotesque mask.

Anthony's mouth was open but the only sound that emanated was an aberrant groan. He was stumped. How could he have answers? He didn't even know the questions. He didn't even know if he was really standing in Lew's study or adrift in a dream—a nightmare. And that's what he hoped it was—an incubus testing his sanity. He was dangling in slow-motion time that was heavy and plodding and thick and tiresome. After a few eternal minutes he managed to eke out enough energy to pull himself together, walk to the wide open window and fan the cordite odor away from the room and out the window. But he still felt nauseated. He glanced at the inert form. He looked away and back again. His eyes must be lying.

He was stunned. His training allowed him little latitude, he was on automatic and in control because he knew he had to be. Anthony pulled out his handkerchief to pick up the phone. He dialed with a pencil he pulled from his jacket breast pocket that he always kept hidden with his fountain pen behind the ornamental handkerchief. "Dicky," he said in a voice he hardly recognized, "get the forensics and Doc Appleby over here on the double. It looks like another murder. There is no sign of a struggle and no sign of a weapon." He gave him the address on Berkeley Street. "And, Dicky, keep it under wraps for the time being, please."

Speaking with Dicky helped to clear his mind and he turned his attention back to Edward who was standing, dumb, in the middle of the room. He led him to a chair across the room from the grisly scene. "Sit down." He didn't want to leave him alone for even a second, but he had to check out the rest of the house. Maybe the murderer was still here. The gun couldn't have been fired more than a few minutes before they arrived. Where had he gone? They had seen no one and heard nothing but the twittering of birds through the open window. "And don't touch anything, please." After he said it, he realized that Edward was not going to touch anything or even move. He was in shock.

Anthony left the study and started for the stairs. He held onto the railing for support. He put one foot in front of the other, climbed the stairs and then opened each closed door to search. He found no one and nothing out of place. No bureau drawers pulled out or upturned, no beds torn apart, no slashed or torn upholstery or toppled furniture. Everything looked as though it had just been cleaned and tidied.

In Lew's study, Edward sat. He couldn't do anything else. He certainly could not look at what used to be his beloved friend, but he couldn't keep his eyes away either. He glanced around the room without getting up, moaning. Who is doing this? And why? Lew was no more a controversial figure than Canfield had been. They both led quiet unassuming academic lives. Like me, thought Edward. And his hands clutched his shaking head. His moaning gave way to sobbing.

Anthony was back and had regained some of his composure while he was searching the upstairs rooms. "Edward," he said, "you should go home. I'll let you know as soon as Appleby has made his pronouncement. And I'll let you know what we find."

Edward looked up and seemed quietly resigned now. "I know what I need to know. Lew is dead. Whoever could have done this? Whoever did this has killed part of me, too. Why?" He was distraught and babbling. "How could this happen? Who will be next?"

Anthony pulled his handkerchief out and picked up the phone again. He dialed. "Cat, I'm glad I caught you. Could you come over to Lew's—no—on second thought, don't come over. I'm bringing Edward around and wonder if you could stay with him for a while. I'll explain in a minute. We'll be right there."

For a moment, Anthony worried about the unsecured scene. But he was more worried about Edward so he simply closed the door behind them. He would only be a few minutes. They walked back down the path, past the lilacs to Edward's house. Cat met them on the walkway.

"What is it? What's wrong?" She took Edward by the arm to lead him and asked Anthony, "What has happened? What?" Her voice was panicky as though she knew it must be something horrible.

"It's Lew. Something terrible. No, don't go over. There's nothing to be done for him now. He's dead. Shot. It has been a ghastly shock for Edward and me, too. Please take him inside, get him a cup of tea or better, a brandy. I could use one too, but I must go back, Doc Appleby is on his way." He knew he sounded too official but he couldn't seem to think about anything but the macabre scene he would have to face again in a few minutes and didn't want to. Right now, he wished he had become an engineer like his father had wanted him to.

". . .And two was all he counted (one he missed)"

from THE GOLD HESPERIDEE
Robert Frost

CHAPTER 30

The slow-motion time warp had subsided leaving only the immediacy of reality. Anthony wanted to be alone for a few minutes before he had to gear up for the intrusive forensic crew and Dicky. He sat in the leather wing chair across from the desk and held his head in his hands. He knew it was unprofessional, but he wept anyway. Across the room was what was left of a man with whom he had shared intimate thoughts and happy moments. A true sympatico. Lew had been a good friend and now he's gone in a flash of . . . what could it have been? greed? anger? envy? to have snuffed out that good life.

Anthony closed his eyes to give his mind over to nothingness but his thoughts went to Isobel. He could see her sitting cross-legged on the floor with her eyes closed, palms up, shutting out all the distractions of the day. He had wanted to understand this practice that was so vital a part of her and so alien to him; so he joined her and learned meditation. Now it was one of his choice tools and whenever he meditated, he remembered Isobel and the gifts she had brought to him. Now, he could blank out muddled worries and clear his mind. It helped him gain perspective at a crime or orderless scene. After a few minutes of hollow quietness, he relaxed and began compiling his thoughts, making lists in his head. It was Lew who had taught him how to use his own mind systematically.

Outside, Dicky parked on the street and looked around to make sure Doc Appleby could park close, too. Otherwise Appleby would blame him for having to carry his little black bag a few extra steps. He wouldn't have to worry about that today. There was plenty of parking space. He, too, walked by the lilacs and sniffed in appreciation. The door was closed but not locked so he pressed the bell and entered.

"Dicky, down here," Anthony called, blew his nose and prepared himself for Dicky who followed his voice to the study. The short meditation had helped Anthony recover his professionalism. He was across the room at the open window when Dicky arrived. There was no screen in the window to hamper his fanning the cordite odor and he used a folder from the desk to help push the ugly smell outside. It was still noticeable in the air and preempted the nicer scent of the lilacs outside the window. The two Cambridge police representatives nodded at each other. Dicky gasped when he saw the desk. He turned away. He hadn't known what to expect. It certainly wasn't what he saw.

"I'll get a sheet from the car," Dicky said as he hurried back out and down the walk. He didn't know if he had a plastic sheet in the trunk or not but it didn't matter because fortunately the forensic crew was driving up and parking. He asked them to be sure to bring one in with them. They had everything that was needed to hide the reality of terrible, gruesome crimes--sheets, body bags, and antiseptics.

"Do you know where we go?" one of the crew asked and Dicky led them through the house to the study. His eyes averted, he started recording in his book. It was 9:30 in the morning. What a way to start a day. What a way to end a life.

When the doctor arrived a few minutes later, the investigation took on an officious air and Doc Appleby bumbled through routine. Anthony stood impatiently to one side, scrutinizing his every move. And though Appleby seemed a klutz, he accomplished his task without incident. Dicky noted everything Appleby said, starting with the time of death: between eight and nine in the morning. Dicky glanced at his watch; it was only a little after ten. Cause of death: gunshot wound to the head. Entrance through the left temple. Exit through the right temple. Dicky wrote: "The exit hole was the rest of the head." The corpse's arms had fallen to the sides, over the arms of the chair as though he were feeling for something on the floor.

Dicky wrote that Lew had been fully dressed in a suit and tie. It looked as though it had been just another day in the string of a lifetime of days.

The forensic crew left at about one o'clock, taping and securing the premises after filling plastic bags with bits of wood, bits of bone and any other bits they deemed evidential. Anthony was relieved to sit down quietly by himself. He had been going through the practiced motions for three hours without crossing the personal boundary that delimited his relationship with the deceased. He needed to untense and think. He needed to understand what had happened.

The crew had searched and found a 35-caliber bullet embedded in the binding of a copy of Keynes, *The General Theory of Employment, Interest and Money* that was in a bookcase on the wall next to the window. It looked like the other silver bullet that had been retrieved from the Canfield murder. Anthony was not surprised; just horrified that another dreadful happening was insinuating its way into his life.

Anthony was quickly assembling data in his head: the silver bullet almost assuredly tied the murder of Canfield and the Wadsworth burglary to this new crime. What did it mean? First, there must be some method to this madness. The connection of the pistol was loose at best. Even so it was undeniable that this all happened in a close circle. Lew had said it must have been a random coincidence that the stolen pistol and the Canfield murder weapon were both 35-caliber weapons. And here he was a victim of what appeared to be a continuation of the same tie-in of the theft and murder of Canfield. He felt his head was filled with cotton, rags and hay; he had to get away and think about something else but his mind kept returning to conversations the troyka had.

Anthony remembered the dinner at Tonio's when the troyka had enthusiastically embarked on commiserating about the Wadsworth theft. At the time, he had been glad Lew had forsaken making plans for taking a few weeks' holiday with Edward. The investigation gave Edward a new and engrossing focus and it was something that he had direly needed. And, now, Lew was dead. He wished now that he had gone away on that holiday.

"Dicky!" Anthony called and Dicky was at his elbow in a flash. "Here's what we know." Dicky was already writing.

"It happened between eight and nine o'clock this morning as Appleby confirmed.. Make a note of the date. Lew was at his desk when he was killed. There are some proofs over there on the corner of the desk." He motioned to a neat pile of manuscript that had escaped the splatter. "He may have been going over his new book to give the printer the o.k. to go ahead. In any case, the notation on the manuscript is that he had checked it and that it is ready for the printer. See, it says, and I'm quite sure that's Lew's writing—it wouldn't be anyone else's—'complete and o.k.' and there's today's date and his initials, LEW." He pointed to the markings.

"He may have been expecting someone else, but I don't see anything on his calendar other than Edward's and my names. We had agreed to meet here sometime around nine. I was going to present the twins' confession of the Wadsworth theft to them and hoped that together we could figure out some answers on how to proceed." He shook his head and said, "I really don't think either of the twins had anything to do with Canfield's death, but they certainly have the odds stacked against them. Rennie, in particular. And now, this murder must be connected. It's those pistols. I wish I knew the answer, and I wish we had that other pistol."

Anthony shifted back to the present scene, "At any rate, Lew was probably surprised by someone he knew; the door was unlocked and there appears to have been no struggle. Nothing has been upset, either here or upstairs, and the proofs are in order and the desk is neat--except for the. . .

"Right," Dicky said. A plastic sheet now covered part of the desk hiding the blood-splattered evidence. The body had been slipped into a generic black body bag, zipped up, and taken away.

"It was a silver bullet. Remember, James Wadsworth said he thought there was at least one in the chamber of each pistol, but there have been two murders which takes up two silver bullets. And this murder that left the bullet embedded in the bookcase—he pointed to the bookcase—appears to be silver. Odds on, this was done by the missing pistol." Anthony tapped on his knee with a pen. "It seems strange to me that whoever it was it was shot him from the left side and the trajectory of the bullet is from low to high." He pointed to the bookcase where the bullet was found after it had passed through part of Lew's skull. It was easier to talk with the body gone. "Ordinarily, I would think anyone standing beside someone would aim from high to low." He stood beside the chair and pointed with his finger. The natural position was, as he had indicated, from high to low. "See. That would mean that whoever did it was either kneeling or a midget." He threw the pen across the room in frustration and disgust. "I'm kidding; nothing really makes sense at all."

"Do you think it could be suicide?" Dicky was eager to help and wanted to understand, too.

"Not without a weapon. He couldn't shoot himself and then get up and surreptitiously dispose of the weapon. And besides, Lew was right handed. This bullet entered from the left and that wouldn't be a natural action for him." Anthony was deep in thought, "Those antique pistols have been nothing but a confounding mystery. I suppose it must be that the pistol that did in Canfield was almost certainly the other antique pistol from the Wadsworth collection. It couldn't be the one we recovered because that one hadn't been fired in years. Without it, we can't know for sure. I hope we'll know more after the tests on the body and the bullet but, I don't think we'll be surprised." Anthony paused, "You know, Dicky, when Edward and I arrived a little after nine this morning, the cordite was still very heavy in the air. If we had come a few minutes earlier maybe . . . maybe we could have prevented this."

"You can't ever know that. It wasn't your fault, or Professor Whitman's. It would be crazy for you to think you could have prevented it or seen into the future. It happened." Dicky started closing the notebook and looked at his watch; it was two o'clock. "I'll drive you to the station or would you like to stop for a bite somewhere?"

"I'm not through here yet. You go. I have my own car and I must go next door when I finish here. I'll see you later." Anthony wasn't looking forward to seeing Edward and trying to explain something that he could not explain to himself. He glanced around the scene of forensic trappings--plastic sheet, tapes, and powdery residue and closed the window and shut the door on the grim sight. He heard the outside door click locked as he slowly walked to Edward's house past the lilacs once more.

Edward had regained some of his composure but sat silently and despondent at the small table where he had shared breakfast so often with his friends. Cat had coffee and sandwiches made and waiting under waxed paper on the table. It was just what Anthony needed. Nothing was going to undo the scene next door. The best he could do now was to reassure everyone that he wasn't going to let it happen again. He hoped he could pull that off because right now he wasn't sure of anything. This was another clueless crime. Though, now that he thought of it, the Canfield murder was not entirely without clues and he thought they were getting closer to a solution even though he didn't see a resolution on the horizon.

Rennie had not yet followed up on his alibi for the time of the Canfield's murder. He certainly had had the opportunity to hide that pistol. And where was he this morning? Why he would want to do such a thing was beyond reason but so were most of Rennie's deeds. He didn't show remorse. Of course, thought Anthony, if he didn't commit any crime why should he show remorse?

He said nothing as he sat at the table. Cat uncovered the plate. He picked up a ham and cheese sandwich and ate. He was hungry and eating was a good ordinary, human thing to do.

"That though there is no fixed line between wrong and right, There are roughly zones whose laws must be obeyed

from THERE ARE ROUGHLY ZONES Robert Frost

Chapter 31

Anthony left Edward and Cat with apologies saying he had to get back to the station to start the paperwork on this most unwelcome case. There were always time-consuming arrangements and detectives to brief. He made his way to the station with a heavy heart. With the next step he had no choice: the twins had to be brought in, at least for further questioning. There was no time for logistics now. Another murder had been committed and he needed to take some action, even if he didn't fully believe in that action. Rennie was located at home about six o'clock. Teddy was not with him and Rennie said he didn't know where he was. Hadn't seen him all day, he said.

It turned out Teddy went on a job interview at eight o'clock in the morning at one of the independent schools in Cambridge. They asked him to stay for the remainder of the day to acquaint him with the scope of the sports program. He came home late, happy with his news, only to find the note from Rennie saying that he was with Anthony at the police station.

This was good news, he thought: Rennie must have decided to come clean about the theft and gone to Anthony on his own to confess his part in the theft. He couldn't help thinking he was glad to be putting all that behind them. Teddy picked up an apple then he hurried down the street and into the station. He had lunch in the school cafeteria but with meeting with everyone in the sports department and also other faculty, he hadn't eaten much; he was hungry. He was finishing off the apple as he knocked on Anthony's door and pushed it open. He nearly choked when he saw Rennie seated on a straight-backed chair in handcuffs.

"What's going on here?" Teddy demanded; he was bewildered. "You don't have to handcuff him. And everything has been returned!" It didn't occur to him that it might be in Anthony's capacity as arresting officer that Rennie was here.

"Not everything," said Anthony. "And burglary is not what Rennie is here for. Today's . . . incident . . . is much more serious."

"What are you talking about? What incident? What is going on?" Teddy put his face close to Rennie's, "Say something! What is he talking about? What have you done?" Teddy was primed to hear some half-baked scheme of Rennie's gone awry. "Is it that Central American. . . plan? Is it the partnership with Celeste? That certainly is not criminal; in fact, that's one of your more lucidly hatched schemes—it sounded like it should succeed." He stood back. "So what is it?"

Rennie stammered. There were paths of dried tears down his face. "Uncle Lew is dead. Someone killed him with that pistol we lost. It wasn't me!"

Teddy sank into an empty chair, put his head in his hands and cried. It was as though this news blew a hole in the dam of his emotions and the floodgates opened. Anthony put his hand on Teddy's shoulder and stood silently for a few moments. Then he walked to the door and gently closed it, leaving the three of them alone in his office. Dicky Cronin had been about to enter and Anthony folded and unfolded his fist three times— fifteen minutes. Dicky understood. When Anthony returned to his desk he started speaking in subdued tones.

"I don't think Rennie did it. He's our only lead right now and had opportunity both this morning and when Canfield was murdered. And he had access to the pistol. We're assuming about the pistol as it seems evident that it was the one used in Canfield's death and the fact that a silver bullet was retrieved at Lew's makes it almost certain that it was used today. Your brother has not been forthcoming with an alibi." The twins were both staring at Anthony now. Teddy fished in his pockets for a handkerchief, found a Kleenex, and blew his nose. Rennie wiped his nose on his sleeve.

"First, tell me about Uncle Lew. How did it happen and where?" asked Teddy.

Briefly and with as little emotion as possible Anthony related the discovery of Lew in his study about nine o'clock in the morning. He left out the details as he had when he told Rennie. There was always the possibility that a suspect would say something that he shouldn't know if he were innocent. Anthony didn't like thinking this way. He let the silence continue for a few minutes. Then he returned to the timing of the murders: where was Rennie then and where he was this morning.

"I told you. I was with Celeste all that night" Rennie whined. He didn't look like such a wise guy with his hands cuffed and his head down. "And I was just walking around down by the river this morning. Is that a crime?" With his brother as audience, he was gaining courage. A slight growl replaced the whine.

Anthony didn't pay attention to the outburst and said to Teddy, "We had the shopkeeper from the pawn shop come in a few minutes ago and he identified Rennie as the person who pawned the pistol. So, you can see that the circumstantial evidence is beginning to mount up."

"No one denies that Rennie pawned the pistol," said Teddy. "But as the experts said, the pistol found in the shop hadn't been fired in years. Anyone could have found the other pistol and used it. Have you spoken with Celeste? She'll tell you where Rennie was that night." He glared at Rennie, "Can't you think of someone who saw you this morning?"

Dicky Cronin, his jacket off and tie askew, knocked and entered. He carried three cups awkwardly by the handles and looked as though he were counting the cups and then the people. He put the cups down, carefully, on the desk and left. "I'll be right back," he said as he gave a pull to close the door after him. Seconds later he returned with another cup and a few donuts in a pink and white box. Outside, the church clock across the street struck six o'clock. It had been a long day and it wasn't close to over yet.

"Dicky," said Anthony, "this is what we're going to do. First," pointing to Rennie, "take those ridiculous cuffs off him." The next forty-five minutes were spent ironing out the details to enable Rennie to be released on bail. Anthony would have to call Edward with this distressing news, but it would have to be. It just was not possible for Anthony to take care of bail himself—conflict of interest, he said.

It was questionable whether or not Teddy should be included in the warrant. In the end, Anthony gave Teddy a lecture about aiding and abetting and told them both that the slightest infraction of the bail agreement would land them both in jail. He made an appointment to meet with them the following day. "One important job for Rennie's defense," said Anthony, "besides getting a lawyer to advise you, is to locate Celeste and get a statement from her as to your whereabouts the evening Canfield was killed. Another is to strain your brain and try to remember anyone who might have seen you on your walk this morning." It looked like an afterthought when Anthony added, "And if you would please tell me about that other pistol, things would be easier for me."

"We've told you before. There is no other answer. We, or rather I," Teddy said, "lost it!"

Anthony looked at Dicky, took a gulp of coffee and shook his head a little, as if to say, he didn't know why they were being so stubborn about this.

Then Anthony called Edward. It was a distressing conversation for both of them. Edward was still in shock over Lew's death and the fact that Rennie, his son, Lew's namesake and godchild, could stand accused of his murder was almost more than he could bear. Anthony explained that Rennie was being released with Teddy as soon as bond arrangements could be made. "No," Anthony said, "don't come down to the station. Call your lawyer. He can take care of it. It shouldn't take long. Then Dicky Cronin will drive them to your house. Please see that they stay there."

"We may as well go patiently on with our life,"

**from ON LOOKING UP BY CHANCE AT
   THE CONSTELLATIONS
Robert Frost**

Chapter 32

As always, he was grateful for Cat and the ease with which she took command of a sticky situation. The usual breakfast fare of coffee and toast was on the table. Edward poured a cup of coffee and sat down to gaze out the window. Cat had already left, saying she had some arrangements to see about. Edward assumed it had something to do with a memorial service for Lew, but she hadn't said and he hadn't asked.

Until now, Edward had always thought the blackest day of his life was the day Ann died. Pondering it, he knew that was wrong. Those last months, when he wondered each morning on awakening if Ann were going to see the sunset that day, were such a blur that though he lumped them together in a one-time-day thought, he had time to get used to the dreaded realization that one day soon she would be gone. He had known that Ann was dying and that nothing could change it. How he had lived through it he couldn't fathom, or remember. It had been a time continuum in a vacuum. He thought of fitting a whole yardful of raked leaves into one waste barrel. One knows, by logic, they won't all fit but one keeps piling them in and they keep tamping down leaving room for more.

But, yesterday supplanted the misery of Ann's final days and he could honestly say it was the very worst single day he had ever lived through. His best friend of forever was gone without so much as a warning. Not even a chance to avert it or postpone it, or to say good-bye, made the done deed all the more disconcerting. Lew, who had always been there; Edward couldn't even think about his not being next door. He tried to imagine a vacant chair and could not. Lew's image was eternal. Losing Lew was like having his own arm cut off. Lew had been his alter ego, his rock, his advocate--everything that personified loyal unwavering friendship. Paradoxically, he kept thinking about airing these feelings with Lew, knowing that he couldn't.

It was even worse to have Rennie and Teddy taken in for questioning. He knew they were not guilty—neither of them: of any crime. That they broke into the Wadsworth's he did not doubt, but he didn't consider it a real crime either. After all, he argued to himself, James and Barbara would have invited them in if they had been there. It was the pistols that snarled things up. Those pistols! It was a dreadful coincidence that one of them had been lost, but it wasn't the twins' fault that it was found by a murderer.

They were upstairs sleeping right now. Last night when they came in with Dicky Cronin, they were subdued but there was no mark of guilt on them. Of course, Edward remembered, he had never seen guilt in the past either. They had always looked innocent to him. He stared off across the room, stirring his coffee. He hadn't even brought in the paper.

A stumbling sound outside caused Edward to blink and bounce back into the present. Anthony opened the door and blundered into the kitchen with the morning paper in one hand and a box of donuts in the other. He had faintly rapped his usual tattoo, but he wasn't his usual cheery self, either. Who would be? with two unsolved murders--one of them a great personal loss, and the sons of his best friend under suspicion for having committed the deeds?

He started off by accepting a cup of coffee and sitting across from Edward at the kitchen table. He gave a little sniff-sneer at Cat's burnt toast and jam and pushed the toast aside as he opened the box of donuts. He picked up a powdered sugar one and kept it over the table as he took a bite, shaking the sugar onto the table. Before he went into detail about the charges against the twins, he smiled and said, "The good news is that the Fragonards have been found undamaged by their trip to the museum. Edward nodded and, eschewing the toast and jam, picked a donut out of the box.

Anthony had faced the twins' involvement in the Wadsworth theft but because of Lew's death he hadn't had the opportunity to broach the subject with Edward. That had been the intent of the appointment with Lew yesterday morning. The horrifying discovery had pushed the theft and the Canfield murder out of the limelight. But it was still in the front of Anthony's mind and he had been giving it some thought.

As he couldn't put it off any longer, Anthony told Edward about the confession the boys had made about the theft at the Wadsworth's and that the Wadsworths didn't intend to press charges and he was grateful for that, but he would rather be charging them on a theft charge than a murder charge. He did say that thirty-year-olds were not usually as easily forgiven as twelve-year-olds and that though they may just have dropped in for a snack, they did remove the books and cause some havoc; not to mention the theft of the paintings and the pistols. So they are not completely innocent.

No matter how he looked at it, it didn't look good. "We're lucky that the Wadsworths are so understanding about the theft. If it had been anyone else, they probably would have pressed charges. And don't forget there is still one pistol missing." Anthony pushed the donut box across the table after he took another. The room was quiet. He swallowed and said, "Those antique pistols have kept me awake too many nights and I know there is a connection between the theft and the murders

Edward listened. He tried to make it easier for Anthony by saying he knew the twins' plight wasn't Anthony's doing and that, while he understood the warrant, he was going to do all he could to see that they didn't spend time in jail. "I guess I was afraid of this all along," he said. "The coincidences seemed to mount up on one side against them. I know they didn't kill anyone. They loved Lew and they didn't even know Canfield. I'm going to ring up Adam Warshoditz and get some legal advice on how we should proceed." This was a new agenda for him but he assumed the burden without a second thought. He said, "The best thing to do is to get professional advice before we really need it." Anthony nodded in agreement silently confirming it was the best approach. Warshoditz was well known not only in Cambridge but nationwide for his defense of defendants with shaky alibis. Edward said, "I'd rather be over-prepared than the reverse and end up wishing we had called in experts sooner."

Anthony took a gulp of coffee, finished off the donut, and said that his mother used to say bad things came in threes and this was the third. Though he didn't believe in those old adages, he hoped there was some basic mathematical truth in it and that there would be no more thefts or murders or anything else.

He picked up another donut, took a bite, and wished aloud that Rennie would tell him what he did with the other pistol because he was sure it hadn't been lost. "Though most of the fingerprints on the pawnshop pistol were smudged, there was a clear thumbprint on the barrel. It was Rennie's. And," Anthony reasoned, "he must have had access to the other pistol—the one that killed Canfield. . . and probably Lew too." It was clear to him at least, that Rennie was still an instigator of malicious machinations. And, though he didn't tell Edward, he and Dicky had discussed the possibility that Teddy could be an accessory at least after, if not before, the fact. "If only we had that pistol," he said again, "we could start to sort things out."

"I know Rennie did not kill Lew," Edward repeated with conviction. "I just wish I knew who did. It can't be anyone in his immediate circle, but it can't be anyone else either. I'm going back to Lew's to search for clues."

"No, don't do that. Anyway, you can't. The whole place has been secured until we can go over the bits and pieces we have. The crew will be finished soon and we can go in then." A little more hopefully Anthony said, "Perhaps you could make some of your lists. You know, the ones with the positives and negatives or pluses and minuses or whatever." Anthony's weary voice drooped and faded, as though his energy had all leaked out. "It's as good a place as any to start."

"I wish we had that pistol!" he repeated.

"You walked a way beside me
To make me sad to go."

from FLOWER-GATHERING
Robert Frost

Chapter 33

The funeral service was at ten o'clock in the morning.

Colleagues from the University and friends and neighbors paid their respects. Lew would be buried with Sarah at Mt. Auburn Cemetery in a corner of the Woodridge plot under a flowering lilac bush. There was a place for his name on the granite monument that had noted the passing of his ancestors for more than one hundred years.

Ames and Ames, lawyers for the deceased, requested that Edward, Anthony, Cat, and the twins be in attendance for the reading of the will the following day.

The disposition of the major part of his and Sarah's estate was to provide a scholarship in their names to be administered by the University. The surprise was that Lew left his house and its contents to Edward. He requested that Anthony be executor and rewarded him with a small legacy. To Cat and each of the twins he left the proceeds of a trust fund while they lived, to be administered by his lawyers, and used for enriching their lives. The restriction was that they must exhibit a yearly earned income to be eligible. There were various other small legacies. It was an impressive document.

Edward was baffled by the gift of the house, "Why? I don't need another house. I suppose he didn't want strangers to go through his private spaces and papers. And I will do that and separate the papers for archives from the personal ones." He was rubbing his forehead in a reflective gesture, and said to Anthony. "I do welcome help." He sighed, "What will I do with another house? One is more than I really want. I can't just sell it and I don't want to."

Anthony shrugged, thinking he was glad he didn't have to cope with another house either, "Sure," he said, "I'll be able to spend some time in the evenings going over his files and book shelves with you." He knew that the evenings were going to be the hardest for Edward; he would miss the chess, and dinner conversations--and Lew's desserts. And so would he.

They had left the lawyers' offices and were strolling along Brattle Street. There was little traffic, as though by some agreement, the hustle and bustle of the Square was shut off out of courtesy for Lew.

Edward said again, "What do you think I should do with the house? I wonder what he had in mind? Do you have any ideas?" They walked in silence for a way. Then he stopped short. "You know, I believe I have an idea," then his speech quickened along with his step, making Anthony first stop and then hurry along beside him. "I'll have to ask the lawyers, but what if we deed the property to the University to be used to house the graduate poetry staff and the poetry chairs?" He smiled. "We've never really had a home in the English Department. Those offices in James Hall are cramped and there is no real conference room or library." He started to list a few changes to the physical structure that would need to be made. "There are houses all over Cambridge that house small departments of the University," he said.

"Lew would have liked it," Anthony said. "The location might be a problem being so far from the rest of the English Department, but those things can be worked out with lawyers and department heads working together to find a way to agree on all those legal and logistical issues necessary in such dealings. It made them both feel better to think something good might come of this tragedy. First though there was the difficult task of going over Lew's personal effects.

They could start in Lew's study that afternoon. The forensic crew had returned and finished their final scraping and packaging, taken down the "do not enter" and "secure premises" tapes. "It won't take long to organize everything," Edward said, "if I spend a few hours each day and you come over once in a while whenever you can," he looked thoughtful, "You never can tell what insignificant bits of paper might give us the clue we need to figure out what happened."

"With his ordered approach to everyhing, Lew would have left his desk and files in good condition I'm sure. He was like that. He never complained about loose ends and always kept things neat and tidy." It was obvious that Edward was rising out of the doldrums that had socked him in since Lew's death. His voice showed some animation as he talked and swung his arms in rhythm with his steps.

They went straight to Lew's house, unlocked the door with the key hidden in a fake rock by the doorstep and went into the study. Anthony breathed a sigh of relief when he saw that the room had been cleaned and straightened. The crime scene had been neutralized but the vision would be haunting the minds of these two friends for a long time. The first thing they dealt with was the posting of Lew's manuscript to the editor. Edward wrote a short explanatory note. There would be some legal complications with the published book itself, but the lawyers could deal with that later. The publisher must have had things like this happen before, they concurred.

It was tough going. Being there in their beloved friend's sanctum, they both felt uneasy. "It's as though someone's watching us, and I feel like I'm prying and making mistakes," admitted Anthony.

After some sorting and stacking, Anthony sighed and sat back, "I'm ready for a change. More than once I've thought about stopping and smelling the roses." He laughed, "Do you think they'd make my nose itch?" He stopped sorting papers, "How about a trip? We could take a long holiday, maybe two months--or more! and visit Italy. I've still got relatives there." A pause, "Maybe we could go to Greece too. I've always wanted to see Athens and the Acropolis rising in the middle of the city, and Delphi, and Crete, the Temple at Knossos. I could go on and on. I've never traveled enough and I think the time is right. What do you say? I mean when everything's sorted out and the twins are exonerated and the murders are solved."

"It sounds good to me," Edward said but didn't sound like he meant it nor did he enlarge on the proposal. "I know I have no right to ask," he was sorting Lew's books into two piles, "but, if there is more pressure to do something more serious with the twins, will you let me know. I don't want to spirit them away or anything like that. I just want to be prepared. I made an appointment with Jay Warshoditz, the noted defense lawyer who will see the twins and start his defense notes just in case.

Anthony told Edward, "I don't believe for one minute that either of them had anything to do with either murder. But we have to sort out the alibis. Mainly, Rennie has to make an effort. There must be someone who saw him and can swear to it. And, Edward, I promise you that no one will come and take them away in the middle of the night. Just impress upon them how important it is for them not to go off without letting us know. They should stay right here, for their own sakes."

Teddy and Rennie had only ventured out of Edward's house, to attend the funeral and the reading of the will, since the evening of Lew's death. Teddy was still hoping to start his new job the following week. He had some organizing to do and said he was glad for the uninterrupted time to outline a proposed course to present to the head of the sports department. He was so looking forward to this step in his journey to normalcy. Rennie, subdued for a change, pulled the TV out of the hall closet and watched some of his favorite programs. They were so depressing, they made him feel better, he said.

Anthony sorted while they talked and pulled some paperback books out from one of the shelves. He turned them over a few times. They weren't important or valuable so he put them in a box that was marked, "Walpole Prison." There was always a need for books at the prisons. "Why don't you call it a day and spend some time with the twins? This is a hard time for them too. No one knows what to do with themselves, and for them it's worse because they're just on the edge of returning to their old lives and they're not sure about where it's all leading." He tossed a couple more books into the prison box. "They might open up, if you didn't push it and just let them talk. It is a long time to bridge under the best of circumstances and," he raised his voice and accented his words, "these are the worst of circumstances. Getting them back into the mainstream should be our first priority now. Maybe, just maybe, they have some information that they don't even know they have that will help."

Edward nodded and prepared to leave after taping one box shut and marking it in big black letters. "All right, I'll do that. That's enough for today anyway. There's only a shelf or two of paperbacks and some encyclopedia to pack up from this wall." As an afterthought as he was almost out the door, Edward turned and said, "Come to dinner tonight." he looked at his watch, "It's only five o'clock now. That'll give you plenty of time to stop at the station if you have to and still get back by seven."

Anthony looked up and nodded as he watched Edward close the door. He took his time and packed the encyclopedia into another box, taped and labeled it. Then he reached his hand into the bookcase and pulled out a few things that had fallen behind some of the volumes. There were a couple of paperbacks he placed in the box for Walpole. Among the wayward pieces, was a thick manila envelope with his name, Anthony, on it. How strange, he thought and opened the envelope after holding it in his hands and testing its weight. It was a journal.

He reached to turn the desk chair around so he could sit. The date on the first page was thirty years ago. He thumbed the pages and he could see that it wasn't something that had been written in every day, but the handwriting was pretty much the same he noticed as he glanced through the pages. He started to read.

When he turned the last page it was a little after seven o'clock; he had forgotten about the dinner invitation and hadn't called to apologize. He reached for the phone but stopped mid-reach. No. Edward would assume he was hung up at the station and would forgive him. He couldn't see him now or even talk to him. He couldn't see anyone right now. He needed the night to think about the next step.

The manila envelope was on the desk. He replaced the journal into the envelope and placed it in the top drawer of the cleaned out desk that now held only a couple of pencils and paperclips. Then he went home and to bed without having any supper at all. Brandy was all he could keep down.

**"Then all I need to do is run
To the other end of the slope,
And on tracts laid new to the sun,
Begin all over to hope."**

**from IN TIME OF CLOUDBURST
Robert Frost**

Chapter 34

Anthony had wrestled with his conscience most of the night before coming up with his solution. It wouldn't have been everyone's solution and he wasn't exactly sure it was even the right one for him. But it was the one he was going with, and to have it settled was like lifting a mountainous burden from his shoulders. It was a dilemma that had no clear-cut answer. Truth is not absolute.

At the station he had a raft of ends to tie up and busied himself with his door closed so there would be no interruptions, not even Dicky. At about eleven o'clock in the morning, Anthony picked up the phone and dialed Edward. Cat answered and told him that Edward must have gone out; she hadn't seen him since breakfast. Ordinarily, she said she wouldn't be there either but she had an interior decorator coming to help with the choices of paint and paper and renovations. Anthony apologized for not having gotten back to her and Edward to apologize for missing dinner. He had been held up, he said.

"Cat, do you have a few minutes," Anthony had made up his mind in a split second to confide in Cat. "I'd like to try something out on you; a theory, that is."

"You're in luck! I am on my way to the office and have about an hour before my appointment with Ambrose. I could stop by now."

"Great. I'll make coffee!"

Ten minutes later Cat burst through the door looking like she was walking on clouds. She had an envelope in her hand and thrust it at Anthony. "Look! I've been accepted. At Oxford. With a nice stipend."

He read the letter and stared at Cat. He was happy for her, at least he thought he was; he would miss her. She was the only one who would understand. The only one he was even considering letting into his confidence. But he kept quiet for now.

"I guess I didn't realize you were really going to do it. Do you think it's the right time?"

"Yes, I really do. I wanted to think it out before I got their acceptance or rejection. And I did. It was hard. These last few years here in Cambridge, while nice and comfortable, have been inhibiting. I've felt the limits of an ordered life and I'm not sure I like it. When Edward needed me I didn't mind the restraints, but Edward is going to be involved up to his ears in family and doesn't need me anymore." She sat down. "Anthony, I can't be a housekeeper all my life. I'm looking forward to another dimension where I can start fresh with no ties or limits. I have so much to accomplish before I can think about being boxed in a life. I need to be free. My book is finished. I will always be grateful to Edward for that. And I will always think of you as my dear friend. Who knows how our paths will cross in future?" She was being a little reserved but it was necessary; she didn't want to cry.

Anthony walked around the desk and put his arms around Cat as she stood up. He thought about the wonderful times they had enjoyed as part of a special affinity. He would miss her redressing him and chastising him for small infractions of "Cat's Rules." An image of trying to beat her to the last piece of Lew's dessert flashed across his mind and he smiled.

"It's the right thing to do, Cat." Though he said it without conviction, he nodded and said with enthusiasm, "You'll wow them right out of their staid seats!"

"Now, what was it you wanted to talk about?" Cat asked.

"Oh," said Anthony, "it was nothing." He hesitated for a moment, "Actually, I'm thinking about taking a long trip for myself, by myself."

"Yes. . . I can see that. You deserve some holidays. These last weeks have been a strain on everyone except Edward, who seems to have risen above all his problems." She walked to the window and paused to take in the street scene down below. Handsome Harry was stopping a pedestrian for a chat and, probably a handout, amid the honking traffic of noontime. "Isn't it funny," she said, "how no two people react in the same way to the same stimulus. That's what Lew always said."

The telephone rang. "It should stop after three rings and switch over to the machine," Anthony explained. It did, but then it started up again. It annoyed him, but he picked it up. "Hello," he sounded short. Then his voice changed completely. "I tried to call you earlier but Cat told me you were out. I was about to try again. What's up?"

Edward must have answered with a few words. Cat looked at her watch, signaled to Anthony it was time for her to go, and left.

"I have some good news," Anthony said to Edward on the phone. "Our worries about alibis are all but over. That woman, Celeste, definitely has given Rennie an alibi. She came in with her lawyer and left a statement defining the critical time of Canfield's death. It seems there were three others who were with them having dinner from about six o'clock on. The others left sometime after midnight. About one o'clock was as close as they could, separately, remember. And Rennie," he cleared his throat, "stayed with her, in her bed, all night long. I asked her how she knew he hadn't slipped out at some point, and she told me in no uncertain terms. I signed the affidavit for Teddy's time with us at the Youth Center. So that lets them both off the hook. The charismatic Mr. Warshoditz thinks that'll end it as far as the twins are concerned." Relief echoed in his words, "And, Rennie remembered stopping at the Dunkin' Donuts in Central Square the morning Lew was killed. He had spilled his coffee all over the counter, and in typical Rennie fashion demanded not only that someone clean it up but that he be given another cup of coffee in a hurry. The very busy counter person had nothing nice to say about him, but he sure remembered him. It was around eight-thirty which is their busiest time of the morning.

"I can't tell you what a burden has been lifted from my shoulders," said Edward on the other end of the line. "I never was worried that they did it; just that they wouldn't be able to prove that they didn't." In the same breath, he happily declared, "Now Teddy can to go to Guanajuato, speak with her folks and make arrangements for Marie-Elena and Edwina to come home. They could be here before long. I am really looking forward to their coming. I never thought I would be excited about being a grandfather, but I am. I can think of all kinds of things I want to do with her and show her." He paused. "Maybe I'll be a better grandfather than I was a father. I couldn't be any worse." And he chuckled at what he now considered a joke.

It was not lost on Anthony. He was as glad as anyone to have Edward focusing on his granddaughter. The twins were emerging from the snarl of events with a little sensitivity. He hoped for a change in Rennie's selfish, self-serving attitude. He seemed to be at least a little repentant about his past. That might be going a bit far, though. Maybe no one had ever scared him before, thought Anthony. It was Rennie's emotional capacities that worried Anthony and should worry Edward. He didn't seem capable of empathy or for that matter, love. But perhaps that would come when he finally found acceptance and contentment. if that were possible.

And Teddy. He had faith that Teddy's sense of honor would rise to the top. He had seen in him a willingness to learn and to make amends. It was he who had confessed the Wadsworth fiasco and he who had devoted time to the Youth

Center. Just the fact that Marie-Elena and Edwina had been on his mind all this time showed his more thoughtful stance.

Anthony said, "I'm really sorry about not getting over last night. I lost track of the time."

"We missed you, but that's o.k I started some of my lists and only came up with positives. We all, in some way benefited from Lew's death, though none of us knew his plans. The legacies were surprises to us all. You didn't know, did you?"

"No. I was surprised, too." Anthony said he'd stop by the next day for his usual morning chat and coffee.

There was still trouble. Anthony knew it was his problem to figure out how to use the information he had in the most beneficial manner. And he felt the conflict of love and honor battling within him. He knew where his duty to the Commonwealth was. It was his duty as a friend that was superimposing itself on the picture and confounding the issue.

"And I ask all to try to forgive me. . ."

from A RECORD STRIDE
Robert Frost

Chapter 35

This will be my last entry.

To leave you, Anthony, with this, is something that though I wish not to burden you, I can see no other way. I leave the quandary of the ultimate choice to you. My hope is that you will be able to leave Edward's memory of me at least somewhat undiminished, if not untarnished. You may have suspected that I've always wanted to eat my cake and have it too!

I have put my things in order, as they say, and hope that my small fortunes will do some good. I am happy to have seen the twins and to know that their lives will not be completely wasted. Their involvement, or non-involvement, in the Canfield fiasco will be laid to rest when this bit of prattle is found. (What will you do with it? I can't imagine!) Though Rennie always will be amoral, he is too much of a coward to involve himself in anything like this. You probably saw that.

I was right those few weeks ago (it seems now like years) when I thought I saw one of them in the Quad. I wish now I had gone right up to him and welcomed him back, but how was I to know the chain of events that would be set off by the pistol I found in the grass that day? The same pistol I picked up that I suspect, he dropped. The pistol that will probably never be found or if it is, whoever finds it will wonder how it got in the lilac bushes.

That I happened to find the pistol that was stolen from the Wadsworths' was fortuitous. It has made a taxing puzzle and has kept everyone (Edward!) involved. I do think the pistol was the impetus that pushed my plan out of my imagination and into reality. The antique pistol made it easier and more confounding. Of course, it was my intent was to create an absorbing puzzle. But, I conjured up a monster that I could not contain. There is only one way to stop it.

But maybe the germ was planted even earlier, before I found the pistol. One might ask, why else would I have kept those keys to Canfield's office. I really just forgot them . . . at first. Then, I liked having them in my pocket. I am not being completely truthful. I knew, in the dark recesses of my mind, what I would use them for. Finding the pistol was the stroke of luck that put the fuzzy outline into focus.

It wasn't merely the fact that I found the pistol at the right time that made me decide to pursue the malefic deed. I have always wanted to plan (though I never thought I would execute) the perfect crime. Hasn't everyone? A crime with such a hidden, obscure motive that no one would recognize it and, therefore, be rendered unsolvable.

I think I have succeeded. I am both excited and horrified!

You said once to appease me, that of course, motive is everything, as though I were a fool. That was before I had committed myself to action but I think it was spinning around in my head then as a fantasy. For a while now, fantasy and reality have become blurred. There are times, like now, when I can see the folly of my thinking. But, I think, the euphoria of lofty vision tricked me into imagining myself a savior instead of the fiend I was, smiling and hiding deadly fangs.

Where was my compassion? Where was my love? Where was my honesty and integrity? Gone with illogical and uncontrollable fancies. I loathe the path that led me to this vile plateau of revolting conduct and ultimate self-hatred.

It wasn't until that defining visit to Dr. Aldorf that I knew this was the last spring I would see, the last time I would walk through Cambridge in April. Anything I wanted to accomplish would have to be done soon. I saw the sands running through the hourglass with awesome speed. I needed to hurry and it was not easy to carry on normally. But I did well, didn't I, Anthony?

Dr. Aldorf will tell you, if you ask him, about the horrid disease that is disintegrating my insides. He will tell you that I would have had only a few months left and those months would have been in a drugged stupor. Even now the morphine is a godsend and makes my days, and nights, bearable. The euphoria of Morpheus--I always wondered what exactly that meant. Now I know. It's a lovely spot where I can think clearly? and imagine a different world and a different self.

When you read this, it will clear up certain procedures that have been confounding Cambridge's finest. I felt smug whenever you, dear Anthony, cursed the one who gave you no clues.

It was the Wadsworth burglary that started the
formations in my mind. Edward's demeanor turned on a dime
when there was an engrossing conundrum to sink his teeth into.
He became a live organism again. He started thinking again.
How could I not wish that to continue? My brainstorm was to
give him something even more mysterious and intriguing.

See how convoluted?

The sick body and mind become one. Even when I am
sure I have approached a question with method and system I find
that the next day my scribblings are fit only for the fire. So, I
have burned my previous compunctious apologies in the study
fireplace. A warm blaze flared with the amende honorable *of a*
burnt sacrifice. Who would have thought that the romantic
conscience would be so consumed by guilt? Certainly, not I; but
I am pleased to know that it is so. Sometimes I wish I could undo
the whole absurd vagary.

Some Roman once said, "temptation has music for all
ears."

May God forgive me!

I was merely testing the key that evening I stopped in at
James Hall. I had seen Dr. Aldorf late in the afternoon and had
stopped at the Wursthaus for a bite. It was a nice evening for
walking and I took the long way. I think I knew where I was
going to end up, though I hadn't planned it. I can't remember
everything. I do know my feet felt light and my head was happy
and in the clouds. Had Dr. Aldorf given me an injection? I can't
remember.

I had left the pistol in my briefcase where it had been since I found it. I had examined it thoroughly at home, but I returned it to the briefcase under the pretense to myself that I was going to return it. James Wadsworth had been diligent about keeping it oiled and in good working condition. I liked the feel and the heft of the metal and polished wood in an intricate balance, and the rubies in the handle made me feel like d'Artangan. There was a silver bullet in the firing chamber. Probably hand poured in a special mold; I think that's the way they're made.

I've always wondered how guns could be left around, loaded and lethal, without a thought. But it's easy.

I found myself outside James Hall. Curious, I fit the key into the lock on the side door and turned it. It was an augury bidding me deeper into a conspiracy with the devil. Canfield's light was on and he greeted me with an air of anticipation, as though he had been waiting for me. We chatted amiably about the poetry contest. I should have told Cat how he admired her work as he was full of compliments. When he asked about the Wadsworth theft I reached into my briefcase, pulled out the pistol and pointed it at him. I didn't mean to alarm him. I think I was just showing him the pistol. But he got rattled and when he went to stand, his foot must have gotten tangled in the maze of desk and chair legs and telephone wires because he tripped and fell and hit the bookcase with his head. His forehead had started to bleed and I was going to wipe it off and help him up when something overtook me. I saw he was stunned by the fall. The plan burst like a firecracker in my head and became crystal clear. I stood back, the pistol still in my hand, aimed and fired. I was surprised that the report was not loud. Just a little "pop" and it was over. He had such an awful look on his face I didn't want to see it again so I turned him over, face down. Then I locked the door and left. I dropped the keys into a sewer just like a criminal covering his tracks.

That's all there was to it. It was so easy. I was shaking with excitement. I don't remember the walk home, but when I awoke the next morning, I felt like I had been drinking and a fuzzy head and throbbing temples bothered me all day.

Plans for my own demise are much more complicated and interesting. I did a great deal of research. In the end, I got my idea from a Sherlock Holmes story with a murder that took place on a bridge. It was really a suicide made to look like murder. Did you think that all along, Anthony? The pistol was tied to the branch of an overhanging tree with a long cord pulled taut. After the pistol was fired, the gun flew from his hand into the high branches of the tree and was concealed by the leaves. Not that anyone would think to search the tree anyhow. It was subsequently found and puzzled over until Sherlock explained step-by-step the intricacies of the plan; but there is no Sherlock Holmes around here!

Except, maybe you! Have you read Conant Doyle? Maybe you can find a copy of his collected works in the Wadsworths' library! Dear Anthony, am I teasing you?

Getting back to the story, of course, the motive was different. I think the Conant Doyle's character was a victim of unrequited love. My motive is the same as the one for which I killed Canfield: to make an interesting, unsolvable and engrossing puzzle. (And, though I sometimes reject it, I cannot live with myself any longer; even for a few drugged months. I have turned into a Mr. Hyde that I do not understand or like.)

The plans occupied my every waking minute. It was my most exciting venture. I had palmed a silver bullet from the pistol case at the Wadsworths on one of our visits, and that was easy. No one noticed as I picked it up out of the case, scrutinized it, and instead of putting it back, put it in my pocket. At the time I didn't know the use I would have for it—or perhaps I did.

The hardest-to-find item was the super-long bungee cord. I finally located one at Brine's in the Square. I will have to hold the pistol in my left hand, though, to ensure that it will fly out the window without incident. I tested it over and over again using a stapler in place of the pistol. It worked each time and I retrieved it from under the lilacs. It was well hidden each time so I had to scrabble around in the leaves beneath the lilacs. The leaves aren't cleaned out from season to season but allowed to mulch in place so it's a perfect hiding place. I am sorry for the pain Edward will endure. But it has to be.

I was lost anyway.

post script
I have put your name, Anthony, on the envelope and sealed this journal inside not to leave you a dilemma but to ensure firstly that no one else will see it before you and secondly that someone for whom I have the greatest love and respect will do the right thing. Though I cringe now, I will be gone when you are left to

make the decision and I won't have to think anymore. Peace and love/ Lew

"That life is only life forevermore
Together wing to wing and oar to oar."

from THE MASTER SPEED
Robert Frost

Chapter 36

"Edward don't even try go in. Please stay here. There's no sense in trying to save anything now. The fire department will save whatever they can of the house. At least we know no one is inside." Cat was trying to comfort Edward. "There's nothing to be done. Maybe it's just as well. With Lew gone, it may be the best way to start over."

It was about five o'clock in the morning and the sun had not started to lighten the night skies. By now the worst of the ordeal was over.

Cat had been awakened about three o'clock in the morning by an acrid odor invading her sensitive nostrils. As she tried to get away from it in her sleep, an inner alarm told her to wake up; it was smoke. She darted from her bed and dashed down the stairs. She switched on lights and yelled to Edward and the twins to wake up—the house was on fire! She made her way into the kitchen dreading what she might find and she found nothing ablaze or amiss—except the horrid smell of smoke. Then she saw through the kitchen window the flames across the yard next door. Moments later Edward entered the room looking confused as he listened to Cat calling the fire department. The twins came stumbling down the stairs and raced out the door. Edward heard the rush of water and saw through the window that they had the hose unfurled from the holder on the side of the house and were dousing as far as the hose would reach. The lilacs were wilting.

The fire trucks were there in a flash and the men started watering down the neighboring houses as they put out the flames in Lew's house.

Much later, after the fire had been extinguished and the charred remains had cooled enough to venture inside, Edward and Anthony made their way into what was left of Lew's study. Some of the ashes still held the shape of their pre-fire forms, but as soon as they were touched, they too fell into a sooty disarray. The back of the house was a soggy, burnt shamble. The kitchen, the small hallway leading to the study, the study itself, and the downstairs bathroom had been pretty much destroyed by the fire. The front of the house would have been next, but the door at the end of the study hallway had been closed and that saved the front stairs and the rest of the house. It could have been a lot worse.

Edward looked for anything in Lew's study that was in tact and there was nothing. All of Lew's personal things: desk, book and display cases, University chair, files, everything. "It certainly is fortunate we mailed Lew's book to the editor," Edward said as he viewed the devastation.

Anthony nodded and poked a finger on the shelf of the charred bookcase behind Lew's desk. He watched as a few burnt book remains disintegrated and fell to the floor with the other ashes.

Edward stood among the ruins, sighed and wondered aloud, "Has some evil aura settled around me. First, the theft, then Canfield's senseless murder. and then the even more senseless murder of Lew. Now this."

Later after the fire squad had investigated they determined that the fire had started in the kitchen. A faulty wire in the toaster was the culprit. "It probably wasn't so much a faulty wire," the Chief had told them, "as it was the fact that the toaster had been plugged in. Toasters work on a hinge mechanism and sometimes the hinge arbitrarily releases, turning the toaster on—particularly if the toaster is old and worn. If the toaster is next to kitchen curtains or paper napkins, for example, as it was here, the results can be disastrous. It's a major cause of kitchen fires after grease fires, of course." He paused for effect, and continued, "It happens more often than you would think. The best thing to do is to always unplug the toaster when you've finished using it."

Edward murmured, "So there is no mystery to this. It was an accidental catastrophe and bears no evil undertones."

Anthony nodded but had his own thoughts. That it was an accident, he had no doubt. But that didn't dismiss the significance and gravity of what was destroyed in the fire. What he didn't know was how to, or even if he should, reveal what he knew. He had felt he would have to. But now there was no evidence. The journal with its confession was a charred memory seen only by him. Why he had ever left it in Lew's study, he couldn't fathom.   He could have taken it home with him and put it in a safe place. He should have! He was back on the merry-go-round. He wasn't entirely sure he, himself, would have believed the journal if he hadn't seen it, held it, and turned the pages himself. If he presented his story, without the defining evidence, it would look like a feeble attempt to wrap things up neatly at the expense of someone who could no longer defend himself. He couldn't help thinking that he wished they had waited to start sorting through Lew's things. One more day and he wouldn't have found the journal and he wouldn't have known the truth.

Anthony was still staring beyond the devastation when Edward left and went home. He looked around at what was left of the room. Without real conviction, he turned over ashes of books that fell apart as he touched them.   The beautiful rosewood desk was demolished. The top desk drawer had fallen through to the floor and charred remains of pencils and a manila envelope crumbled as he edged the burnt remains with his toe.

As Commissioner he was sworn to uphold the law and truth; as a friend he was obliged to uphold a cherished memory. There were already several unsolved crimes, two of them murders, that had been on the books for years in Cambridge. Adding a couple more would be no big deal. People tended to forget about such things after the original hew and cry has subsided.

In the final analysis, he did what he had to do.

The moving finger writes, and having writ,
Moves on, nor all your piety nor wit
shall lure it back to cancel half a line,
nor all your tears wash out a word of it.

From THE RUBAIYAT OF OMAR KHAYYAM
Edward FitzGerald

EPILOGUE

"Cafe? . . . Ouzo?" The young waiter in crisp white shirt and carefully pressed, black trousers smiled down at Anthony—his eyebrows raised in question and his neatly trimmed moustache twitched as he cocked his head toward the empty chair. Stavos was used to Anthony's visit and a familiar routine. The small umbrella-shaded, outside table close to the balcony railing overlooked the sparkling Aegean and proved a comfortable repose where Anthony had spent two or three hours each day for the past week. Usually—in fact always—Anthony was alone. Today the September late-afternoon ambience felt welcoming though the intensity of the summer's dazzling sun had hardly abated. He said, "I've got a date."

The ubiquitous blue-and-white Greek flag waved lazily over the outdoor bar at the market's edge. The small space was comfortably crowded with not enough people to make Anthony feel he had to hurry but enough so that he didn't feel alone or conspicuous as the summer crush of vacationers, mostly students, eased with university terms beginning soon. Crete had become manageable. Browsing the museum and the Temple at Knossos was much more pleasant without anyone breathing down his neck. He was still in his exuberant, exploring mode; and it was not only that he was happy to be free from those dark worries, everything was exciting and new to him and he was ready to prolong his stay. Another month was a good idea and as he had no constraints—why not? He loved everything: the friendly hoi polloi, the amazing history and myths that informed everyday life, the wonderful cuisine: tzatziki, moussaka, pastitiso, kabobs, he was even used to Retsina—he loved it all. And his nose had stopped sneezing and itching.

More than anything he loved the glorious panorama stretched out before him. From his little table he had full view of the busy harbor with its small fishing boats, larger sailing boats, and still larger excursion boats all gracefully afloat in the sparkling, azure Aegean. The backdrop of a cumulus-dotted horizon melting into the sea completed the *mise en scene*. Maybe he'd take up the artist's brush to see and experience the "springtime" writers and artists sketch: the almond trees in bloom and the daffodils and crocus and the flora that Greece is home to. Yes, he would stay for a while, so he could take exploring visits to other near-by islands only an excursion-boat trip away. This part of the ancient world boasted a super-abundance of venues; there was so much to do and see, so many sites to explore, and history to ponder, so many people to meet and share a café or ouzo, or Retsina. To Anthony everything was new and exciting and he was going to gather it up and stuff his very being with experience.

He nodded at the waiter and put up two fingers as he saw his date wave and stride toward him across the narrow market walkway. The waiter was back before she arrived at the table and set down two small glasses of ouzo and two cups of steaming espresso. "I feel like a truant' Anthony said as he motioned to the seat across the small table. "I never would have ordered ouzo in Cambridge. Certainly not in the afternoon." He smiled his broad smile and picked up his glass. "But this isn't Cambridge and this is a special day!"

His last few weeks in Cambridge were pushed to the periphery of his mind though he knew he could never completely forget. Just getting through his job and tying up the loose ends was traumatic. His goal had been to maneuver those loose ends into granny knots that he hoped no one would ever be able to untangle. The unsolved and unresolved stamp had been put on both the deaths of Canfield and Lew, so it was as finished as it ever would be. At least, he hoped those files would be forgotten and relegated to mothballs.

Even though he knew the course he had chosen was the right one for him, he was not happy with it. In an attempt to bring closure to an unsatisfactory chain of events, he had written and dated everything he knew about the incidents until he was satisfied and read it over many times. Then he set the whole thing afire in his East Cambridge fireplace and watched the final burst of flame until it blackened and the sheaf crumbled. His last paragraph had read: "The exercise of compiling these unexplainable events and conclusions has served a cathartic purpose for me, and the burning of the pages will symbolize the passing of malfeasance where it will vanish forever into the eternal vapors that surround us." I sound like Lew, he thought as he wrote the words.

In one of his many solo debates, he reasoned: nothing would be served by disclosing, at this time, what he had read in an unsubstantiated, now destroyed, journal. It could be that Lew's state was such that the drugs and medications played tricks with his mind—most certainly they did—and that he had written a mostly contrived, not to say, false, distorted version of the facts.

What Anthony hadn't wanted to admit, even to himself, was that he knew the journal was pretty much a true chronicle.

His conscience wouldn't allow him to sit in the commissioner's chair with an omission tantamount to a lie hanging over him. In his second-floor, lop-sided office at the station, behind closed doors, he thoughtfully hand-wrote the letter resigning his post. When he finished, he called Dicky in. "Here, read this," he said and passed the letter across the desk:

Dicky sat down, read, looked from the letter to Anthony and shook his head. "Why?"

"Because I think you're ready for it," said Anthony.

"Not, why the recommendation? Why the resignation? You're not old enough to retire and I know you love this work. So? Why?" Anthony yawned and leaned back in his chair, "I need some time for myself. I've never had any, you know and I'm not getting any younger. My first foray into retirement is to take a trip around the world and take more than eighty days. And then, maybe I'll try my hand at being a cowboy."

Dicky thought there must be more to it but he also knew his boss well enough to let it be. "Well, I'm grateful for the recommendation and all I've learned working with you. I really will miss you, both as a boss and a friend, not to mention the basketball practices."

When the resignation was made public a few days later, there were protests from all quarters, but Anthony's mind was made up, he said. Arrangements for his around-the-world trip were exciting and engrossing. He was looking forward to going alone. He couldn't ask Edward to accompany him because he knew he would not be able to see Edward every day and keep his secret. Maybe with time. . . but in his soul he knew he would never be able to reveal to Edward what he knew.

Shortly after Lew's funeral, Anthony dug up some lilac shoots from his own backyard in East Cambridge to replace the lilacs between Edward's and Lew's houses that had wilted and died from the smoke and heat of the fire. He had insisted on digging and planting the lilacs himself. He said it was a labor of love, but it was more. He had easily found the missing ruby-handled pistol in the dead leaves and tangle of roots. He cleaned and polished it and sent it anonymously back to the Wadsworths where, after the initial commotion, it was put to rest with its mate in the specially made rosewood case. There were no silver bullets to rattle around and after James Wadsworth remarked that he wondered where they were, nothing more was said.

When Anthony returned from this trip, he decided, he would settle in another part of the country. Maybe North Dakota or Wyoming—he really would like to try Western living. Maybe that was unrealistic, but he meant to pursue it anyway. In any event, the trip would take upwards of a year and who knew what could happen. Maybe he'd look up relatives in Sicily and stay there where they needed a fresh outlook on the Mafia problem. England was a possibility too. He would like to know more about Scotland Yard. And he'd like to see Oxford and walk some of Inspector Morse's paths. Maybe he would find a chorus to sing with, too. Of course, being near Cat would be a plus. If there were anyone, he thought, who would understand his quandary it would be Cat.

The possibilities for the future were endless.

Before starting the Oxford term Cat wanted to see some of her history-book sights and maybe gain a new perspective for her next book, so she bid farewell to Edward and Cambridge early in August. Her poetry had won acclaim not only in academic circles but as well, in the popular realm. Her aim had always been to infuse joy into relating everyday happenings in the tradition of Robert Frost. Edward was sad she was leaving but he was elated, he said, to see her on the road to realizing her potential. There would always be a place for her on Berkeley Street, he said.

Robert Ambrose left another door open for her return to Cambridge. Though he was happy in the Robert Frost Chair right now, "You can never tell what the future might bring," he had said to her with a gleam that hinted he just might support the nomination of Cat someday.

Mark won the FROST-ing cover job, and it made him a sensation in the photographic-art world. He was written up in the *Globe*, and the *Times* too, as "a young Cambridge artist that deserved watching." His work on Cat's book was hailed as extraordinarily sensitive and unique and he was invited to show at the Heineken. He seemed to be very involved with both his new acclaim and a young *protégé*, named Marianne, who followed him about with adoring admiration.

Teddy loved his new job and family life. He settled in easily and he was ready for it and his responsibilities. Rennie moved in with Celeste to be closer to his new business. Celeste was smart and Rennie seemed to be learning from her. Together they made a trip to Central America that was written up in the **Chronicle** and appeared along with ads for "new and unique treasures from untapped Central American sources."

As for Edward, he was totally immersed in family— Edwina was the shining light of his life. Everything now interested Edward. Nothing was too small to notice and nothing too big to overcome or see around. It was a complete reversal of the Edward of last year. His regret was that Lew was not here to enjoy this vitalized life too. If only he could have foreseen the future. If only they had been a few minutes earlier maybe they could have saved Lew. If only . . . but that was unproductive thinking. Things are as they are and in life there is no changing the past. However, the future: that's a different story and starts a new page just as Ann had said.

Anthony stood as Cat plopped her pack down so she could give him a hug and peck on the cheek. She glanced around, "So this is what artists and poets rave about. Now I know why! It's too beautiful for words." She picked up the ouzo, turned it around a few times, looked at Anthony with her familiar mischievous smile. "Salute," he said and Cat added, "To a brilliant day on Crete with my good old friend before we both set off exploring uncharted waters."

They both drank the ouzo down in one noisy gulp, reached for the espresso, and sat down to enjoy a scintillating afternoon in the dazzling and absorbing history of myth and beauty that surrounded them.

The End and the Beginning

Made in the USA
Monee, IL
21 September 2019